THE COZY
COOKBOOK

THE COZY COOKBOOK

More than 100 Recipes from Today's Bestselling Mystery Authors

AVERY AAMES/DARYL WOOD GERBER,
ELLERY ADAMS, CONNIE ARCHER,
LESLIE BUDEWITZ, LAURA CHILDS, CLEO COYLE,
VICTORIA HAMILTON, B. B. HAYWOOD,
JULIE HYZY, JENN McKINLAY, PAIGE SHELTON

BERKLEY PRIME CRIME, NEW YORK

THE BERKLEY PUBLISHING GROUP
Published by the Penguin Group
Penguin Group (USA) LLC
375 Hudson Street, New York, New York 10014

USA • Canada • UK • Ireland • Australia • New Zealand • India • South Africa • China

penguin.com

A Penguin Random House Company

Berkley Prime Crime Books are published by The Berkley Publishing Group.
BERKLEY® PRIME CRIME and the PRIME CRIME logo are trademarks of Penguin Group (USA) LLC.

Library of Congress Cataloging-in-Publication Data

The cozy cookbook : more than 100 recipes from today's bestselling mystery
authors / Julie Hyzy, Laura Childs, Cleo Coyle, B. B. Haywood, Jenn McKinlay,
Avery Aames, Daryl Wood Gerber, Connie Archer, Ellery Adams, Leslie Budewitz,
Victoria Hamilton, Paige Shelton.
pages   cm
Includes index.
ISBN 978-0-425-27786-7
1. Cooking, American.   2. Cooking in literature.   3. Detective and mystery
stories, American.   I. Hyzy, Julie A.
TX715.C8729 2015
641.5973—dc23
2014044235

PUBLISHING HISTORY
Berkley Prime Crime trade paperback edition / April 2015

The recipes and excerpts in this volume first appeared in books published by Berkley Prime Crime Books.

Contents

A Note from the Editor...vii

BREAKFAST...1

BREADS, MUFFINS, AND OTHER BAKED GOODIES....................31

SOUPS, SALADS, AND SANDWICHES......................................77

DRINKS...115

APPETIZERS..143

MAIN COURSES...169

SIDE DISHES..215

DESSERTS...239

Index..349

Series Lists...365

Author Bios..369

A Note from the Editor

Welcome to *The Cozy Cookbook*! If you're looking for a side of mystery with a heaping helping of some truly delectable recipes, you've come to the right place. Within these pages you'll find scrumptious offerings for breakfast, lunch, and dinner, as well as delicious desserts, appetizers, sides, and drinks. You'll also get to spend a little time with your favorite cozy mystery characters and meet some new ones as you peruse over a hundred mouthwatering recipes from our bestselling authors.

We are delighted to be able to bring this collection to you and hope that you enjoy every page. Be sure to check out the series lists from the featured authors and devour the titles you haven't yet sampled.

We wish you happy reading and, of course, bon appétit!

Breakfast

Delilah's Grilled Breakfast Sandwich..................................3

    EXCERPT FROM *STATE OF THE ONION* BY JULIE HYZY..........5

Eggs Benedict..8

A Fat-Free, Cheese-Free, Yolk-Free, High-Fiber Omelet...........10

San Simon Frittata...12

    EXCERPT FROM *PECAN PIES AND HOMICIDES* BY ELLERY ADAMS.........14

Charmed Bacon-Lattice Breakfast Pie............................16

Spinach Quiche...17

Charmed Pancetta and Gruyère Tart..............................19

    EXCERPT FROM *A SPOONFUL OF MURDER* BY CONNIE ARCHER..........21

French Toast Sandwich..23

Jenna's Monte Cristo Sandwich..................................24

Pancakes with Gouda and Figs
(and Grandmother's Pancake Mix)................................26

Maggie Tremont's German Strawberry-Apple Pancakes..............28

Skillet Potatoes...30

Delilah's Grilled Breakfast Sandwich

~ From *Clobbered by Camembert* by Avery Aames ~

MAKES 1 SANDWICH

2 eggs

Dash of Tabasco

3 grinds of the pepper mill

2 tablespoons butter

1 green onion, green ends only

2 slices white bread

2 slices (at least 1 ounce each) Tomme Crayeuse cheese
  (may substitute cream cheese or Brie)

First prepare the eggs. Crack the eggs into a bowl; whisk to blend. Add a dash of Tabasco and three grinds of the pepper mill.

Heat sauté pan on medium-high heat. Grease the pan with ½ tablespoon butter. Chop the green onion ends. Drop the onion ends into the heated butter. Cook for 1 minute. Add the whisked eggs. Reduce heat to simmer. Stir the eggs until cooked through.

Heat griddle to 400° F. Butter the outsides of each slice of bread using the remaining butter.

Set the bread, butter side down, on the griddle. Top each side with half of the cheese. Mound the cooked eggs on one side of the bread with cheese. Set the other side of bread with cheese on top. Cook for

2 to 3 minutes until the bread is a medium brown. Using a spatula, flip the sandwich and cook another 2 to 3 minutes.

Note: More cheese may be added, to your liking. After all, it is a grilled cheese sandwich.

State of the Onion

by Julie Hyzy

"Ollie, are you okay? What's happening?" Henry walked in moments later, talking up a storm. "I just passed the president in the corridor. Was he in here with you?"

I opened my mouth to speak, but stopped myself as Cyan and Marcel appeared behind Henry. Not thirty seconds before, the president of the United States of America had asked me not to discuss this with anyone, and here I was about to spill the spaghetti with my coworkers.

"Yeah," I said, "he'd like scrambled eggs for breakfast."

Henry glanced in the direction the president had exited and gave me a thoughtful look. "He came down here to tell you that in person?"

I nodded.

Although he was set to retire on his sixty-seventh birthday, Henry was still one of the most vibrant and quick-witted people I knew. He was also the most talented chef I'd ever worked under. It was just in the past couple of years that I'd noticed him taste-testing more often, as evidenced by his expanding waistline, and delegating the more physically demanding tasks to us. His light brown hair had started to thin and go gray at the temples, but his voice was just as resonant as it had been when I'd joined his staff during the administration immediately prior to this one.

Cyan's eyes widened. "That's all he said? Why did he have to talk with you in person, then? Alone? I bet it had something to do with all the commotion outside this morning. Did it? Hey, you must have been outside when it happened, weren't you?"

Henry picked up on Cyan's comment, but she didn't seem to notice her gaffe. "What commotion? You were outside, Ollie?"

I shook my head, "I forgot my keys down by the staff entrance." I hated lying to Henry, but between the president's words and the need to keep my errand secret if we were to pull off our surprise, I didn't think I had much choice.

He smiled. "Maybe you should tie those keys around your neck." He let out a satisfied sigh. "As for the commotion, I'm sure we'll hear more about it later."

Cyan moved closer. "So, what did the president really say?"

"Not much." I pointed to the computer monitor. "President Campbell said he was looking forward to the big dinner tonight. And that he hadn't had breakfast and he's hungry. We should probably get those scrambled eggs started."

"Oh, come on. He must have wanted something. What was it?" Cyan took a deep breath, which, I knew, heralded another slew of questions.

Henry raised his hand, silencing her. "Less talk, more work." To me, he said, "Say no more, Ollie. The president's meals are our first responsibility. Scrambled eggs it is."

We set to work on a second breakfast. The timing was tough because of the official dinner tonight, but it wasn't anything we couldn't handle.

In addition to the scrambled eggs, we prepared bacon—crisp—

wheat and rye toast, fruit, coffee, orange juice, and Henry's Famous Hash Browns. More than just pan-fried potatoes, Henry used his own combination of seasonings that made my mouth water every time he prepared the dish. The president and First Lady were so impressed with the recipe that they insisted we serve them at every official breakfast function.

Henry wielded the frying pan with authority, flipping his special ingredients so they danced like popcorn, sizzling as bits landed back in the searing hot oil. "Work fast, my friends. A hungry president is bad for the country!"

After the meal was plated and sent to the family quarters, we cleaned up the kitchen and began preparations for lunch. Then it was time to pull out the stops as we got the official dinner together for India's prime minister. This wasn't as significant an event as a state dinner, where guest lists often topped one hundred, and we were required to pull in a couple dozen temporary assistants to help. This was a more sedate affair; it required a great deal of effort, but it was certainly manageable for a staff of five.

I'd designed a flavorful menu, and the First Lady, after tasting the samples we provided, had approved. We'd feature some of the best we had to offer: chilled asparagus soup; halibut and basmati rice with pistachio nuts and currants; bibb lettuce and citrus vinaigrette; and one of Marcel's show-stopping desserts. We'd done as much as we could in advance without sacrificing freshness or quality, but the time had come to marshal the troops and get everything in the pipeline for the big dinner.

Eggs Benedict

From Eggsecutive Orders by Julie Hyzy

SERVES 4

8 eggs

4 egg yolks

2 tablespoons cream

Juice of ½ lemon (around 1 tablespoon)

½ teaspoon kosher or sea salt

Pinch cayenne pepper or paprika (optional)

1 cup (2 sticks) butter, melted and still hot

4 English muffins, fork-split, buttered, and toasted

8 slices warm Virginia ham (or Canadian bacon, if you
prefer) cut to fit the muffins

Chopped parsley, for garnish (optional)

Bring a medium saucepan full of salted water to a rolling boil. Reduce heat to a gentle simmer. Crack 1 egg into a small bowl, taking care not to break the yolk. Gently slip the egg into the saucepan, and repeat with 3 more eggs. (You can usually fit 4 eggs at a time in the hot water. Too many, and the eggs won't poach correctly.) Gently coddle to doneness, about 3 minutes, until the whites are set and the yolks remain runny. Remove the eggs from the hot water with a slotted spoon. Set on warmed plate to hold. Repeat with remaining 4 eggs.

MAKE HOLLANDAISE SAUCE:

This blender recipe takes a lot of the angst out of the process of making the sauce the traditional way, which is over a double boiler with a wire whisk. I find it's a lot easier for home cooks to get perfect hollandaise sauce this way. Place egg yolks in a blender container. Add cream, lemon juice, salt, and a pinch of cayenne or paprika (optional, but it adds a nice bite). Cover and pulse on low until blended. Remove the middle insert from the lid, and while continuing to blend on low, slowly and gently add the hot butter to the egg mixture, in a gradual stream. The sauce should thicken and smooth about the time the last of the butter goes in. (The hot butter cooks the egg yolks and the blender emulsifies the lemon juice and melted butter with the yolks.)

On warmed serving dish, top each toasted English muffin half with a warm slice of Virginia ham. Place a poached egg gently on top of the ham. Pour Hollandaise sauce over eggs. Sprinkle with paprika and chopped parsley to garnish. Serve warm.

Note: This recipe sounds a lot more complicated than it is, and it's a restaurant favorite because it used to be a lot harder to make at home. In fact, eggs Benedict used to be a bear to make—especially getting the sauce right. Doing it on the stove, the sauce had a tendency to curdle in inexperienced hands. Thanks to the wonder of modern blenders and a good stove, you should be able to have this on the table in less than 20 minutes.

A Fat-Free, Cheese-Free, Yolk-Free, High-Fiber Omelet

~ From *Eggsecutive Orders* by Julie Hyzy ~

Given that almost every recipe in here is likely to send a cardiologist into palpitations, here's the exception.

SERVES 2

½ cup broccoli florets, cleaned and chopped

1 cup fresh spinach leaves, cleaned and de-stemmed

½ cup fresh mushrooms, thinly sliced

1 plum tomato, chopped

1 green onion, rinsed and thinly sliced

¼ cup fat-free ham, cubed

1½ cups egg substitute

Salt and pepper, to taste

Coat a nonstick skillet with nonstick cooking spray and place over medium-high heat. Add the vegetables and the ham to the skillet. Sauté until the veggies are cooked through, the spinach has wilted, and the broccoli is tender, about 3 to 5 minutes. Remove from heat to a warmed plate and set aside.

Rinse and dry the skillet. Spray again with nonstick cooking spray. Add egg substitute to pan. Roll the pan around, spreading the egg substitute evenly across the skillet surface. Cook over medium heat until bottom is well set, about 2 to 3 minutes. Flip egg in pan to cook other side. Place vegetable-ham mixture on half of the egg's surface. Fold cooked egg round gently over veggies. Slide out of skillet onto warmed plate.

Season with salt and pepper, to taste. Serve warm.

San Simon Frittata

〜 From *Clobbered by Camembert* by Avery Aames 〜

SERVES 4

4 eggs
½ cup Parmesan cheese, shredded
½ teaspoon salt
½ teaspoon white pepper
1 tablespoon plus 2 teaspoons olive oil
1 (4-ounce) turkey sausage, diced
2 teaspoons rosemary
¼ cup red onion, diced
¼ cup scallions, diced
½ cup chopped Roma tomatoes
3 ounces San Simon cheese, sliced (may substitute
　　other cow's milk cheese)

Preheat oven to broil.

Mix eggs, Parmesan cheese, salt, and pepper in a bowl and set aside.

In an 8-inch skillet, heat 1 tablespoon of oil. Toss in diced turkey sausage and rosemary. Sauté on medium-high heat for 3 to 4 minutes. Drain.

Wipe skillet. Add 1 teaspoon of oil. Toss in onion and scallions. Sauté on medium-high heat for 3 to 4 minutes, until tender.

Add turkey sausage and egg mixture.

Cook, using spatula to lift cooked edges and allow uncooked eggs to ooze underneath, 3 to 5 minutes.

In a separate 8-inch skillet (that can be safely put into the oven), heat remaining 1 teaspoon of oil. Place hot-oiled skillet upside down on top of egg mixture skillet. Flip. Cook eggs in new skillet for 2 more minutes.

Pour chopped Roma tomatoes in center of the frittata; spread to edges. Arrange San Simon cheese on top. Broil frittata in oven for 3 to 5 minutes. (Be careful not to burn the cheese.)

Remove from oven (remembering to use a pot holder for hot handle.) Slide frittata onto serving plate.

Pecan Pies and Homicides

by Ellery Adams

After washing her face and brushing the tangles from her hair, Ella Mae descended the stairs. The sound of clanking dishes and the aroma of coffee and bacon drew her into the kitchen.

"I made a pie," Reba said upon seeing her. "Your mama looked like she needed a big dose of protein, so I fixed her a breakfast pie with eggs, cheese, and sausage. Then I added this bacon lattice on top. What do you think?"

Ella Mae looked at the crisscrossed strips of oven-baked bacon and smiled. "Very creative. Can I steal that idea for the pie shop?"

"Let's see how it tastes first." Reba waved in the direction of the sunroom. "Your mama and your coffee are in there. Chewy too. I went over to fetch him after I got up. Hugh was already gone. He made the bed, neat as a pin, but left no signs of havin' been in the lake last night. Nothin' I could find anyway."

"I'll stop by Canine to Five later and try to get a read on him." Ella Mae sighed. "But I can't make Hugh a priority today. I gave the Gaynors a deadline. If Rand Dockery doesn't turn himself in, Verena will have to call a meeting of the Elders. Then they'll have to figure out what to do with him."

Reba cut into the breakfast pie. "How will they punish him if he doesn't show up at the police station? The grove is self-sufficient now. There's no Lady. That means there's no one to penalize folks who break the rules."

Ella Mae had never stopped to consider the negative consequences of injecting the grove with an unwavering source of power. She'd been so caught up with saving her mother that she hadn't imagined she could be making a mistake.

Charmed Bacon-Lattice Breakfast Pie

~ From Pecan Pies and Homicides by Ellery Adams ~

SERVES 8

10 strips black pepper bacon

4 large eggs, beaten

1½ cups half-and-half

1½ cups shredded Colby and Monterey Jack cheese
   (can substitute shredded Cheddar or Swiss)

1 cup breakfast sausage, cooked and crumbled

1 unbaked deep-dish piecrust

Preheat oven to 400° F. Line a baking sheet with parchment paper and create bacon lattice by lining up 5 strips of bacon from top to bottom and then weaving in 5 more strips from side to side (follow same method as making a lattice piecrust). Bake until crisp, approximately 25 minutes. Drain the grease from tray and set aside. Reduce oven to 350° F. In a large bowl, blend the eggs and half-and-half. Add the cheese and sausage crumbles. Pour into the unbaked piecrust. Bake until the eggs are set and a toothpick inserted into the center comes out clean, approximately 1 hour. Remove the breakfast pie from the oven, carefully transfer the bacon lattice from tray to the top of pie, return the pie to oven, and bake for 5 more minutes. Serve warm.

Spinach Quiche

~ From *Eggsecutive Orders* by Julie Hyzy ~

SERVES 6

½ cup butter

3 cloves garlic, smashed, peeled, and finely minced

1 small onion, trimmed, peeled, and finely chopped

1 pint fresh mushrooms, cleaned and thinly sliced

1 (10-ounce) package frozen chopped spinach,
    thawed and drained

4 ounces herbed feta cheese, crumbled

8 ounces good-quality Cheddar cheese, shredded, divided

½ teaspoon kosher or sea salt, or to taste

¼ teaspoon ground black pepper

1 deep-dish piecrust, unbaked

4 eggs

1 cup milk

Preheat oven to 400° F.

Melt butter in a large skillet over medium heat. Add minced garlic and onion. Stir gently and cook until onion is soft and slightly browned on the edges, about 5 minutes. Add mushrooms and stir until warmed through and reduced, about 3 minutes. Add spinach, feta cheese, and half of the Cheddar cheese. Add salt and pepper, to taste.

Place mixture into unbaked pie shell. In a medium bowl, whisk eggs until blended. Add milk, and whisk to combine well. Pour into pie shell over vegetable mixture. Place filled pie shell on cookie sheet to keep it from overflowing.

Place into preheated oven. Reduce oven heat to 375° F. Bake for 20 minutes. Top quiche with remaining Cheddar cheese. Return to oven and bake for an additional 30 to 40 minutes. Quiche is done when the eggs are set and firm in the center.

Remove from oven and let sit for 10 minutes. Serve warm.

Charmed Pancetta and Gruyère Tart

~ From *Pies and Prejudice* by Ellery Adams ~

SERVES 8

Butter and flour for prepping tart pan

1 Charmed Piecrust (recipe makes 2 crusts so you can
    freeze the extra for another time) (page 315)

1 Charmed Egg Wash (page 316)

2 teaspoons vegetable oil

3 ounces pancetta or any other type of bacon,
    cut into small pieces

5 eggs, lightly beaten

½ cup mascarpone cheese, at room temperature

2 cups shredded Gruyère cheese

3 green onions, thinly sliced

½ teaspoon ground pepper

Preheat oven to 400° F. Butter and flour the bottom and sides of a 9-inch tart pan.

Place piecrust in the tart pan. Carefully press crust into the bottom and sides of the pan. Trim excess crust using kitchen scissors. With the tines of a fork, prick the pastry a few times. Using a pastry brush, coat the crust with Charmed Egg Wash. Put the pan on a baking sheet and bake for 10 minutes or until the egg wash has set. Allow the crust to cool.

In a medium skillet, heat the oil. Add the pancetta and cook until brown and crispy (like regular bacon). This will take 8 to 10 minutes. Transfer to a plate covered with a layer of paper towels. Let drain.

In a medium-size mixing bowl, combine the beaten eggs, mascarpone cheese, Gruyère cheese, green onions, pepper, and pancetta. Mix gently. Pour filling into the piecrust and bake until the mixture has set and the top has a nice, golden bark, about 18 to 20 minutes. Cool tart in pan for 15 minutes before removing.

Note: For a meatless tart, substitute mushrooms for the pancetta.

A Spoonful of Murder

by Connie Archer

By the time she reached Snowflake's main street, Lucky's face was numb with cold. She pulled her woolen scarf up to her nose, hoping to reach By the Spoonful, her parents' soup shop, without running into any more old friends and acquaintances. Everyone had been so kind, but whenever condolences were offered, she felt as if she would burst into sobs. She missed her parents terribly. They had always been there for her. She had never considered the day when that would not be true.

The streetlights had already blinked on in the darkening evening, and holiday lights in the shape of large snowflakes hung at each pole all the way down Broadway. Local shops had closed, but the windows of By the Spoonful Soup Shop were brightly lit and fogged from the warmth inside. Lucky stood across the street as if seeing the restaurant for the first time. The old blue-and-yellow neon sign her dad had been so proud of still hung in the front window. For a moment, she imagined her parents, Martha and Louis Jamieson, would be inside. She could rush into the warmth and throw her arms around them, as she did when she was very young.

Her grandfather Jack stood at the cash register now. It was dinnertime, and the simple restaurant was filled to capacity with tourists and locals alike. The menu was a rotating variety of soups, stews and sandwiches, depending on the time of year. Hearty meat-filled soups or thick lentils for winter, lighter ones for the summer. Each soup was served with a generous hunk of crusty bakery bread or ladled into a bread bowl. Tonight's special was an original created by Sage, the Spoonful's talented chef.

Her parents had hired Sage DuBois while Lucky was at college, and his expertise kept the menu delicious and unique. His special tonight was a soup based on yams, potatoes, carrots and red peppers in a creamy broth with white pepper. Lucky had worked up an appetite walking all the way from the cemetery and looked forward to a large bowl of the new soup as soon as she could take a break.

She hadn't intended to stay away from the restaurant so long. Her grandfather was sometimes overwhelmed by the rush of customers and became confused. She couldn't imagine herself taking over the business her parents had left to her, but she also couldn't imagine the end of By the Spoonful either. Her grandfather Jack had made it clear he was only holding on, running the shop until she was ready to take over—if that was what she wanted to do. He had been very patient and hadn't pressured her, but Lucky knew he was waiting for a definite answer. She wondered how much longer she could delay.

French Toast Sandwich

~ From *A Spoonful of Murder* by Connie Archer ~

MAKES 1 SANDWICH

1 egg
⅓ cup milk
2 slices white or whole wheat bread
1 or 2 sliced mushrooms
1 slice Swiss cheese
Worcestershire sauce

Whisk egg in a shallow dish, adding milk to the egg mixture. Dip each slice of bread in the mixture, coating both sides. Using cooking spray or a small amount of butter, place bread slices in a pan, cooking over medium heat until both sides of the bread slices are browned.

Layer mushrooms on one slice, add a layer of cheese, cover with other slice of bread and, flipping over, heat both sides until the cheese has melted. Drizzle Worcestershire sauce over the top.

Jenna's Monte Cristo Sandwich

~ From *Inherit the Word* by Daryl Wood Gerber ~

The Monte Cristo sandwich is a classic. It was one of my mother's all-time favorite sandwiches. She used to serve it for brunch on Sundays. It's such a perfect combination of sweet and savory, and you know, it's not too hard to make, even for me. It looks like it has a lot of ingredients, but don't panic. The whole thing layers together like a regular sandwich. The hardest, or messiest, part is dipping the whole shebang in the egg mixture and setting it in the hot oil. Again, don't panic. It's easy once you get the hang of it. Make sure you have plenty of confectioners' sugar on hand to make it pretty! Savor!

MAKES 2 SANDWICHES

2 eggs

2 tablespoons milk

¼ teaspoon cinnamon

4 slices bread (white or a brioche-style bread works great; gluten-free bread works, too)

1 tablespoon spicy mustard

2 slices cooked turkey

4 slices Swiss cheese

2 slices ham

2 tablespoons butter or vegetable oil (canola preferred)

Confectioners' sugar, for decoration

2 tablespoons jam

In a pie plate, whisk together the eggs, milk, and cinnamon.

To assemble the sandwiches: Place the bread on a cutting board. Spread mustard on each piece of bread. Place turkey on 2 slices of bread. Top the turkey with 2 slices of cheese. Then add the ham. Put the remaining pieces of bread on top.

To cook: On medium-low heat, heat the butter in a large, nonstick skillet. Dip each sandwich into the egg mixture. Turn the sandwich to coat both sides. Set the sandwiches in the skillet. Cover with a lid and cook 3 to 4 minutes, just until the underside begins to brown. *Make sure you don't burn the bread.* Flip the sandwich with a spatula and press down to compress the sandwich. Cook for another 3 to 4 minutes or until the underside begins to brown. If necessary, turn once more and cook until the cheese has melted completely, about 1 to 2 minutes.

Transfer to a plate, and sprinkle with confectioners' sugar. Cut diagonally and serve with a spoonful of jam alongside.

Pancakes with Gouda and Figs

~ From *Clobbered by Camembert* by Avery Aames ~

SERVES 2

Grandmother's Pancake Mix (see recipe below)
Maple syrup
4 ounces Gouda cheese, cut into 12 to 16 very thin slices
4 to 6 figs, stems removed, and then sliced

Make the pancake mix according to directions. Warm the maple syrup by heating a pot filled with water. Set the syrup carafe into the boiling water. Turn off the heat.

Heat griddle to 400° F. After flipping the pancakes, top each with a piece of Gouda cheese. Cook until the underside of the pancake is desired color of golden brown.

Set the pancakes on 2 plates. Top with sliced figs. Drizzle with warm maple syrup.

Grandmother's Pancake Mix

MAKES 16 PANCAKES

1¼ cups milk
1 egg
½ teaspoon salt
3½ teaspoons baking powder

1 tablespoon sugar

4 tablespoons butter, melted

1½ cups flour

Mix together the milk, egg, salt, baking powder, sugar, and butter. Blend in the flour until smooth.

Heat a frying pan or griddle over medium heat. Using a large spoon or ladle, pour about ¼ cup pancake mix onto the griddle. Let pancake heat to warm brown and flip with a spatula. Brown the other side. Serve hot.

Note: This recipe is not gluten-free. To make it gluten-free, substitute 1½ cups gluten-free flour of your choice and keep the rest of the ingredients the same.

Maggie Tremont's German Strawberry-Apple Pancakes

∽ From *Town in a Strawberry Swirl* by B. B. Haywood ∽

MAKES ABOUT 8 PANCAKES

1 cup milk

3 eggs

¾ cup flour

3 tablespoons sugar

2 tablespoons butter

1 medium to large apple, peeled, cored, and chopped

6 to 8 medium-size strawberries, hulled and chopped

¼ teaspoon cinnamon

Preheat the oven to 375° F.

In a bowl, whisk together the milk, eggs, flour, and 2 tablespoons of the sugar. Set aside.

In a large ovenproof skillet, melt the butter over medium-high heat.

Add the apple, strawberries, and cinnamon, and the remaining 1 tablespoon of sugar.

Reduce the heat to medium and cook, stirring often, for 2 to 3 minutes, until the fruit is soft.

Remove the pan from the heat.

Pour the batter from the bowl over the fruit mixture in the pan.

Place the pan in the oven.

Bake for 30 minutes, or until the pancake is light brown and fluffy.

Cut the pancake into wedges and serve.

If you do not have an ovenproof pan, put the cooked fruit into a casserole dish or pie pan, pour the batter over the fruit, and bake the same as above.

This is a wonderful recipe for brunch!

Skillet Potatoes

<hr>

~ From *If Mashed Potatoes Could Dance* by Paige Shelton ~

Skillet potatoes are like most breakfast potatoes you get at restaurants, but they aren't hash browns, which are, of course, a whole different shredded idea. I make these with bacon and cheese most of the time, but once in a while, I just make the potatoes. Notice I don't peel the potatoes.

SERVES 4 TO 5

4 slices bacon

1 onion, chopped

2 pounds Yukon Gold potatoes, thinly sliced

1 cup shredded Cheddar cheese

6 tablespoons sour cream

Cook bacon in a skillet over medium heat. Once it's crispy, remove the bacon from the pan, drain it on some paper towels, then crumble it and set it aside.

Keep about 3 tablespoons of the bacon grease in the skillet. (I've found that the 4 slices of bacon usually render just the right amount of fat for this recipe!)

Add the onions to the skillet and cook for about 5 minutes, stirring frequently. Stir in the potatoes and cover the skillet.

Cook covered on medium-low heat for 20 to 25 minutes, until the potatoes are tender, stirring occasionally.

Top with the cheese and crumbled bacon. Cook covered for 1 to 2 minutes more.

Serve topped with sour cream.

Breads, Muffins, and Other Baked Goodies

EXCERPT FROM *HAIL TO THE CHEF* BY JULIE HYZY.....................33

Cinnamon Bread.....................37

Holly Holliday's Pumpkin Chocolate Chip Bread.....................39

Betts's Best Banana Bread.....................40

EXCERPT FROM *TOWN IN A BLUEBERRY JAM* BY B. B. HAYWOOD.........41

Blueberry Gingerbread.....................43

Cliff's Pear Bread.....................45

Zucchini Bread.....................46

EXCERPT FROM *BRAN NEW DEATH* BY VICTORIA HAMILTON.....................47

Golden Acres Banana-Bran Muffins.....................49

Clare Cosi's Doughnut Muffins.....................51

EXCERPT FROM *A BREW TO A KILL* BY CLEO COYLE.....................53

Clare Cosi's Classic Coffee Cake Muffins with Streusel
Topping and Vanilla Glaze.....................54

Jake's Favorite Blueberry-Orange Muffins.....................57

EXCERPT FROM *MUFFIN BUT MURDER* BY VICTORIA HAMILTON.........58

Fit for the King Muffins (Banana–Peanut Butter–Chocolate
Chip Muffins).....................60

Bacon-Cheddar Muffins.....................62

Savory Herb Muffins.....................63

EXCERPT FROM *IF BREAD COULD RISE TO THE OCCASION*
BY PAIGE SHELTON.....................64

Gram's Instant Miracle Rolls..65

Rosemary Biscuits 66

Gluten-Free Popovers 67

Old-Fashioned Crumpets 68

Easy Cream Scones 69

    EXCERPT FROM *SWEET TEA REVENGE* BY LAURA CHILDS 70

Dandy Devonshire Cream 72

    EXCERPT FROM *SHADES OF EARL GREY* BY LAURA CHILDS 73

Haley's Lemon Curd 75

Cherry Scones 76

Hail to the Chef

by Julie Hyzy

I pulled biscuits out of the freezer, set them on the counter, and fired up one of the ovens. Sean hadn't struck me as despondent or suicidal. And yet the Secret Service had mentioned a note. That made no sense.

So acute was my concentration on Sean, and on preparing breakfast for what would be a long, grueling day for the First Family, that I didn't notice one of the butlers come in until he was almost next to me.

My head jerked up. "Red!"

His pale eyes widened in alarm. "I'm sorry," he said, taking a step back.

Red had been here forever, and though the man was spry, he'd crossed the line to elderly at least a decade ago. Along the way he'd lost the hair color that had given him his nickname. I hadn't meant to shake him. Waving off his apology, I pointed up, toward the residence. "How is she?"

"Bad times here," he said, with a sad shake of his head. "And no one is stopping long enough to grieve."

My puzzled expression encouraged him to explain.

"The president returned last night. He'll be taking breakfast early with his wife," he said. "Then he will depart for a meeting in New York."

I hoped that didn't mean the First Lady would be left alone at a time like this. "Is Mrs. Campbell going with him?"

Lines bracketing Red's eyes deepened. "The First Lady will remain in the residence to host the Mother's Luncheon this afternoon."

"What?"

"The luncheon will proceed as scheduled."

This couldn't be right. "But, after the news. After what happened to Sean . . ."

He stopped me with a sigh. "Yes," he said, "the family has much to deal with today. And on top of everything else, Gene Sculka's family is holding his wake tonight."

Dear God, I'd almost forgotten about that. I was about to ask if the president and First Lady were planning to attend, but Red anticipated my question.

"The president will not return to the White House until Saturday. The First Lady has called the Sculka family to pay respects."

I made a mental note to make an appearance myself this evening. But right now only one thing was on my mind. "I thought they would cancel the luncheon."

Red sighed. "Mrs. Campbell doesn't want to disappoint all the women and kids who have flown from all over the country—at their own expense—to be here today."

"But surely people would understand—"

"You know our First Lady."

I did. Selfless to a fault, she was notoriously stubborn but always looking out for the greater good. I admired her—and I hoped to achieve that serenity someday myself. "Well, then, I suppose I'd better move a bit faster here."

Cyan arrived moments later, followed by Bucky, Rafe, Agda, and a few more SBA chefs we'd hired for the day. I was glad I hadn't canceled the extra staff. Even if today's luncheon had been scrapped, we had a great deal of work ahead of us. The holiday season officially began Sunday afternoon—two days from now—when the president and First Lady would attend a presentation at the Kennedy Center. Extra hands in the kitchen were never a waste.

While managing breakfast and cleaning up, we got to work on the afternoon's event. Buffets were so much less stressful than plated dinners—for us, and for the waitstaff. We'd prepared as much as possible ahead of time, but there was still a lot to be done before the guests arrived.

More than two hundred moms and tots were expected, and we'd been careful to include plenty of kid-friendly fare in our offerings. One of the president's favorite sandwiches, peanut butter and banana, was on the menu today. We would offer a choice: served on plain white or on cinnamon bread. In fact, the staff had taken bets on which would be more popular with the kids.

Rafe expertly sliced away the crusts from a peanut-butter-on-white sandwich. "Kids will go for plain, every time."

"Cinnamon tastes better," Cyan said, singsong.

Rafe raised his own voice up an octave, continuing the singsong cadence. "Won't matter if they refuse to try it."

Shaking her head so her ponytail wagged, Cyan slathered peanut butter on yet another slice of cinnamon bread. "They'll try these."

I was happy to hear their chitchat. Although normalcy was not to be expected—not so soon after the two unexpected deaths—any little bit of happiness was worth grabbing.

Cinnamon Bread

From *State of the Onion* by Julie Hyzy

MAKES 2 LOAVES

1 package active dry yeast

¼ cup warm water

2 cups milk (any kind will do nicely—the richness of the dough will
increase as you add fat)

½ cup sugar

½ cup unsalted butter

2 teaspoons salt

1½ tablespoons cinnamon

6 to 7 cups flour

2 eggs, beaten

Cinnamon sugar, for garnish (optional)

Preheat oven to 375° F. Grease 2 standard loaf pans (either 9 × 5 or 8 × 4) and set aside.

Mix the yeast and water in a medium bowl.

While the yeast is proofing, gently heat the milk, sugar, and butter in a saucepan over low to medium heat until the butter melts; do not boil. Remove from heat and set aside.

Sift salt, cinnamon, and 3 cups of flour together into a large bowl. Add the frothy yeast and milk mixtures and beaten eggs to the dry ingredients. Mix until a soft, doughy ball forms. Turn dough out on floured board. Knead until dough is smooth and has the soft and rubbery texture of your earlobe. In the course of this process you may need to add up to 4 more cups of flour to get a nice, springy dough. Knead for 10 minutes.

Cover dough loosely with either a damp towel or greased plastic wrap and leave to rise for 1 hour. Punch down and then divide into two balls of dough. Form into loaves, place into loaf pans, cover, and then leave to rise about 30 minutes, or until doubled in size.

Dust the tops with the cinnamon sugar, if desired, and bake for 35 to 40 minutes. If the loaves start to brown too quickly, cover with foil for the remaining cooking time.

Note: Excellent served buttered for breakfast, or as a base for peanut butter and jelly sandwiches.

Holly Holliday's Pumpkin Chocolate Chip Bread

~ From *Town in a Pumpkin Bash* by B. B. Haywood ~

MAKES 1 LOAF

1½ cups flour

½ cup sugar

½ cup brown sugar

1 teaspoon baking soda

1 cup pumpkin (fresh or canned)

½ cup vegetable oil

2 eggs

¼ cup water or milk

¼ teaspoon nutmeg

½ teaspoon cinnamon

1 cup chocolate chips

½ cup walnuts, chopped (optional)

Preheat the oven to 350° F. Grease a 9 × 5-inch loaf pan and set aside.

Mix together the flour, sugars, and baking soda.

In a second bowl, mix together the pumpkin, oil, eggs, water, and spices.

Combine the pumpkin mixture with the dry mixture.

Add the chocolate chips and nuts.

Bake for 50 to 60 minutes, until a toothpick poked in the center comes out clean.

Take out of the pan and cool on a rack or board.

Holly Holliday made this bread for Candy's birthday every year. Happy fortieth birthday, Candy!

Betts's Best Banana Bread

～ From *If Bread Could Rise to the Occasion* by Paige Shelton ～

Betts has been making this for years. Even Gram admits it's the best banana bread she's ever tasted.

MAKES 1 LOAF

1 cup sugar

⅓ cup margarine or butter, softened

2 eggs

1½ cups mashed ripe bananas (3 to 4 medium—Betts
   uses really ripe bananas)

⅓ cup water

1⅔ cups all-purpose flour

1 teaspoon baking soda

1 teaspoon salt

¼ teaspoon baking powder

Preheat oven to 350° F. Grease bottom only of an 8- or 9-inch loaf pan, and set aside.

Mix the sugar and margarine in a medium bowl. Stir in the eggs until blended. Add the bananas and water and beat with a mixer for 30 seconds.

Stir in the remaining ingredients just until moistened.

Pour into prepared pan.

Bake 55 to 60 minutes for a 9-inch loaf, or 75 minutes for an 8-inch loaf, or until wooden pick inserted in the center comes out clean.

Cool 5 minutes in pan, then loosen the sides of the loaf from the pan and remove the loaf. Cool completely before slicing.

Town in a Blueberry Jam

by B. B. Haywood

Candy Holliday stood in the kitchen of her farmhouse at Blueberry Acres in Cape Willington, Maine, and surveyed her handiwork. She'd cooked herself into a frenzy, and had prepared an impressive array of goodies.

Ready for sale at the town's Blueberry Festival the following day were a dozen large blueberry pies, three dozen mini pies, half a hundred blueberry scones, and an equal number of oversize blueberry cookies—a popular seller with the kids. There were jars upon jars of blueberry jam, blueberry honey, and blueberry syrup, lined up in neat rows like soldiers on parade. Toward the end of the counter were twenty squat jars of blueberry butter, an experiment this year, and more blueberry muffins than she cared to count, neatly packed into battered tins that had once belonged to her mother.

On the floor by the back door were two large cardboard boxes stuffed with a hundred blueberry tie-dyed T-shirts of various sizes, another favorite with festival-goers. Next to those was a smaller box filled with bars of blueberry soap, also a hot seller. Then there were the empty baskets she still had to fill with a variety of carefully arranged homemade products—the Blueberry Acres gift baskets were her most profitable items.

She also had a few dozen pints of fresh blueberries ready to go, though there would be so many of those available at the festival tomorrow that she wasn't counting on selling too many of them. Most tourists preferred something a little more exotic than the pure and simple fruit itself.

And, of course, there was the last batch of pies, still warming on the stovetop. And the chocolate-covered blueberries, which had to be packed into small cellophane packages and tied up with blue and green ribbons. Some of the items still had to be labeled. She had to pack everything up for transport into town in the morning.

She felt exhausted just looking at it all. She had spent the better part of three weeks getting it all together, and there was still so much to do . . .

Blueberry Gingerbread

From *Town in a Blueberry Jam* by B. B. Haywood

Soon to be sold at Melody's Café!

MAKES 1 LOAF

½ cup butter

½ cup dark brown sugar

1 cup molasses

1 egg

2½ cups all-purpose or white whole wheat flour

1 teaspoon baking powder

1 teaspoon ginger

1 teaspoon cinnamon

½ teaspoon salt

1½ cups Maine wild blueberries (fresh or dried blueberries only)

1 cup hot water

Preheat oven to 350° F. Grease an 8-inch-square pan and set aside.

In a large bowl, cream together the butter and sugar.

Mix in the molasses.

Stir in the egg.

In a separate bowl, combine the dry ingredients.

Take out 1½ tablespoons of the dry ingredient mixture and add to the blueberries in a measuring cup or small bowl; set aside.

Add the dry ingredients and the hot water alternately to the butter mixture, beating after each addition. Continue beating until mixture is smooth.

Fold in the blueberries.

Bake for 35 minutes, or until a toothpick inserted in the center comes out clean.

Cliff's Pear Bread

~ From *If Bread Could Rise to the Occasion* by Paige Shelton ~

Cliff's favorite!

MAKES 1 LOAF

½ cup vegetable shortening

½ cup packed brown sugar

½ cup sugar

1 egg

2 cups all-purpose flour, sifted

1 teaspoon baking soda

½ teaspoon allspice

¾ teaspoon cinnamon

½ teaspoon salt

2 cups chopped canned pears, drained

Preheat oven to 350° F. Grease a 9 × 5-inch loaf pan, and set aside.

Cream the shortening and sugars. Add the egg and beat well.

Sift together the flour, baking soda, allspice, cinnamon, and salt. Blend into the shortening mixture.

Stir in the pears. This is a crumbly batter, but that's okay.

Pour into prepared loaf pan. Bake for 1 hour.

Cool completely in pan before removing.

Zucchini Bread

From *A Roux of Revenge* by Connie Archer

MAKES 1 LOAF

- 1½ cups flour
- 1 cup dark brown sugar
- ½ teaspoon baking soda
- ¼ teaspoon salt
- ¼ teaspoon baking powder
- 1 teaspoon cinnamon
- ¼ teaspoon nutmeg
- 1 cup peeled, shredded zucchini
- ¼ cup vegetable oil
- 1 egg
- 1 cup water
- ¼ teaspoon shredded lemon zest
- ¼ cup chopped walnuts

Preheat oven to 350° F. Grease an 8 × 4-inch loaf pan, and set aside.

In mixing bowl, combine flour, sugar, baking soda, salt, baking powder, cinnamon, and nutmeg. Mix well. Add shredded zucchini, oil, and egg. Mix well and add 1 cup of water to the mixture. Stir the batter until completely mixed and add the lemon zest and chopped walnuts, stirring again to evenly distribute the walnuts.

Pour the batter into a prepared loaf pan. Bake for 60 minutes or till a knife inserted at center comes out clean. Remove from pan and cool on a wire rack. Once cooled, wrap and store the bread overnight in the refrigerator before slicing.

Bran New Death

by Victoria Hamilton

"Oh, you've started her up now! Prepare to be lectured. You've just enrolled in Muffins 101."

"Huh?" he said, looking back and forth between us.

I bit my lip to keep from laughing at the tragic look on my friend's face. She's just heard the lecture once too often, I thought. "You go feed your bunny, or something, while I tell McGill all about it." I got the other three sets of my brand-new muffin tins out of the bag—I think I had wiped out the town of Autumn Vale where muffin tins were concerned—and washed them, then dried and lined them with paper cups as I answered McGill. "It's easy. Most people think that if it's frosted or iced, then it's a cupcake, but that's not so. Some muffins can be frosted, too. Instead, think of the difference between a banana cake and a loaf of banana bread."

"Okay," he said. "I got that."

"Well, with the batter of a banana cake, you can make cupcakes, and with the batter for banana bread, you can make banana muffins. You can do the same with any cake batter or quick-bread batter."

"Ah!" he said, his eyes lighting up. "Cakes are to cupcakes as, uh, what did you call it?"

"Quick bread," Shilo, who had not gone to feed Magic, filled in.

"Right . . . cakes are to cupcakes as quick breads are to muffins!"

"Correct!" I scanned my pile of ingredients. I hadn't been able to find bran at the general store, so I'd bought a big box of bran cereal. "In general, muffins are denser and a little less sweet. They're a whole lot easier and less finicky than cupcakes, let me tell you, but right now I'd give my right arm for my cookbooks." Why hadn't I thrown them in the car instead of in a bin at the self-storage? Because I hadn't foreseen a retirement home full of seniors needing bran muffins.

"Well, here goes."

"Feel free to experiment on me," McGill said. "But right now, I'd better get back to work."

Golden Acres
Banana-Bran Muffins

~ From *Bran New Death* by Victoria Hamilton ~

MAKES 12 MUFFINS

1½ cups bran flake cereal

1 cup (2 to 3 large) mashed ripe bananas

½ cup milk

1 egg

3 tablespoons vegetable or canola oil

1 cup all-purpose flour

¼ cup sugar

2 teaspoons baking powder

½ teaspoon baking soda

⅛ teaspoon ground nutmeg

¼ teaspoon cinnamon

¼ cup chopped pecans (optional)

Preheat oven to 400° F. Grease or paper line muffin cups. If greasing, use cooking spray.

Combine cereal, banana, milk, egg, and oil in a bowl, and mix well. Let stand at least 10 to 15 minutes, stirring occasionally to break up cereal.

Combine flour, sugar, baking powder, baking soda, spices, and nuts (if using) in a separate bowl.

Add flour mixture all at once to cereal mixture, stirring until just moistened.

Divide evenly among prepared muffin cups.

Bake 20 to 25 minutes until toothpick poked in center comes out clean, or until muffin springs back when top is pushed down.

Clare Cosi's Doughnut Muffins

~ From *Roast Mortem* by Cleo Coyle ~

Tender and sweet, these muffins taste like an old-fashioned cake doughnut, the kind you'd order at a diner counter with a hot, fresh cuppa joe. They'll pair beautifully with your favorite coffee, too.

MAKES 12 MUFFINS

FOR THE BATTER

¾ cup (1½ sticks) unsalted butter, softened

1 cup white, granulated sugar

2 large eggs, lightly beaten with fork

1 cup whole milk

2½ cups all-purpose flour

2½ teaspoons baking powder

¼ teaspoon baking soda

¼ teaspoon salt

½ teaspoon ground nutmeg

FOR THE CINNAMON TOPPING

½ cup white, granulated sugar

1 teaspoon ground cinnamon

2 tablespoons butter, melted

Step 1—Prepare the batter: Preheat the oven to 350° F. Using an electric mixer, cream the butter and sugar until fluffy. Add in the eggs and milk and continue mixing. Stop the mixer. Sift in the flour, baking powder, baking soda, salt, and nutmeg and mix only enough to combine ingredients. Do not overmix at this stage or you will develop the gluten in the batter and toughen the muffins.

Step 2—Bake: Line cups in muffin pan with paper holders. Fill each up to the top. Bake for 15 to 25 minutes, or until the muffins are lightly brown. Remove muffins quickly from pan and cool on a wire rack. (Muffins that remain in a hot pan may end up steaming, and the bottoms may become tough.)

Step 3—Prepare the topping: Mix together the sugar and cinnamon to create the cinnamon topping. Brush the tops of the cooling muffins with the melted butter and dust with the cinnamon topping.

EXCERPT FROM

A Brew to a Kill

by Cleo Coyle

Matt had kindled a fire in our shop's brick hearth, and I was glad to see it. The night breeze off the Hudson had grown colder, and the crackling flames warmed my skin and spirit.

When it was time to close, we cleaned and restocked, secured the outdoor tables, and bid the last of our customers good night. Then I locked the entrance, dimmed the lights, and shut our wall of French doors tighter than a Gallic fortress.

Now Matt and I were alone in the coffeehouse, just like the old days. He waved me over to the espresso bar, and I weaved through the tables and chairs of our darkened shop.

Suddenly I couldn't stop appreciating how sturdy the Blend's wood planks felt beneath me, how vivid the flickering firelight appeared, how darkly sweet the shop's beans smelled.

When Death rattles your windows, jams a foot in your door, something cracks you open. Colors seem brighter, angles sharper, noises louder. Quinn attributed this sort of thing to adrenaline. But he was a street-hardened detective. With me it was something more. . . .

Clare Cosi's Classic Coffee Cake Muffins with Streusel Topping and Vanilla Glaze

～ From *A Brew to a Kill* by Cleo Coyle ～

These truly are classic muffins, and they're especially delicious paired with coffee. Clare was only too happy to share a fresh-baked batch of them with Madame at the story's end, right before she hopped on a train to visit her beloved Mike in D.C.

MAKES 12 MUFFINS

MUFFINS

1½ cups Streusel (Crumb) Topping (page 56)

½ cup (1 stick) butter, softened

½ cup sugar

½ cup light brown sugar

¾ teaspoon salt

½ teaspoon cinnamon

1½ teaspoons vanilla extract

2 large eggs, lightly beaten with fork

¾ cup sour cream

¼ cup brewed coffee or espresso,
    cooled (see Note, below)

2 cups all-purpose flour

1½ teaspoons baking powder

½ teaspoon baking soda

(OPTIONAL) VANILLA GLAZE
2 tablespoons butter
1 cup confectioners' sugar
½ teaspoon vanilla extract (for a whiter glaze, use clear vanilla)
1 tablespoon milk (more or less)

Step 1—Preheat, prep pans, mix streusel ingredients: First make the streusel filling and topping (recipe follows). Now preheat your oven to 350° F and place paper liners in 12 muffin cups.

Step 2—One-bowl mixing method: In a large bowl, use an electric mixer to cream the softened butter and sugars. When light and fluffy, beat in the salt, cinnamon, vanilla, eggs, sour cream, and cooled coffee or espresso. Continue beating for another minute. Stop the mixer and measure in the flour. Sprinkle the baking powder and baking soda over the flour. Mix everything until you have a batter that is smooth, but do not overmix or you'll develop the gluten in the flour and your muffins will be tough instead of tender.

Step 3—Layer muffin cups and bake: You will now need the streusel topping that you prepared ahead. Into your paper-lined muffin cups, drop a generous dollop of batter. Sprinkle streusel onto the batter and top with more batter. Finish with a generous sprinkling of streusel. Bake for 18 to 20 minutes. Muffins are done when a toothpick inserted comes out with no wet batter clinging to it. Remove from oven and take muffins out of the hot pan promptly or the bottoms may steam and toughen.

Step 4 (Optional)—Glaze the cooled muffins: In a small saucepan, over medium-low heat, melt the butter. Sift in the confectioners' sugar (or sift the sugar first and then add). When all of the sugar is melted into the butter, remove from heat and stir in vanilla. Finally stir in the milk, a little at a time, until the glaze is the right consistency to drizzle over the muffins. To finish the muffins, dip a fork in the warm glaze mixture and drizzle it in a back-and-forth motion over the cooled muffin tops.

Note: Whole milk or buttermilk (regular or light) may be substituted for the coffee.

Streusel (Crumb) Topping for Any Muffin or Coffee Cake

MAKES ABOUT 2 CUPS OF STREUSEL

¾ cup all-purpose flour
½ cup light brown sugar
¼ cup white, granulated sugar
1 teaspoon cinnamon
5 tablespoons butter (unsalted is best), cubed
⅛ teaspoon table salt

In a food processor: Place all ingredients in the processor and pulse until you see coarse crumbs.

By hand: Using your hands and/or a fork or pastry blender, work the butter into the dry ingredients until you see coarse crumbs. Store any extra in the refrigerator.

Jake's Favorite
Blueberry-Orange Muffins

~ From *If Bread Could Rise to the Occasion* by Paige Shelton ~

This is a really easy recipe, and fresh blueberries make it a perfect treat.

MAKES 18 TO 24 MUFFINS

3 cups all-purpose flour
4 teaspoons baking powder
¼ teaspoon baking soda
¾ cup sugar
1½ teaspoons salt
2 cups blueberries
2 eggs
¾ cup milk
½ cup butter, melted
1 tablespoon grated orange peel
½ cup orange juice
1½ tablespoons lemon juice

Preheat oven to 425° F. Grease muffin tins, and set aside.

Sift together the flour, baking powder, baking soda, sugar, and salt. Add the blueberries and toss until coated.

In another bowl, mix the remaining ingredients. Pour the liquid mixture into the dry ingredients, and stir.

Fill greased muffin tins two-thirds full. Bake for 20 minutes.

Let cool in muffin tins for 5 minutes and then remove. Serve.

Muffin but Murder

by Victoria Hamilton

The next day was going to be a busy one. They were having a Halloween party at Golden Acres, and I was supplying treats for it, as was Binny. I was also supplying some cookie-and-square platters to a meeting at the Brotherhood of the Falcon meeting hall, which was going to be a new client for me. I awoke early and baked a few dozen muffins as well as several batches of cookies, chocolate chip and peanut butter. I made lemon squares, too, a simple and delicious addition for those strange beasts who don't like chocolate or peanut butter.

I actually had a new muffin recipe that was so good, it was sinful. I worked it out to honor Hubert Dread, one of the old guys at Golden Acres who had told me a long story about his meeting with "the King" in some kind of undercover operation. He claimed that Elvis was actually an undercover agent for the FBI. It was clearly one of Hubert's highly embroidered and fanciful tales, but fun. My own knowledge of Elvis, which was sketchy, related mostly to his food preferences; I knew he loved peanut butter and banana sandwiches. So I baked a couple dozen Fit for the King muffins, which were peanut butter, banana, and chocolate chip. Delectable! I also made a batch of Pecan Pie muffins and, while I was at it, a couple of batches of bran muffins and carrot muffins.

Fit for the King Muffins (Banana-Peanut Butter-Chocolate Chip Muffins)

~ From *Muffin but Murder* by Victoria Hamilton ~

MAKES 12 MUFFINS

1 cup all-purpose flour

½ cup whole wheat flour

1 teaspoon baking soda

1 teaspoon baking powder

½ teaspoon salt

¼ cup sugar

¼ cup brown sugar

¼ cup (½ stick) unsalted butter, softened

2 ripe bananas, mashed

½ cup creamy peanut butter

1 teaspoon vanilla extract

1 egg

1 cup milk chocolate chips

1 tablespoon turbinado sugar

Preheat oven to 375° F. Coat a muffin tin with cooking spray, and set aside.

Mix together the flours, baking soda, baking powder, and salt in a small bowl. In a second bowl beat sugars and softened butter. Add the mashed bananas, peanut butter, vanilla, and egg.

Stir the flour mixture into the banana mixture until just combined;

add ¾ cup of chocolate chips to the batter and mix. Spoon batter evenly into the prepared muffin cups.

Sprinkle the tops of each muffin evenly with the remaining chocolate chips and turbinado sugar.

Bake in preheated oven for 13 to 15 minutes until a tester inserted into the center of a muffin comes out clean.

Remove from the oven and let cool for a few minutes before removing from the tray and placing on a wire rack to finish cooling. Enjoy.

Bacon-Cheddar Muffins

~ From *Bran New Death* by Victoria Hamilton ~

MAKES 12 MUFFINS

½ to 1 pound bacon

⅓ cup bacon drippings

1 egg

¾ cup milk

1¾ cups all-purpose flour (use half all-purpose
    and half whole wheat, if desired)

¼ cup brown sugar

1 tablespoon baking powder

2 cups Cheddar cheese, shredded

Preheat oven to 400° F. Lightly grease a 12-cup muffin tin, and set aside. Cook bacon in a skillet over medium-high heat until crisp.

Remove the bacon from the pan, and drain on paper towels.

Reserve the drippings and measure out ⅓ cup. Once the bacon is cool, crumble it. In a medium mixing bowl, combine the egg, milk, flour, sugar, baking powder, and bacon drippings.

Stir until combined. There will still be some lumps.

Stir in the bacon and cheese until evenly distributed. Divide the batter among the cups of prepared muffin tin.

Bake for about 15 minutes, until golden brown. Remove from the pan and cool or eat warm.

Savory Herb Muffins

From Muffin but Murder by Victoria Hamilton

MAKES 12 MUFFINS

2 cups whole wheat pastry flour, or unbleached all-purpose flour

1 tablespoon baking powder

1 teaspoon baking soda

½ teaspoon salt

1 tablespoon fresh oregano, chopped (or 2 teaspoons dried oregano)

1 tablespoon fresh thyme leaves (or 2 teaspoons dried thyme)

1 tablespoon fresh basil, chopped (or 2 teaspoons dried basil)

2 eggs

1 egg white

1 cup nonfat buttermilk

2 tablespoons mildly flavored vegetable oil or canola oil

2 teaspoons sugar (less if you like)

¼ cup grated Parmesan cheese

Additional oil for muffin tin, or cooking spray

Preheat oven to 400° F. Lightly oil or spray a 12-cup muffin tin, and set aside.

Combine flour, baking powder, baking soda, salt, oregano, thyme, and basil in a large mixing bowl.

In another bowl, combine eggs, egg white, buttermilk, oil, sugar, and Parmesan.

Add the liquid mixture to the flour mixture, stirring briefly, then spoon into prepared muffin cups, filling two-thirds full.

Bake for approximately 25 minutes; check at 20. Let cool slightly, then remove from tins.

If Bread Could Rise to the Occasion

by Paige Shelton

"Come on in, sweetie. We'll figure it out. There's not a thing we Winston women can't handle."

A few moments later we were both sitting on Gram's couch, sipping some of her fresh-brewed iced tea and snacking on some sugar cookies she'd baked recently.

Just sitting on the couch next to her, drinking iced tea and eating sugar cookies, had the same effect it always had. I felt better, perhaps even a little silly about my true concern, but I still had some questions.

"I know it's possible for more than one ghost at a time to come back. I saw that when Sally was here," I said. Gram nodded. "But . . . well, I have a sense that a ghost—Jerome, in fact—is partially here."

Gram's Instant Miracle Rolls

〜 From *If Bread Could Rise to the Occasion* by Paige Shelton 〜

Gram calls these her instant rolls because the dough can be stored, covered, in the refrigerator for several days and used as needed. It seems she always has some of the dough in her fridge. You just never know when you'll need some homemade rolls.

MAKES 3 DOZEN ROLLS

3 (¼-ounce) packages active dry yeast

½ cup warm water

5 cups unsifted self-rising flour

¼ cup sugar

1 teaspoon baking soda

1 cup vegetable shortening

2 cups lukewarm buttermilk

Preheat oven to 325° F.

Dissolve the yeast in warm water and set aside while mixing other ingredients. In a large bowl, mix the flour, sugar, and baking soda. Cut in the shortening. Add the buttermilk and yeast, mixing well.

Cover the dough and chill for 2 hours. Place the dough on a floured cloth, roll out, and cut with a biscuit cutter. Set aside until the dough reaches room temperature.

Bake rolls for 10 to 15 minutes. If desired, brush with melted butter before baking.

Rosemary Biscuits

From A Roux of Revenge by Connie Archer

MAKES 12 BISCUITS

2 cups self-rising flour

½ teaspoon salt

1 teaspoon baking powder

2 tablespoons chopped fresh rosemary or 1 tablespoon
dried rosemary (if using dried rosemary, soak the
leaves in hot water for a few minutes to soften)

¼ cup butter or margarine, melted

⅔ cup milk

1 egg, beaten

Preheat oven to 450° F. Grease a baking tray with a small amount of butter or cooking spray, and set aside.

Mix flour, salt, and baking powder together. Add the chopped rosemary, butter, and milk and mix thoroughly to form a soft dough. Knead the dough lightly on a floured surface. Roll it out to approximately ¾ inch thick, and cut out biscuits with a biscuit cutter. Brush the tops of the biscuits lightly with the beaten egg, and bake for 8 to 10 minutes until golden. Cool the biscuits for a few minutes on a wire rack.

Gluten-Free Popovers

From *To Brie or Not to Brie* by Avery Aames

MAKES 6 POPOVERS

¾ cup tapioca flour

¼ cup potato flour

¼ cup sweet rice flour

1 teaspoon whey powder

½ teaspoon salt

1 cup half-and-half

2 large eggs, room temperature

Preheat oven to 450° F. Liberally grease a popover pan with vegetable oil, and set aside.

Combine tapioca flour, potato flour, sweet rice flour, whey powder, and salt in a small mixing bowl. Combine half-and-half, eggs, and gluten-free flour mixture in a large blender pitcher. (IMPORTANT: Add the items in that specific order.) Blend at high speed for 30 seconds. Scrape down the sides of the pitcher and pulse briefly, 15 seconds. The batter should look like thin pancake batter.

Place popover pan in preheated oven for 3 minutes. Carefully remove pan and fill each popover cup one-half to two-thirds full. Place pan back in oven and bake for about 15 to 20 minutes. Reduce oven temperature to 300° F and bake an additional 5 to 7 minutes, or until the popovers are deep golden brown. Serve warm.

Note: I made a batch using a cupcake tin instead of a popover tin. It doubled the amount of popovers, and you need to cut the baking time to a total of 15 minutes. They cook fast!

BREADS, MUFFINS, AND OTHER BAKED GOODIES

67

Old-Fashioned Crumpets

⌒ From Scones and Bones by Laura Childs ⌒

MAKES ABOUT 14 CRUMPETS

2 teaspoons honey

½ cup warm water

1 tablespoon active dry yeast

2½ cups all-purpose flour

1 teaspoon salt

½ teaspoon baking soda

1½ cups milk

In a large mixing bowl, stir the honey into the warm water. Sprinkle the yeast in and let it sit for about 5 minutes, until it bubbles. Stir in the flour, salt, baking soda, and milk. Cover and let sit for 30 minutes in a warm place. Grease a frying pan as well as several round cookie cutters or biscuit cutters. Place the cutters in the pan and preheat over medium-low heat. Pour 2 to 4 tablespoons of batter into each cutter and cook until set, about 10 minutes. When the top is full of holes, the crumpet is ready to turn. Now carefully turn the crumpet and brown the other side for about 1 minute. Repeat the process until all of the batter is used up. Serve warm with butter and jam, or slice the crumpets and fill with chicken salad.

Note: These are also known as griddle scones.

Easy Cream Scones

~ From *Shades of Earl Grey* by Laura Childs ~

MAKES 8 TO 10 SCONES

1 cup all-purpose flour

3 teaspoons baking powder

½ teaspoon salt

¼ cup (½ stick) unsalted butter, chilled

2 eggs, beaten

½ cup cream

2 tablespoons sugar

Preheat oven to 375° F.

Sift flour, then add baking powder and salt and cut butter into dry mixture. Combine eggs and cream and add to dry mixture. Pat to ¾ inch thick. Cut in squares or triangles, sprinkle with sugar, and bake until lightly brown, about 20 minutes. Serve hot with jam or preserves.

Sweet Tea Revenge

by Laura Childs

"Great," said Theodosia. She was frantically busy and didn't have time to drop everything and take a look this instant. So she said, "How about you sit down and have some lunch first?"

Glass narrowed his eyes. "You really mean it? Usually you're trying to give me the bum's rush."

"I don't do that," said Theodosia. She grabbed his arm and steered him over to a vacant table in the corner, where she hoped he wouldn't be too intrusive. "You relax here and I'll be back with some scones and sandwiches."

"Jeez, thanks," said Glass.

"Haley," said Theodosia, as she squirted around the doorway and into the kitchen, "I need a quick plate for Bill Glass."

"What?" said Haley. "What's that jerk doing here?"

"He took photos the day of Delaine's wedding," said Theodosia. "He's going to let me look at them."

"Oh."

"Just throw a scone and a couple of sandwiches on a plate; that'll be good enough."

"Hold everything," said Haley. "If we're going to do this, we have to do it properly." She mounded a citrus salad on a plate, then added a scone, two sandwich wedges, and a brownie bite.

"Perfect," said Theodosia.

"Wait," said Haley, as Theodosia snatched it up. "What about a cup of Devonshire cream, too?"

"No. We don't want to make him feel *that* welcome."

Dandy Devonshire Cream

~ From Sweet Tea Revenge by Laura Childs ~

MAKES 2 CUPS

8 ounces heavy whipping cream
1 tablespoon sour cream
1 teaspoon confectioners' sugar

Beat the whipping cream for 2 to 3 minutes, until stiff. Mix in the sour cream and confectioners' sugar. Serve as a topping for your favorite scones.

Shades of Earl Grey

by Laura Childs

H aley cast an appraising eye at the yellow froth that bubbled in the top pan of her double boiler. It looked good, she decided, was sticking together nicely. Grabbing a wire whisk, she added the last of the sugar and lemon zest, then continued to whisk the mixture as it cooked. Finally, when her concoction began to thicken, she removed the pan from the stove and began to add soft fresh cream butter, feeding it in a little at a time.

"My goodness, Haley," marveled Drayton as he stepped into the kitchen, "it smells absolutely divine in here. What magic are you whipping up this morning?"

She held up the pan for him to see. "Lemon curd. And it *does* smell wonderful, doesn't it?"

"You're making *real* lemon curd?" he asked in amazement.

"Sure. It's a snap, really. Just four simple ingredients. Eggs, lemon, sugar, butter."

"Yes, but you have to know exactly what to *do* with the ingredients. And it's not just proportions, the cooking times are quite exacting, too. And then there's the double boiler thing."

"Are you saying I don't know how to make fresh lemon curd?" Haley demanded with a crooked smile.

"No, I'm just saying it's a tricky proposition at best."

"Proof's in the tasting," said Haley as she held up a wooden spoon with a swirl of yellow gracing the end.

Obediently, Drayton tasted the dollop of lemon curd. "Oh my goodness!" he exclaimed. "This *is* good. Sweet but subtly tart, too. Layers of flavor."

"My grandmother's recipe," explained Haley. "And if it's any consolation to you, those are the same things *she* said. Awfully tricky, got to get the proportions just so, and a double boiler is a must."

"But you mastered it," said Drayton, still impressed.

"Of course."

Haley's Lemon Curd

From Shades of Earl Grey by Laura Childs

MAKES ABOUT 2 CUPS

3 large lemons
5 eggs
1 cup sugar
½ cup (1 stick) unsalted butter, softened

Grate the lemon rind and set aside. Squeeze the juice and put into a blender or food processor. Add remaining ingredients and process until smooth. Pour the mixture into the top half of a double boiler. Stir about 10 minutes, until thickened. Stir the mixture with a wire whisk if it appears lumpy. Chill the lemon curd before serving (it thickens as it cools). Spread on scones, crumpets, muffins, or toast.

Cherry Scones

~ From *Lost and Fondue* by Avery Aames ~

MAKES 6 TO 8 SCONES

½ cup dried cherries

¼ cup (½ stick) unsalted butter, softened

⅔ cup milk

2 tablespoons orange juice

⅓ cup sugar

1 egg, beaten

2¼ cups flour

1 teaspoon baking powder

Confectioners' sugar, for garnish

Whipped butter, for serving

Presoak dried cherries in ½ cup hot water for 10 minutes. Drain and discard the water. Meanwhile, preheat oven to 375° F.

Mix butter, milk, juice, sugar, and egg. Add in flour and baking powder. Beat until all flour is incorporated. Add in cherries. Mix well.

Drop large dollops onto a cookie sheet. Bake for 15 to 17 minutes until golden brown.

Dust with confectioners' sugar. Serve with whipped butter.

Soups, Salads, and Sandwiches

EXCERPT FROM *LADLE TO THE GRAVE* BY CONNIE ARCHER 79

Chicken Pot Pie Soup with Dumplings 81

Cauliflower and Cheddar Soup 83

EXCERPT FROM *A ROUX OF REVENGE* BY CONNIE ARCHER 84

Potato-Yam Soup 86

Beet-Mushroom-Barley Soup 87

Wild Mushroom Soup 88

Tomato-Spinach Soup 89

Chilled Mango Summer Soup 90

EXCERPT FROM *A BROTH OF BETRAYAL* BY CONNIE ARCHER 91

Cucumber, Yogurt, and Walnut Soup (Chilled) 93

Caprese Salad 94

Watermelon, Basil, and Feta Salad 95

Erin's Two-Bean and Pesto Salad 96

Chicken, Apricot, and Almond Salad 98

Max's Blue Cheese, Apple, and Walnut Salad 99

Fennel and Blood Orange Salad 101

EXCERPT FROM *INHERIT THE WORD* BY DARYL WOOD GERBER 103

Aunt Vera's Brie, Apple, and Turkey Grilled Cheese 105

Goat Cheese and Pancetta Sandwich 107

Delilah's Grilled Cheese with Bacon and Fig Jam 108

Avocado and Roasted Red Pepper Sandwich 110

Torpedo Sandwich 111

    EXCERPT FROM STEEPED IN EVIL BY LAURA CHILDS 112

Ladybug Tea Sandwiches 114

Ladle to the Grave

by Connie Archer

Sage looked up. "I'm doing an onion soup today, and something kind of different—watercress and pear. What do you think?"

"Sounds very different."

"I thought it might be a good choice for a spring soup. I'm trying to decide on a couple of others. I can do the potato-kale again, I know you like that one, and then maybe a sausage and pasta stew or . . . how about a chicken pot pie soup with dumplings?"

"Mmm. That sounds great, so comforting, chicken pot pie with dumplings. Great range of choices," Lucky replied as she joined them at the tall butcher block and pulled up a stool.

"Okay, I'll do that one today then."

"Save me a big bowl."

"Isn't he brilliant?" Sophie grinned from ear to ear as she turned to Lucky.

"I think he is," Lucky replied seriously.

Sage whacked Sophie's arm gently with a dish towel. "Stop that. I'll get a big head."

Sophie laughed in response. "Just kidding. Don't be so serious."

Sage looked across the worktable at Lucky. "Sophie told me about Brenda and what she had to say last night. I don't like this one bit."

"Me neither," Lucky offered. "No way to prove it but it looks like real down-and-dirty intimidation to me."

"The more I mull this over," Sage said, angrily slamming his knife into the worktable as he chopped, "I really don't want Sophie going back there."

"To the resort?"

Sage nodded.

"Hey." Sophie reached over to touch his shoulder. "I know you worry about me but I'm a big girl. I'm not afraid of those goons."

"One goon. At least from what I've heard. And I'll tell you what I'm gonna do to him if he even says one word to you. If he even looks at you or breathes funny around you. Around either of you," he said, indicating both Sophie and Lucky. "In fact, I may not even wait for him to make a move. Maybe I'll just have a word with him now."

Chicken Pot Pie
Soup with Dumplings

~ From *Ladle to the Grave* by Connie Archer ~

SERVES 4

1 large or 2 small skinless boneless chicken breasts

4 cups chicken broth or bouillon

4 carrots, peeled and sliced

4 celery sticks, chopped

1 medium onion, chopped

2 cups frozen peas

¼ cup half-and-half (or milk)

Dumplings (see recipe below)

Chop chicken breasts into small, bite-size pieces, add to large pot with chicken broth, carrots, celery, and onion. Cook over medium heat for 15 minutes or until carrots and celery are tender. Add peas and cook 1 minute more. Add half-and-half and stir. Prepare dumplings and reheat soup, drop dough into the bubbling soup, and cover. Cook 10 to 15 minutes more, until dumplings are cooked.

DUMPLINGS

⅔ cup all-purpose flour

2 tablespoons chopped parsley

1 teaspoon baking powder

¼ teaspoon dried thyme

⅛ teaspoon salt

¼ cup milk

2 tablespoons vegetable oil

In a bowl, mix flour, parsley, baking powder, thyme, and salt. In a separate bowl, mix milk and oil, and pour into flour mixture. Stir with a fork until combined.

Cauliflower and Cheddar Soup

From Muffin but Murder by Victoria Hamilton

SERVES 6 TO 8

1 medium head cauliflower, broken in florets

1 medium onion, chopped

2 cups chicken broth (homemade or commercial)

2 tablespoons butter

2 tablespoons all-purpose flour

3 cups milk

2 cups (8 ounces) shredded Cheddar cheese

1 tablespoon dried parsley flakes

1 teaspoon salt

¼ teaspoon ground nutmeg

⅛ teaspoon pepper

In a large saucepan, combine the cauliflower, onion, and chicken broth. Cover and cook over medium heat until the vegetables are tender.

Meanwhile, in a medium saucepan, melt butter; stir in flour until smooth. Gradually add milk. Cook and stir until bubbly. Cook, stirring, for 2 to 3 minutes longer, or until thickened.

Reduce heat; add cheese and seasonings. Pour into cauliflower mixture.

Simmer slowly for 30 minutes: do not boil! Serve with Savory Herb Muffins (page 63).

A Roux of Revenge

by Connie Archer

Barry looked up. "What do you have for specials today, Lucky?"

"We have three new soups—Sage has a pumpkin rice with Persian spices, he tells me. I haven't tried it yet myself, but it smells delicious. And a zucchini leek with potatoes, and a beet mushroom and barley soup. I've tried that one, I really love it."

"Hmm. I'll have to sample every one of those this week," Barry said. "We're going over to the Harvest Festival later. I want to pick up some vegetables from the farmers' market but I'll be sure to come back for lunch. Make sure you save me a bowl of that pumpkin soup today."

"I will, and Jack should be back by then." Lucky turned back to the counter. Janie was staring out the window again. Lucky walked closer and stood behind her. The same man stood under the awning across the street. He had disappeared for a short while and now was back.

"You're right. He does seem to be around a lot," Lucky whispered.

Janie had lost her father quite suddenly only four months earlier, just as she was about to graduate from high school. Doug Leonard had been a kindly man who adored his only child. When he died of a massive coronary, Janie was at first inconsolable. Lucky felt a deep empathy for the girl, especially since her own parents had also been taken in an equally sudden fashion. Given Janie's youth, she knew how much more difficult the loss must have been. Lucky tried to always do her best to look out for Janie and make sure she was on an even keel.

"I wonder who he is," Lucky said.

Janie, a troubled look on her face, didn't answer. She turned away from the window and hurried into the kitchen.

Potato-Yam Soup

∽ From *A Spoonful of Murder* by Connie Archer ∽

SERVES 4

1 red pepper

4 carrots

2 large potatoes

1 yam

4 cups chicken stock or 4 cubes of chicken bouillon

½ teaspoon white pepper

½ cup heavy cream

Dash of paprika

Remove seeds from red pepper, and chop pepper into cubes. Place pepper cubes in soup pot, cover with water, and simmer for 10 minutes. Peel and slice carrots and add to pot. Peel potatoes and yam, cut into cubes, and add to pot. Add chicken stock to cover vegetables. Bring to a boil and reduce heat. Let simmer for 20 minutes. Add white pepper and stir. Potatoes should be quite soft. Continue stirring until potatoes have softened completely and soup is thickened. Add cream and stir again. Serve with a dash of paprika in each bowl.

Beet-Mushroom-Barley Soup

~ From *A Roux of Revenge* by Connie Archer ~

SERVES 4

1 teaspoon olive or vegetable oil

½ medium onion, chopped

6 mushrooms, sliced

4 cups chicken broth

3 beets, peeled and cubed

1 apple, peeled and cubed

½ cup pearl barley, uncooked

½ cup crumbled feta cheese, for garnish

In a large pot, heat olive oil over medium heat. Sauté chopped onion and sliced mushrooms for five minutes or until mushrooms and onions are tender.

Add chicken broth. Add the beets, apple cubes, and barley to the pot. Bring to a boil, reduce heat, and simmer for 20 minutes. Remove from heat and let the soup sit for 30 minutes, making sure barley is thoroughly softened.

Garnish each bowl with crumbled feta cheese.

Wild Mushroom Soup

~ From *A Spoonful of Murder* by Connie Archer ~

SERVES 4

2 cups dried porcini mushrooms

1 cup warm water

2 tablespoons olive oil

2 leeks, finely sliced

2 shallots, chopped

1 clove garlic, chopped

8 ounces fresh wild mushrooms

5 cups vegetable stock

½ teaspoon dried sage

Salt and ground black pepper, to taste

½ cup light cream

Fresh thyme, for garnish

Add dried porcini to 1 cup warm water and soak for 30 minutes. Remove from the liquid and finely chop, reserving the liquid for later.

Heat oil in large pot over medium heat. Add leeks, shallots, and garlic, cooking for 5 minutes, stirring until softened. Chop fresh mushrooms and add to pan. Stir mixture over medium heat for 5 more minutes. Add vegetable stock and bring mixture to boil. Add the porcini mushrooms, sage, and reserved mushroom soaking liquid. Season with salt and pepper, to taste.

Simmer gently for 20 minutes, stirring occasionally.

Allow soup to cool for 15 minutes, then puree soup in food processor or with an immersion blender. Stir in cream and reheat gently. Garnish with a sprig of thyme.

Tomato-Spinach Soup

From A Spoonful of Murder by Connie Archer

SERVES 4

2 cups jumbo pasta shells
1 tablespoon olive oil
½ medium onion, coarsely chopped
1 clove garlic, chopped
1½ pounds tomatoes (or substitute 1 [16-ounce] can
    crushed tomatoes)
6 carrots, peeled and chopped
3 cups frozen or fresh spinach
2 tablespoons dried oregano
2 tablespoons dried basil (or 6 fresh shredded
    basil leaves are even tastier)
6 cups vegetable broth
Salt and pepper, to taste
½ cup grated Parmesan cheese, for serving

Bring salted water to boil in a large pot. Add jumbo pasta shells to the boiling water with a few drops of olive oil. Stir and lower heat slightly. When pasta is only slightly al dente, drain and set aside.

In same pot, heat olive oil over medium heat. Sauté the onion and garlic for 5 minutes, then add the tomatoes, carrots, spinach, oregano, and basil. Add vegetable broth to the mixture. Bring to a boil, lower heat, and simmer for 20 minutes. Ladle soup over the pasta shells and serve with grated Parmesan cheese for garnish.

Chilled Mango Summer Soup

~ From Steeped in Evil by Laura Childs ~

SERVES 4

2 mangos, peeled, seeded, and diced

¼ cup sugar

1 lemon, zested and juiced

1½ cups cream (or half-and-half)

Place mangos, sugar, lemon juice, lemon zest, and cream into a blender or food processor. Cover and whip until smooth and creamy. Serve chilled.

A Broth of Betrayal

by Connie Archer

A family approached with their bill in hand. Jack smiled at them and rang up their charges. Lucky went to the counter and glanced at the blackboard, where Sage had listed his specials for the day. There were three different soups, one hot and two chilled, in deference to the heat. Her favorite salad was on the menu today too—romaine with thinly sliced red onions, small cubes of sweet potato and apple with caramelized walnuts, served with a sun-dried tomato vinaigrette dressing. Her stomach growled in response.

Jack must have read her mind. He called over to her, "Have you eaten anything today?"

Lucky had to think a minute before she replied. "Just a piece of toast this morning, I guess."

"And to think you try to baby me! Sit right over there at the counter. I'll bring you one of those salads."

Janie finished her break and took over the cash register while Jack put together a salad for Lucky. He served it to her at the counter with a flourish and slipped another CD into the player. It was soothing music, a new age kind of synthesizer. She dove into the salad, eating ravenously. Jack returned to his seat by the cash register, and Janie slipped onto the stool next to Lucky.

"I'm going on one of the search parties tomorrow, as soon as Jack's back. No news?"

Lucky shook her head. "Charlie's been taken care of. Flyers are posted everywhere. It's on the web. The news media is picking it up. Sophie and I are starting very early tomorrow by car. We're going to search every street, road, dirt path and byway we can find for Elizabeth's car. And we'll just keep searching. I can't think what else to do."

"You're right. But try to stay calm. We're all on edge now after what happened to Harry. I just want Nate to catch whoever did that to him." Janie placed a comforting hand on Lucky's shoulder and rose from her stool.

Cucumber, Yogurt, and Walnut Soup (Chilled)

~ From *A Broth of Betrayal* by Connie Archer ~

SERVES 4

1 cucumber
½ clove garlic
½ teaspoon salt
1 cup cooked white rice
1½ cups coarsely chopped walnuts
1 teaspoon walnut or sunflower oil
2 cups plain yogurt
1 cup cold water
2 teaspoons lemon juice
Fresh dill sprigs

Cut cucumber in half lengthwise and remove seeds, and peel one half of the cucumber. Dice both the peeled and unpeeled cucumber and set aside. Blend garlic and salt together in a food processor.

Add cooked rice, peeled cucumber, and 1 cup of chopped walnuts to food processor and blend again. Transfer the mixture to a large bowl. Slowly add the walnut or sunflower oil, stir, then mix in yogurt and unpeeled cucumber. Add the cold water and lemon juice to the mixture.

Pour the soup into chilled soup bowls to serve. Garnish with remainder of chopped walnuts and sprigs of dill. Serve immediately.

Caprese Salad

~ From *Death al Dente* by Leslie Budewitz ~

Serve this as an appetizer or a salad course, with a loaf of crunchy bread.

Ripe tomatoes—any round, meaty variety will do
Fresh mozzarella
Fresh basil leaves
Fruity olive oil
Coarse sea salt and freshly ground pepper (optional)

Slice tomatoes and mozzarella about ¼ inch thick. Arrange tomato slices on a salad plate or an appetizer tray. Top each tomato with a slice of cheese and a basil leaf. Drizzle with olive oil. Season if you like. How many you need depends on whether you're serving other appetizers, but these are a guaranteed hit!

Watermelon, Basil, and Feta Salad

～ From *A Broth of Betrayal* by Connie Archer ～

SERVES 2

2 cups chopped watermelon cubes

½ cup chopped red onion

½ cup crumbled feta cheese

½ cup chopped fresh basil leaves

8 leaves romaine lettuce, washed and chopped

Balsamic vinegar, for serving

Mix all ingredients in a large bowl.

Serve with a sprinkle of balsamic vinegar.

Erin's Two-Bean and Pesto Salad

~ From *Crime Rib* by Leslie Budewitz ~

SERVES 6 TO 8 AS A MAIN DISH, 10 TO 12 AS A SIDE DISH

1 pound fresh green beans (the thin, or French style, called
    haricots verts, works best)
1 (14-ounce) can white beans
1 cup cherry or grape tomatoes, cut in half
1 small white onion, chopped fine (sweet, red, or green onions
    also work well, but a yellow onion will be too strong)
Fresh pesto (see recipe, below)
Sea salt and freshly ground pepper, to taste

Steam beans until tender-crunchy (start checking after about 3 minutes). When steaming, use enough water to reach just below the bottom of your steamer basket. Rinse, drain, and cool, then cut into bite-size pieces, about 1 inch long. Rinse and drain white beans. Mix vegetables and beans in a large bowl and toss with pesto. Add sea salt and freshly ground pepper to taste. Serve at room temperature or chilled, by itself or on a bed of greens.

Pesto

In a small (2-cup) food processor, loosely chop about ¼ cup fresh basil leaves. Toss in 1 or 2 cloves of garlic—the pesto will blend more easily if you slice or chop the cloves first. Drizzle in olive oil and pulse. Add oil and pulse until you get a good consistency for mixing with other ingredients. Add grated Parmesan and, if you'd like, pine nuts or walnuts, and pulse to mix well.

Chicken, Apricot, and Almond Salad

~ From *A Broth of Betrayal* by Connie Archer ~

SERVES 2

1½ cups cooked, chopped, skinless chicken breast

½ cup chopped dried apricots

2 stalks celery, chopped

3 tablespoons chopped fresh cilantro

1 cup plain yogurt

2 tablespoons spicy mustard

2 teaspoons honey

2 teaspoons orange zest

10 large leaves romaine lettuce, washed and chopped

½ cup sliced almonds

In a large bowl, mix chicken pieces, dried apricots, celery, and cilantro together. In a separate small bowl, mix yogurt, mustard, honey, and orange zest, and add it to the chicken mixture. Add chopped romaine leaves. Mix all ingredients thoroughly and garnish with sliced almonds.

Max's Blue Cheese, Apple, and Walnut Salad

From Crime Rib by Leslie Budewitz

SERVES 2 OR 10—JUST VARY THE AMOUNT OF SALAD GREENS!

3- to 4-ounce chunk of blue cheese
½ cup walnut halves
Mixed salad greens, about 1 cup for each serving
1 Granny Smith apple
Olive oil and balsamic vinegar, for serving, or
    a balsamic vinaigrette (see recipe below)

Toss a chunk of blue cheese (well-wrapped in plastic) in your freezer for about 30 minutes. Toast chopped walnut halves at 300° F for about 10 minutes. Don't overbake as the nuts will continue to brown as they cool.

Place mixed greens in your serving bowl. Slice a Granny Smith apple thinly and layer on top. Add the walnuts. Drizzle with vinaigrette and toss. Use a cheese slicer or potato peeler to curl slices of blue cheese on top.

If you prefer to serve as Max does, serve the salad on individual plates with the walnuts and apple slices on the side, and drizzle with vinaigrette.

Balsamic Vinaigrette

1 cup walnut oil
1 tablespoon balsamic vinegar

1 teaspoon Dijon mustard

Sea salt and freshly ground pepper, to taste

Whisk ingredients together in a small bowl, or combine in a jar with a tightly fitting lid and shake to combine or emulsify the dressing. (Walnut oil is thinner than olive oil, so make sure the jar lid is tight and shake with care, to avoid a leaky mess!)

Fennel and Blood Orange Salad

~ From *Butter Off Dead* by Leslie Budewitz ~

Erin likes this as a complement to sautéed scallops or shrimp, or a salmon burger.

SERVES 4

¼ cup hazelnuts or walnuts, toasted

1 medium to large fennel bulb, leaves and stems trimmed; 1 tablespoon fennel fronds chopped and reserved, for garnish

Juice of 1 lemon

Sea salt and freshly ground black pepper, to taste

2 large blood oranges (the Cara Cara, a red-fleshed navel orange, works well)

1 small shallot, peeled and cut into paper-thin slices

10 mint leaves, chopped

2 tablespoons extra-virgin olive oil

Mixed greens, for serving (optional)

Preheat oven to 300° F.

Toast nuts for 10 minutes, shaking pan occasionally. (Don't overbrown, as nuts will continue to darken after toasting.) Cool. If you use hazelnuts, roll them with a dish towel or paper towel to remove any loose skins, and discard—they are bitter. Coarsely chop the nuts and set them aside.

Slice off the root end of the fennel and discard. Slice bulb thinly, using a sharp knife. (Some cookbooks recommend starting at the flat bottom side, but Erin thinks it's easier to rest the bulb on its side, which is fairly flat, and slice from the end, using the stem end to hold the bulb.) Toss the slices in a mixing bowl with lemon juice, salt, and pepper.

Remove peel and pith from oranges. Cut the oranges in half crosswise, and use a small serrated knife to cut the sections from the membrane. Add the sections to the seasoned fennel. Some orange pulp will remain in the cut orange halves; squeeze juice out by hand or with a juicer, and add juice to the seasoned fennel. Add the shallots, mint leaves, olive oil, and chopped nuts, and toss gently. Serve the salad by itself or on a bed of greens, and garnish with the fennel fronds.

This salad can be made ahead; add the mint and fennel fronds before serving.

Inherit the Word

by Daryl Wood Gerber

I clambered down the ladder in the storeroom of The Cookbook Nook, carrying a stack of cookie cookbooks in my arms. My foot hit something soft. I shrieked. Tigger, a stray kitten that had scampered into my life and won my heart a month ago, yowled. His claws skittered beneath him as he dashed from my path.

"Shh, Tigger. Hush, baby." I had barely touched him with my toe. I knew he wasn't hurt. "C'mere, little guy." I arrived at the floor, knelt down, and spied him hunkering beneath the ladder, staring at me with his wide eyes. "It's okay," I cooed. As I scooped him up, one-armed, and nuzzled his neck, I felt a cool stream of the unknowable course its way up my spine. Tigger was a ginger-striped tabby, not a black cat. Passing beneath a ladder wasn't a bad omen, was it? Why did I suddenly feel like seven years of bad luck was lurking in the shadows?

"Miss Jenna, yoo-hoo," a girl squealed. "Miss Jenna, come quick!"

Fear tickled inside me. We had invited children to The Cookbook Nook for a cookie-decorating event—Aunt Vera's idea. She was a master cookie baker herself, with an extensive personal collection of cookie cookbooks. Had one of the children gotten hurt? Was that the dark cloud I'd sensed in the storeroom? I raced into the shop and skidded to a slippery halt in my flip-flops.

"Look at my killer shark." A girl with frothy orange hair was standing beside the tot-height table in the children's corner, brandishing a deep blue, shark-shaped cookie.

Nothing amiss. Kids being kids. No one hurt. *Thank the breezes*, as my mother used to say.

Aunt Vera's Brie, Apple, and Turkey Grilled Cheese

∽ From *Inherit the Word* by Daryl Wood Gerber ∽

I gave this idea to Katie. Can you see me preening? It's one of my favorite sandwiches. Perfect for lunch or brunch. The cinnamon adds just a hint of flavor. It's like apple pie with a pack of protein, thanks to the turkey. Also, just so you know, cream cheese is a nifty little trick for any grilled cheese. When spread on the inside of a sandwich, it heats up fast and helps the other ingredients melt evenly. Enjoy.

MAKES 2 SANDWICHES

4 slices bread
4 tablespoons butter
4 tablespoons cream cheese
1 teaspoon cinnamon
6 ounces cooked turkey, sliced thinly
6 ounces Brie cheese, sliced, rind trimmed off
1 green apple, sliced thin

Butter each slice of bread on one side. Spread the cream cheese on the other side of the bread. Sprinkle with cinnamon. (Note: This is the inside of the sandwich; the butter side is the outside.)

To assemble: Top two slices of bread, cream cheese side up, with turkey. Place Brie cheese slices on top of turkey. Place apples on top of the cheese. Set the other slice of bread on top of the sandwich and press slightly.

If cooking on a stovetop: Heat a large skillet over medium heat for about 2 minutes. Set the sandwiches on the skillet and cook for 4 minutes, until golden brown. Flip the sandwiches with a spatula and cook another 2 to 4 minutes. You can compress the sandwich with the spatula. Turn the sandwich one more time. Press down with the spatula and remove from the pan. Let cool about 2 to 3 minutes and serve.

If cooking on a panini grill or sandwich maker: Set the sandwich on the grill surface and slowly lower the top. Cook for a total of 4 minutes. Remove from the griddle and let cool 2 to 3 minutes, then serve. Beware—the cheese filling might ooze out the sides. If the lid is too heavy, you might want to consider resorting to the stovetop method.

Goat Cheese and Pancetta Sandwich

~ From A Spoonful of Murder by Connie Archer ~

MAKES 1 SANDWICH

1 tablespoon olive oil

1 tablespoon balsamic vinegar

2 slices crusty bread

⅓ cup goat cheese

3 slices pancetta

3 figs, chopped

Brush olive oil and balsamic vinegar on two slices of crusty bakery bread. Spread goat cheese, then a layer of pancetta and a layer of chopped figs on one slice of bread, cover with second slice of bread and serve.

Delilah's Grilled Cheese with Bacon and Fig Jam

~ From *Days of Wine and Roquefort* by Avery Aames ~

MAKES 2 SANDWICHES

4 slices bread

3 to 4 tablespoons butter

3 to 4 tablespoons cream cheese

2 tablespoons fig jam or preserves

4 ounces (4 slices) Swiss cheese

4 slices bacon, cooked crisply and crumbled

2 tablespoons scallions, diced

For each sandwich, butter 2 slices of bread on one side. Flip the bread over and spread cream cheese on the other side of the bread. Now, spread the cream cheese side of the bread with fig jam. Place a slice of Swiss cheese on top of the jam.

On two of the cheese-bread combos, add the cooked bacon, dividing equally, and then the chopped scallions. Top with the other cheese-bread combo.

Heat up a flat grilling pan or a panini grill. Place the sandwiches on the grill. (If using a grilling pan, grill the sandwich on low to medium for 4 minutes. Flip the sandwich and grill for another 4 minutes, until the bread is a nice golden brown and cheese is oozing. If using a panini grill, cook the sandwich for a total of 4 minutes, until the bread is a nice golden brown.)

Remove from heat and serve immediately.

Note: This can be made on gluten-free bread; it is still amazing. Also, if you prefer another jam, feel free to use it. It's the combination of the salty with the sweet that matters.

Avocado and Roasted Red Pepper Sandwich

From Ladle to the Grave by Connie Archer

MAKES 1 SANDWICH

2 slices sourdough bread

2 tablespoons pesto (see recipe, below, or use store-bought)

8 to 10 strips roasted red pepper (see Note, below, or use store-bought)

⅓ avocado

Spread pesto mixture on 1 slice of bread. Layer with strips of roasted red pepper. Spread softened avocado on the other slice of bread and cover sandwich.

Note: If you'd prefer to make your own, brush fresh or frozen red pepper strips with oil and grill under the broiler until browned.

Pesto

1 cup basil leaves, firmly packed

½ cup parsley sprigs firmly packed

½ cup grated Parmesan cheese

2 cloves garlic, peeled and cut into quarters

¼ cup pine nuts or walnuts

¼ cup olive oil

Combine basil leaves, parsley sprigs, cheese, garlic, nuts, 2 tablespoons olive oil and blend in food processor until a paste forms. Gradually add the remaining oil and blend on low speed until smooth.

Torpedo Sandwich

~ From *Clobbered by Camembert* by Avery Aames ~

Urso's favorite!

MAKES 2 SANDWICHES

2 (6-inch) torpedo-shaped rolls

4 tablespoons mayonnaise (plain; not salad-dressing-style)

2 teaspoons Dijon mustard

2 teaspoons maple syrup

1 teaspoon ground pepper

1 teaspoon salt

2 green onions, white parts only

8 (1-ounce) slices maple-infused ham

8 (1-ounce) slices Jarlsberg cheese

Slice the torpedo-shaped rolls lengthwise.

In a bowl, combine the mayonnaise, mustard, syrup, pepper, salt, and green onion tips.

Slather each side of the torpedo-shaped rolls with the mayonnaise mixture. Top the bottom half with 4 slices of ham and 4 slices of cheese. (At this point, you might desire to heat the bottom half. If so, place under broiler for 2 to 3 minutes until cheese is bubbling.)

Place the top half on the sandwich and cut the roll on the diagonal.

Serve with crispy potato chips.

Steeped in Evil

by Laura Childs

"Who knew Miss Josette could read tea leaves?" said Drayton.

"Who knew?" said Theodosia.

"I don't mean to change the subject . . ."

"Yes, you do," said Theodosia. "Miss Josette's words unnerved you because you tend to be a practical, linear thinker who relies on logic. Kind of like Mr. Spock on *Star Trek*."

Drayton pursed his lips together. "I don't believe I understand that reference at all."

"You can't fool me," she told him.

"Changing the subject," said Drayton as he dug into the front pocket of his apron and pulled out an index card, "Haley deigned to give me our luncheon menu for today."

"I guess we are changing the subject."

Drayton made a big production out of clearing his throat. "Chicken and vegetable soup, crab Rangoon with an Asian slaw, blue cheese and grape tea sandwiches, and . . ." He wrinkled his nose. "Something Haley calls her ladybug tea sandwiches?"

"With cream cheese and cherry tomatoes sliced so they look like

wings," said Theodosia. "You remember, she's made them before."
Haley did enjoy being fanciful and creative.

"Okay," said Drayton. "And you remember about the candied fruit
scones and white chocolate chip muffins?"

"And the poppyseed bread," said Theodosia.

"Right."

Theodosia walked over to the highboy, which served as her gift shop
area. She perused the shelves, thinking about which items might go
into her tea basket. A couple of tins of tea were critical, of course. And
so was a teapot. She had a nice stash of teapots she'd picked up at tag
sales around the area, but maybe she would pop next door to the Cabbage Patch and buy a brand-new one. That might be better. Theodosia
eyed the shelves again. And then, because there was an assortment of
candles sitting right in front of her, Theodosia decided to heed Miss
Josette's words. So she reached out and grabbed a bayberry candle.

"Gee, that smells nice," Miss Dimple commented, once Theodosia
had carried the candle up to the front counter.

"It's going to go in my tea basket," she said. "For the silent auction
at the Art Crawl Ball."

"I've seen those gorgeous baskets you put together," said Miss Dimple. "A person would be lucky to get one."

"You think?" said Theodosia. "You'd bid on it?"

"Sure, I would," said Miss Dimple. "Drayton, wouldn't you?"

Drayton was busy measuring out tea. "Hmm?" he said absently.
"What?"

Miss Dimple chuckled so hard that little mounds of flesh all over
her small body began to tremble and shake. "Don't you just love Drayton when he pretends to be all fussy-busy? Isn't he a stitch?"

"That's our Drayton," said Theodosia. "A laugh a minute."

Ladybug Tea Sandwiches

~ From *Steeped in Evil* by Laura Childs ~

MAKES 18 SMALL (AND VERY CUTE!) SANDWICHES

6 slices white bread
Cream cheese, about 4 ounces
18 cherry tomatoes
18 parsley leaves
18 black olives, pitted

Using a cookie cutter, cut 3 rounds of bread out of each slice of bread. Spread rounds with cream cheese. Slice cherry tomatoes in half and arrange as wings on top of each round. Place a leaf of parsley under tomatoes so it looks like each ladybug is sitting on it. Slice olives in half. Reserve 18 halves. Slice the remaining halves into small bits. Place an olive half in front of wings to form the ladybug's head. Place the small bits on the tomato wings to create the ladybug's spots.

Drinks

Black Orchid Cocktail 117

May Wine 118

    EXCERPT FROM *BUTTER OFF DEAD* BY LESLIE BUDEWITZ 120

Cocktails with the Murphy Girls: Huckleberry
    Martinis and Huckleberry Margaritas 122

Drayton's Green Tea Tippler 124

Summer Tea Sparkler 125

Killer Sweet Tea 126

Coffee Milk and Coffee Syrup 127

Old-Fashioned Iced Coffee 129

The Village Blend's Chilly Choco Latte 130

    EXCERPT FROM *TOWN IN A WILD MOOSE CHASE* BY
    B. B. HAYWOOD 131

Marjorie Coffin's White Moose Hot Cocoa 133

Pumpkin Spice Coffee Blend 134

Fa-La-La-La Lattes! (Gingerbread, Eggnog, White Chocolate,
    Candy Cane, and Orange-Spice) 135

Mexican Coffee 141

Black Orchid Cocktail

~ From *Dragonwell Dead* by Laura Childs ~

MAKES 1 COCKTAIL

1 part blue curaçao liqueur

1 part dark rum

1 dash grenadine syrup

Pour into cocktail shaker over ice, shake well, strain, and serve.

May Wine

~ From *Ladle to the Grave* by Connie Archer ~

May wine is a traditional drink in many cultures to celebrate the coming of spring on May Day. The brew is a combination of white wine, dried or fresh leaves of the sweet woodruff plant, strawberries, and sparkling wine. Sweet woodruff is a perennial herb with dark green leaves and small, star-shaped white flowers growing in shady areas in temperate climates. It blossoms in late April or early May. Its generic name, Galium odoratum, *derives from the Greek word* gala, *or milk.* Odoratum *is Latin for fragrant. Sweet woodruff has had many uses for centuries—medicinally to treat various disorders, as a poultice on cuts and wounds, as fragrant mattress filling, and as sachets to repel moths and insects. Ingesting a small amount of the woodruff leaves is not harmful. However, large quantities can cause dizziness and vomiting. Today, the U.S. Food and Drug Administration considers sweet woodruff safe only in alcoholic beverages.*

MAKES AROUND 8 CUPS

1 bottle white wine (a Riesling is an excellent choice)
½ cup dried sweet woodruff leaves, plus a few fresh leaves for
    garnish
¾ cup strawberries, chopped
1 bottle sparkling wine
Sugar (optional)

Pour the bottle of white wine into a large glass container. Soak dried woodruff leaves in the wine for approximately 1 hour. Add chopped strawberries and stir. Add the bottle of sparkling wine, mix, and garnish with a pinch of fresh woodruff leaves. Add a small amount of sugar, if desired, depending on taste. Serve chilled.

Butter Off Dead

by Leslie Budewitz

"He shouldn't be up there alone," Fresca said now, reaching for one of the truffles she'd spurned.

"He's a grown man, Mom. Let him mourn his own way." My sister's words seemed to take the bone out of Fresca's spine, and she sank into the upholstery, deflated. Pepé hopped up next to her, so attuned to changing moods that she ignored the truffle and rested her snout on my mother's thigh, in easy reach. Like any good pet, she knew that to an animal lover, petting is as comforting to petter as to pettee.

"I bought all the ingredients—we might as well drink." In the kitchen, I got out the blender and mixed a batch of huckleberry margaritas while my sister put together huckleberry martinis. People often mistake us for each other—we've got the same fair skin, dark eyes, and straight dark bobs, though mine's a little longer and at five-five, I'm an inch taller. She's two years older and by far the freer spirit.

"Shaken or stirred?" she asked.

"Doesn't matter," I said. "Either way, you've managed to do single-handedly what Dr. No, Goldfinger, and Oddjob couldn't. Fruit in a martini? You've given James Bond a heart attack and killed him."

Giggling, we carried the cocktail tray out to the living room. Pepé raised her head, saw that it was us, and went back to her nap.

"I can't imagine what you girls can find to laugh about at a time like this," Fresca said.

"Mom, it stinks. It really stinks." My voice got tight, my eyes watered, and my throat swelled—and not from the cat scratch on my neck. "But save it for the killer. Not us."

Chiara—say it with a hard C and rhyme it with "tiara"—poured margaritas into thick glasses rimmed in cobalt blue, souvenirs from a trip to Puerto Vallarta.

"Hard to believe Zayda George would kill anybody," she said.

"At first, she said she waited outside for me, then she had to admit she'd gone inside. She swears nothing happened—the brow ring just fell out." I took a glass. "Doesn't make sense. Why go back outside? If she knew Christine was hurt, why not call for help? If she shot her, why stick around?"

Fresca accepted a drink. "Doesn't seem like the girl we know."

Cocktails with the Murphy Girls

~ From *Butter Off Dead* by Leslie Budewitz ~

MAKES 2 COCKTAILS

Huckleberry Martinis

Commercial huckleberry-flavored vodkas are available. Erin prefers to make her own. This drink is similar to a Cosmopolitan.

HUCKLEBERRY VODKA

3 ounces huckleberries, fresh or frozen

3 ounces vodka

Pour vodka over berries in a Mason jar or mortar; mash the berries with a fork or a pestle and let sit at least 1 hour. Makes 3 ounces huckleberry vodka.

3 ounces huckleberry vodka

2 ounces triple sec

1 ounce lime juice

1 cup ice cubes

1 teaspoon simple syrup (optional)

Combine ingredients in a cocktail shaker. Shake until the outside of the shaker is frosty or your hands are cold. Strain into 2 chilled martini glasses. If you prefer a sweeter drink, add ½ teaspoon simple syrup to each drink.

Huckleberry Margaritas

HUCKLEBERRY TEQUILA

3 ounces huckleberries, fresh or frozen

3 ounces tequila

Pour tequila over berries in a Mason jar or mortar; mash the berries with a fork or a pestle and let sit at least 1 hour. Makes 3 ounces huckleberry tequila.

3 ounces huckleberry tequila

2 ounces triple sec

1 ounce lime juice

Ice cubes

Lime wedges

1 teaspoon simple syrup (optional)

SERVE ON THE ROCKS OR BLENDED, WITH SALT OR WITHOUT

On the rocks: Combine ingredients in a cocktail shaker with 1 cup ice. Shake until the outside of the shaker is frosty or your hands are cold. Strain into 2 glasses with ice. Serve with a lime wedge.

Blended: Add ingredients to blender with 2 ice cubes. Pulse and pour into glasses. Serve with a lime wedge.

If you prefer a sweeter drink, add ½ teaspoon simple syrup to each drink. For salted rims, shake salt onto a saucer. Run a lime wedge around the rim of each glass and dip the glass into the salt.

Drayton's Green Tea Tippler

~ From *The Jasmine Moon Murder* by Laura Childs ~

MAKES 4 COCKTAILS

½ cup sugar

½ cup water

8 ounces vodka

1 cup brewed strong green tea, cooled

½ cup fresh lemon juice

1 teaspoon grated fresh ginger

1 tablespoon sugar syrup

Lemon slices, for garnish

To make sugar syrup, mix ½ cup sugar and ½ cup water in saucepan over low heat and stir until sugar dissolves, about 5 minutes.

For drink, combine all ingredients in a large shaker, then shake and strain into 4 tall glasses with ice, and garnish with a slice of lemon.

Summer Tea Sparkler

~ From *Sweet Tea Revenge* by Laura Childs ~

MAKES 1 DRINK

Jasmine, raspberry, or rosehips tea
Ginger ale
Lemon slices, for garnish

Brew a small pot of jasmine, raspberry, or rosehips tea. Allow to cool, then pour over a glass of crushed ice until half-full. Now add ginger ale and stir. Garnish with lemon slices.

Killer Sweet Tea

~ From *Sweet Tea Revenge* by Laura Childs ~

They say revenge is a dish best served cold. So is this sweet tea!

SERVES 8 TO 10

3 cups water

3 tea bags

¾ cup sugar

6 cups cold water

1 tray ice cubes

Bring 3 cups of water to a boil in a saucepan. Add the tea bags. Simmer for 2 minutes, then remove from the heat. Cover and let steep for 10 minutes. Remove the tea bags and add the sugar, stirring until dissolved. Pour into a 1-gallon jar or pitcher, then add the cold water and the ice. Enjoy!

Coffee Milk and Coffee Syrup

~ From *Decaffeinated Corpse* by Cleo Coyle ~

Coffee Milk is a seventy-year-old tradition in Rhode Island and the official state drink. Our barista Dante Silva explained to me that it's very much like a glass of chocolate milk, except the syrup used is coffee-flavored instead of chocolate-flavored. The origin of the drink is believed to be with the Italian immigrants who settled in the region. At the Village Blend, many of our customers order it made with steamed milk, much like a hot cocoa.

2 tablespoons of sweetened coffee syrup (regular or decaf, see
    recipe below)
1 cup milk

Mix together and enjoy cold or warmed.

Homemade Coffee Syrup

If you wish to make your own coffee syrup, there's the traditional way and a modern method. I would recommend the newer recipe, but if you're adventurous and have a percolator on your stove, give old-school a go.

Step 1: Make super-strength coffee by brewing coffee (regular or decaf) at a ratio of 1 cup—yes, *cup*—of ground coffee to 16 ounces cold water.

Step 2: In a medium saucepan, combine 1 cup of sugar with 1 cup of super-strength coffee.

Step 3: Bring to a boil, stirring constantly to dissolve sugar.

Step 4: Lower heat and simmer for about 3 minutes, stirring often.

Step 5: Let cool and refrigerate. This method will yield 1 cup of thick syrup. Coffee syrup can be stored in refrigerator, in a tightly sealed container, for up to 1 month.

COFFEE SYRUP THE TRADITIONAL WAY

Step 1: Percolate a pot of coffee (regular or decaf), then discard the grounds.

Step 2: Add fresh grounds (regular or decaf), and percolate again, using the brewed coffee as liquid instead of fresh water.

Step 3: Repeat 3 times.

Step 4: Measure the finished coffee mixture. (The amount may vary.) Combine sugar and coffee in a medium saucepan at a ratio of 1 cup of sugar for every 2 cups of coffee. Heat until boiling and sugar is dissolved, stirring constantly.

Old-Fashioned Iced Coffee

From *Murder Most Frothy* by Cleo Coyle

The best tip for making plain old-fashioned iced coffee is to remember that adding ice to regular coffee is not the way to do it! The ice will melt and simply water down your coffee. Either brew your coffee double-strength first, or better yet, create ice cubes out of brewed coffee, then add these iced coffee cubes to your already cooled coffee. Now you won't have to sacrifice the flavor for the chill.

Simple Sugar Syrup

Want to sweeten an iced coffee drink? Do it the way iced tea drinkers do! Create this simple sugar syrup.

1 cup sugar
1 cup water

Combine the water and sugar in a saucepan. Simmer over low heat until the sugar is totally dissolved—probably no more than 5 minutes. Cool thoroughly, then store the mixture in a jar in the fridge.

The Village Blend's Chilly Choco Latte

~ From *Murder Most Frothy* by Cleo Coyle ~

MAKES 2 LATTES

1 cup espresso or strong coffee, cooled

¼ cup chocolate syrup

1 tablespoon vanilla syrup

1 cup milk

6 cups crushed ice

Pour all of your ingredients into a blender and blend on high until the ice is thoroughly crushed. Divide between 2 chilled glasses. Drink as a midday treat on a hot, sunny day or serve as a dessert coffee, topped with whipped cream and chocolate shavings, on a warm summer evening.

EXCERPT FROM

Town in a Wild Moose Chase

by B. B. Haywood

Candy and Maggie started down the street toward the Light-keeper's Inn. The Sleigh and Sled Parade was just about to start, and they wanted to make sure they had a good vantage point for the festivities. Onlookers had gathered on the sidewalks awaiting the arrival of the winter parade, and vendors were walking along the edge of the street, selling lighted necklaces and glow sticks. A group of individuals off to one side was singing Sleigh Bells in three-part harmony.

As Candy and Maggie neared the inn, the crowd thickened, but with a little bit of patience they managed to negotiate their way through the pressing bodies, and reached the inn's porch just as the jingling of bells and the first clip-clops of horse hooves echoed down from Main Street.

"Here they come!" Maggie said excitedly, clapping her hands together.

Ben Clayton, editor of the local newspaper and Candy's boss, had staked out a primo spot on the porch with excellent views up Ocean Avenue and across to Town Park, so they wouldn't miss a thing. And he had a treat for them. "Freshly made hot chocolate with homemade whipped cream, courtesy of Chef Colin," he said as he pointed to a small silver serving tray on a table nearby, with a large steaming pot and several heavy mugs set out. "Ladies, can I interest you in a cup of cocoa?"

Warming their hands around the mugs and basking in the mellow aromas coming off the hot chocolate, they sipped away in deep pleasure as the first sleighs turned down Ocean Avenue.

Marjorie Coffin's White Moose Hot Cocoa

∽ From *Town in a Wild Moose Chase* by B. B. Haywood ∽

MAKES 4 DRINKS

½ cup unsweetened cocoa powder

½ cup sugar

¼ teaspoon ground cinnamon

⅓ cup hot water

4 cups milk

¾ teaspoon vanilla extract

White chocolate chips, for garnish

Combine cocoa powder, sugar, and cinnamon in a saucepan. Blend in hot water.

Bring to a boil over medium heat, stirring constantly, for 2 minutes. Add milk. Stir and heat. Do not boil.

Remove from heat. Add vanilla extract. Stir with a whisk until foamy.

Pour into mugs and sprinkle with white chocolate chips.

Pumpkin Spice Coffee Blend

~ From *Butter Off Dead* by Leslie Budewitz ~

Created by Fresca, in honor of the newest member of Erin's household.

MAKES ABOUT ¼ CUP

2 tablespoons ground cinnamon

2 teaspoons ground nutmeg

2 teaspoons ground ginger

1½ teaspoons ground allspice or cloves, or a blend

Dash of ground cardamom

1 teaspoon dried orange or lemon peel

Mix all ingredients together in a small bowl and store in a jar or tin with a tight lid. For a pot of drip coffee, add ½ to 1 full teaspoon of the spice blend to the ground coffee. For a single cup of espresso, drip coffee, or French press coffee, use ¼ teaspoon to start, until you know how much tastes just right to you.

If you like to sweeten your coffee, turbinado sugar goes well with this blend; add it to the spices or to your cup. Feel free to experiment with the amounts and add other spices, such as a vanilla bean or whole cloves. Trust your own taste buds, and have fun!

Fa-La-La-La Lattes!

~ From *Holiday Grind* by Cleo Coyle ~

Unless otherwise indicated, the recipes that follow are for single servings.

Gingerbread Latte

1 shot hot espresso or strong coffee
1 tablespoon or to taste Homemade Gingerbread
    Syrup (see recipe, below) or bottled syrup
⅔ cup milk or half-and-half
Whipped cream, for serving

Pour the espresso into an 8-ounce mug. Stir in the gingerbread syrup. Fill the rest of the mug with steamed milk. Use an espresso machine steam wand or my rustic stovetop method (see page 139). Top with a dollop of whipped cream.

Homemade Gingerbread Syrup

MAKES ENOUGH FOR 4 LATTES

2 cups water
1½ cups sugar
2 tablespoons ground ginger
½ teaspoon ground cinnamon
¼ teaspoon vanilla extract

In a nonstick saucepan, combine the water, sugar, ginger, and cinnamon. Over medium-high heat, bring the mixture to a boil, stirring frequently to prevent burning. After the mixture comes to a boil, reduce heat to medium-low and continue simmering for 15 to 20 minutes, stirring every so often to prevent sticking or burning. The mixture will reduce and become slightly thicker. Continue stirring for 1 minute. Remove pan from the heat. When the mixture cools a bit, stir in the vanilla. Serve warm in your latte or try it over vanilla ice cream!

Eggnog Latte

½ cup cold eggnog
¼ cup cold milk
1 shot hot espresso or strong coffee
Pinch ground nutmeg, for garnish

Step 1—Combine the eggnog with the milk. Steam the liquid mixture using an espresso machine steam wand or my rustic stovetop method (see page 139). Note that eggnog will scald faster than milk, so watch the steaming process closely.

Step 2—Pour the espresso into your mug. Fill the mug with the steamed eggnog mixture. Top the drink with a bit of foamed eggnog mixture. Garnish with ground nutmeg.

White Chocolate "Snowflake" Latte

½ cup milk
¼ cup white chocolate, chopped, or white chocolate chips
¼ teaspoon vanilla extract

1 to 2 shots hot espresso or strong coffee

Whipped cream, for optional serving

White chocolate shavings, for optional garnish

Step 1—Combine milk and white chocolate in a heatproof bowl and place over saucepan about one-third full of boiling water. (The water level should be under the bowl edge but not touching it.) Stir constantly until the chocolate is melted. (Do not allow this mixture to scorch or the flavor will be subpar.)

Step 2—Using a whisk or electric mixer, whip in the vanilla. Continue to whip about a minute until the warm mixture is loosely frothy.

Step 3—Pour the espresso into a large mug. Add the steamed white chocolate milk and stir to blend the flavors. You can top with whipped cream, but I serve it without. This drink is absolute heaven. It tastes like a rich, warm coffee-infused milkshake! Enjoy!

Candy Cane Latte

⅔ cup cold milk

1 shot hot espresso or strong coffee

1 candy cane

½ tablespoon kirsch (cherry liqueur) or cherry syrup

½ tablespoon crème de menthe liqueur or
    peppermint syrup

Whipped cream, for serving

Finely crushed candy canes (optional)

Step 1—Froth the milk using an espresso machine steam wand or my rustic stovetop method (see page 139).

Step 2—Pour the espresso into an 8-ounce mug and use the candy cane to stir in the kirsch and crème de menthe.

Step 3—Fill the rest of the mug nearly to the top with steamed milk and stir a second time with the candy cane to distribute the flavors. Top the drink with whipped cream and a sprinkling of finely crushed candy canes. Leave the candy cane in the mug for a festive serving touch!

Orange-Spice Yule Latte

⅔ cup cold milk
½ tablespoon orange syrup or Grand Marnier liqueur
½ tablespoon amaretto syrup or liqueur
Pinch allspice
1 shot hot espresso or strong coffee
Cinnamon stick
Whipped cream, for serving

Step 1—Froth the milk using an espresso machine steam wand or my rustic stovetop method (see page 139).

Step 2—Measure out the flavored syrups or liqueurs into an 8-ounce mug, add the allspice, pour in the shot of hot espresso, and stir well with the cinnamon stick to distribute the flavors.

Step 3—Fill the rest of the mug nearly to the top with your steamed milk and stir a second time with the cinnamon stick to mix the flavorings through the drink. Leave the cinnamon stick in the mug to continue adding spiced flavor. Top the drink with whipped cream.

How to Create Latte and Cappuccino Froth *Without* an Espresso Machine Steam Wand

No, it is not the same as professional, coffeehouse-quality foamed milk, and I wouldn't even try to pour latte art with it. For true microfoam nirvana, you should visit your local barista! To have some fun at home, however, my stovetop method allows you to create a rustic version of a coffeehouse cappuccino and latte in your own kitchen.

If you're looking for something higher-tech, you can now find machines designed solely to heat and froth your milk. Just type "automatic milk frother" into an Internet search or shopping engine, and you'll get a variety of affordable models to begin considering. In the meantime, here's a low-tech solution for creating foam at home.

Step 1—Fill a medium-size saucepan about one-third full with water. Place the pan over high heat until the water begins to boil. Turn the heat down to medium and allow the water to simmer.

Step 2—Select a heatproof mixing bowl from your cupboard that is large enough to sit on top of the saucepan. (You are creating a double boiler.) Make sure the simmering water beneath the bowl is not touching the bowl's bottom. Pour fresh, cold milk into the bowl and allow it to warm over the boiling water for 1 minute, no longer! How much milk? About ⅔ cup per serving.

Step 3—With an oven mitt on one hand to hold the hot bowl and a handheld electric mixer in the other, tip the bowl enough to tilt all the milk into one deep, concentrated pool and then whip it. (Whip it good! Use the *fastest* speed available on your mixer and simply hold the mixing beaters in the center of the milk pool—do not move the mixer around.) In a matter of seconds, you'll see the warmed white fluid froth up. Whip the milk 20 to 90 seconds, depending on how much foam you'd like to create, and you're done! Do not overwhip the milk. You won't be able to foam up every molecule of milk with this method, and if you whip it too much, you'll just be breaking down the foam you've created.

Troubleshooting: To make this rustic frothing method foolproof, keep these four suggestions in mind. (1) Never try to re-froth milk that's been whipped and has fallen. It won't work. You must always start with cold, fresh, undisturbed milk. Pour it straight from the fridge to your measuring cup to the bowl. That's it. (2) Don't try to start whipping at a low speed and increase it. Whip it like crazy from the start, using the highest speed possible on your blender—if there's not enough immediate, vigorous whipping action, the milk won't properly foam up. (3) If you want to infuse spices or flavorings into your latte or cappuccino, stir them into your hot espresso shot. Do *not* add syrups, flavorings, or ground spices into the milk before trying to froth it. (4) Finally, do not allow the milk to warm much longer than a few minutes over the boiling water. Steaming milk properly brings out its sweetness. If the milk is overheated, however, your latte will have a terrible, scorched taste instead of a sweet one. That's why my rustic frothing method is done double-boiler style instead of in a pan sitting directly on the stove burner. It's the best way to control the heat and prevent your milk from scorching.

Mexican Coffee

From Assault and Pepper by Leslie Budewitz

MAKES 1 DRINK

1 cup hot, strong brewed coffee
¼ to ⅓ cup vanilla ice cream
½ ounce tequila
½ ounce Kahlúa
Dash of cinnamon (optional)

Make the coffee. Use a clear glass cup if you can, for presentation. Set out the ice cream. You want it partially melted.

Combine the tequila and Kahlúa in the serving cup. Pour in the coffee, add the ice cream, and dash of cinnamon, if desired. Serve immediately. Enjoy!

Appetizers

EXCERPT FROM *DEATH AL DENTE* BY LESLIE BUDEWITZ 145

Fennel and Shrimp Prosciutto Wraps 147

Blue Cheese and Garlic Fondue 148

Crostini Times Two: Olive Tapenade and Morel Sauté 149

Deviled Eggs 151

EXCERPT FROM *BOOK, LINE, AND SINKER* BY JENN MCKINLAY 152

Charlene's Cucumber Cups Stuffed with Feta 154

Baked Crab Rangoon 155

EXCERPT FROM *AFFAIRS OF STEAK* BY JULIE HYZY 156

Pastry-Wrapped Asparagus Spears with Prosciutto 159

Parmesan Crisps 160

Cranberry-Pecan Brie en Croûte 161

EXCERPT FROM *TO BRIE OR NOT TO BRIE* BY AVERY AAMES 163

Ricotta-Stuffed Mushrooms 165

Smoked Salmon Florets 166

Stuffed Cherry Tomatoes 167

Death al Dente

by Leslie Budewitz

I collapsed into the nearest chair. There were a million things I should be checking, but none of them seemed to matter. Or more accurately, to need me. The apron-clad caterers and bartenders knew what they were doing. Let them.

If only I hadn't gone out to the alley, maybe Claudette would be alive.

Foolish thought, and I knew it.

"What about the music?"

"What?" My mother's question broke my trance.

"The music, darling. The quartet should keep playing, don't you think? Soothing tunes."

At my nod, she beelined for Sam, on lead guitar, her hair fanning out over her shoulders.

Ray from the Bayside Grille slid a small plate in front of me, disappearing before I could speak. Mushrooms stuffed with herbed bread crumbs, shallots, and chopped mushrooms, grilled fennel and shrimp wrapped with prosciutto, olive tapenade on crisp bruschetta.

Ohmyohmyohmy.

Old Ned put a sweating glass of white wine on the table. It looked fragile in his meaty hand.

"Such service. Thanks. Aren't you on guard duty?"

He grunted. "Delegated to Ted. Serves him right, showing up late."

I stood and wrapped my arms around him—or part of him. I'd never hugged a bear but imagined this came close. He wiped away a tear.

Behind him, Dean glared, drops of sweat curling his Elvis sideburns. I felt a twinge of sympathy for Linda, one of those women learning too late that looks weren't enough.

"I didn't kill her." His words, slow and deliberate, held a hint of Memphis that no longer rang true.

Being callous and conceited didn't make him a killer. Or rule him out. Too many people within earshot, so to save myself from saying something I might regret, I picked up a shrimp by the tail and took a bite.

"I told you it was pointless," Linda said. The large diamond on her left ring finger flashed as she grabbed Dean's hand and jerked him away.

Fennel and Shrimp Prosciutto Wraps

∽ From *Death al Dente* by Leslie Budewitz ∽

Unusual and tasty!

SERVES 4, ALTHOUGH ERIN HAS EATEN AN ENTIRE
RECIPE HERSELF WITH NO REGRETS

1 fennel bulb
8 thin slices of prosciutto
8 large shrimp, preferably tail-on

Preheat oven to 400° F (or heat your outdoor grill).

Trim the fennel bulb. Cut it in half lengthwise, and core it; cut each half into 4 spears. Wrap each spear in a slice of prosciutto; one wrap is fine, two is even tastier. Wrap the shrimp with the remaining prosciutto.

Place the fennel spears on a baking sheet and roast until fennel is tender and prosciutto is lightly browned, 15 to 20 minutes. Add the shrimp about halfway through the fennel cooking time—they cook more quickly. These can also be grilled on an outdoor grill.

Blue Cheese and Garlic Fondue

～ From *Lost and Fondue* by Avery Aames ～

SERVES 4

2 cloves garlic
½ cup half-and-half
2 ounces Point Reyes Blue Cheese (or your favorite blue cheese)
1 tablespoon tapioca flour

Cut garlic cloves in half. Rub garlic around the inside of a fondue pot. Heat fondue pot to medium heat. Add the half-and-half. Add blue cheese and stir until melted. Add tapioca flour and stir again so there are no lumps. This all takes about 5 to 7 minutes.

Serve warm in a small Crock-Pot with cut vegetables like broccoli florets, celery sticks, carrot sticks, and asparagus. It may also be served with crackers and/or bread cubes.

Note: This tastes delicious as a warm dressing on a green salad.

Crostini Times Two

~ From *Death al Dente* by Leslie Budewitz ~

Olive Tapenade

Erin adores her mini (2-cup) food processor—it's perfect for the home-size version of Fresca's bestselling tasty treat.

MAKES ABOUT 1 CUP OF TAPENADE

1 cup pitted Kalamata olives (Nicoise olives work well, too—the
  flavor will differ)
2 cloves garlic, peeled
2 tablespoons olive oil
2 tablespoons fresh oregano leaves
2 tablespoons fresh flat-leaf (Italian) parsley
2 tablespoons fresh lemon juice

Combine all ingredients in the food processor and pulse until just pureed. The spread should be textured, not smooth. It will keep up to 1 week, covered and refrigerated.

Morel Sauté

2 cups morel mushrooms, fresh, dried, or frozen

2 tablespoons butter

1 small shallot, finely chopped

1 or 2 tablespoons flat-leaf (Italian) parsley, chopped

A splash of red or white wine

Wash morels thoroughly and slice or chop. Sauté with butter, shallots, and parsley to bring out the meaty earthiness. Deglaze the pan with a splash of wine to emphasize the mushrooms' natural sweetness.

~

Serve tapenade and morels with thinly sliced fresh bread, crostini, or crackers. Make your own crostini by slicing a baguette thinly, brushing the slices with olive oil, and toasting lightly. (Erin loves Lu brand Flatbread Crackers, both Herbes de Provence and Pain Rustique varieties.)

For a crostini tray, add a small bowl of creamy goat cheese mixed with herbs—fresh chives are an early-summer favorite—to impress even the hard-to-please.

Deviled Eggs

~ From *Eggsecutive Orders* by Julie Hyzy ~

SERVES 4

6 hard-boiled eggs
3 tablespoons Dijon mustard
½ small onion, very finely minced
1 tablespoon white wine
2 tablespoons mayonnaise
Paprika, for garnish
Chopped chives, for garnish

Cut hard-boiled eggs in half lengthwise. Scoop out yolks into a medium bowl. Set whites aside on serving tray. Refrigerate. Whisk the egg yolks with Dijon mustard, onion, white wine, and mayonnaise. When well blended, pipe or spoon the egg yolk mixture back into centers of cooked whites. Sprinkle with paprika. Top with chopped chives. Serve chilled.

Book, Line, and Sinker

by Jenn McKinlay

"Daisy Buchanan was an insipid, shallow, soulless woman," Violet La Rue declared. "Jay should have found someone else."

"But he loved her," Nancy Peyton argued.

"Why?" Violet asked. She shuddered. "The woman was a horror."

"She was old money," Lindsey Norris said. "She was everything that the new money, like Jay Gatsby, aspired to be."

It was lunchtime on Thursday at the Briar Creek Public Library, where the crafternoon group met every week to work on a craft, eat yummy food and talk about their latest read. Per usual, Violet and Nancy were the first to arrive.

Lindsey was the director of the Briar Creek library and this group had been one of her ideas to boost the popularity of the library in town.

"Buchanan was a bully. Remember when Daisy has that bruise?" Nancy asked. "What kind of man treats a woman like that?"

"Yeah, I'm pretty sure I've dated him, well, men just like him at any rate," Beth Stanley said as she waddled into the room.

Beth was the children's librarian and today she was dressed as a giant green caterpillar, the puffy underbelly of which seriously impeded her ability to walk. Dangling from one arm, she held a large basket of plastic fruit and foodstuffs.

Lindsey lowered the sampler she was attempting to cross-stitch and studied Beth.

"Don't tell me, let me guess," she said. "You read Eric Carle's *The Very Hungry Caterpillar.*"

"What?" Mary Murphy exclaimed as she stepped over the tail end of Beth's costume to enter the room. "I thought we were reading F. Scott Fitzgerald's *The Great Gatsby.*"

"We are," Nancy said. "Beth read the caterpillar book to her story-time crowd."

"Oh, phew, you had me worried there," Mary said as she plopped into the chair beside Lindsey.

Charlene's Cucumber Cups Stuffed with Feta

~ From *Book, Line, and Sinker* by Jenn McKinlay ~

MAKES 18 TO 20 CUCUMBER CUPS

3 large cucumbers, peeled and cut into 2-inch slices

6 ounces crumbled feta

3 tablespoons plain Greek yogurt

10 pitted Kalamata olives, diced

1 tablespoon chopped dill

2 teaspoons lemon juice

Use a melon baller to scoop out the seeds of the cucumber slices, leaving enough behind to create the base of the cup. With a fork, mash together the feta and the yogurt then add the olives, dill, and lemon. When thoroughly mixed, spoon 1 to 2 tablespoons of cheese mixture into each cup. Chill in refrigerator until ready to serve.

Baked Crab Rangoon

From Steeped in Evil by Laura Childs

MAKES 24

1 (16-ounce) package cream cheese, softened
1 can crabmeat, drained and crumbled
2 green onions, chopped
2 teaspoons Worcestershire sauce
½ teaspoon soy sauce
1 package wonton skins

Preheat oven to 425° F. Grease a cookie sheet, and set aside.

Combine first 5 ingredients in a bowl and mix until well blended. Lay out 24 wonton skins. Place 1 teaspoon of crab mixture in the center of each wonton. Moisten the edges of the wonton with water, then fold in half to form a triangle. Pull 2 of the edges in slightly and pinch to seal. Arrange rangoons on prepared cookie sheet and bake for 12 to 14 minutes, or until golden brown. Serve with your favorite sweet and sour sauce.

Affairs of Steak

by Julie Hyzy

Tonight's dinner would be a nice, easy one. Although we were diligent at providing the tastiest and most interesting food for our guests, the kitchen remained relatively calm. This was not the sort of event that made the news. Not an official social gathering. Working dinners for the president and his guests didn't require the crazed, last-minute wildness of preparing a hundred perfect meals all ready to go at precisely the same time.

What was special about this gathering—at least for us in the kitchen—was that we hoped to gauge reactions to a few new items we were considering for the secretary of state's birthday party next month. Pastry-wrapped asparagus with prosciutto topped my list. Now that the event's location was set and its invitation list no longer in flux, I hoped to get cranking on finalizing the menu.

"Where's Virgil?" I asked when I got back.

Bucky gave me a baleful glare. Cyan giggled. "He's upstairs, in the residence."

"Mrs. Hyden and the kids aren't here. The president is taking lunch in his office. What's Virgil doing up there now?"

"I'm ready for my close-up, Mr. De Mille," Bucky said, striking a pose. "He's walking a photographer through some of the rooms to get 'inspiration' for yet another magazine spread."

I hated to point out the obvious. "Shouldn't the magazine be focusing on photos of him working in the kitchen?"

"You'd think, wouldn't you?" Bucky asked.

Cyan wore a mischievous grin. "He prefers photographers and feature writers to capture his 'full essence.'"

"He said that?"

Cyan laughed again. "Word for word."

I was not a person to look a gift horse in the mouth.

"While he's gone—" I said.

Bucky turned. "You've got some dirt on him?"

"Sorry, no," I said, "but I do want your opinions on a matter that just came up, which I'd rather not discuss in front of Virgil."

"Ooh, Ollie, what is it?" Cyan crossed the room to peek around the corner. "The coast is clear."

I beckoned them closer. Keeping my voice down, I told them about the guest list problem and how I believed Sargeant wasn't responsible. "He's asked me to help him find out who might have done it."

"Oh, ho!" Bucky said loudly. "Sure, he comes to you when he needs help because he knows that you find answers. Whenever you've been in trouble in the past though, he's always first in line with a rock in his hand."

"I know, but—"

Cyan winced. "I'm with Bucky on this one," she said.

"He's been nothing but trouble for you from day one. Let him figure this out himself."

"Who do you think has it in for Sargeant?"

Bucky rubbed his chin, pretending to study the ceiling.

"I don't know. Maybe . . . everyone?"

"I know he's been a problem, but I'm stuck working with him—"

"And you feel responsible," Cyan finished for me.

I winced at her spot-on analysis. "Sort of."

Bucky leaned in. "Listen, maybe this is just the thing to get him out of here. You don't *know* he didn't make this mistake. Maybe he's hoping you'll poke around so that he can turn the tables and blame *you*."

I started to protest, but Bucky also had a point.

"Call me insensitive, but all we need are a few mistakes blamed on him and we'll be saying bye-bye to our sensitivity director."

"So you two think I should let this drop?"

Cyan gave me the look. "That's a no-brainer."

Pastry-Wrapped Asparagus Spears with Prosciutto

⟶ From *Affairs of Steak* by Julie Hyzy ⟵

MAKES 24 TO 30 APPETIZER PORTIONS

1½ pounds asparagus

1 (16- to 20-ounce) package puff pastry, thawed

1 (3-ounce) package herbed or garden vegetable cream cheese,
    well softened

½ pound prosciutto or good deli ham, very thinly sliced

Preheat oven to 400° F.

Wash the asparagus and trim off the tough stems at the bottom. Lay the vegetables on a towel to dry.

Gently roll out the puff pastry sheets to smooth them. Spoon half the softened cream cheese onto each sheet, and spread evenly across the pastry. Divide the prosciutto evenly and place half on each piece of puff pastry, covering the cream cheese in a thin layer.

Cut the puff pastry into long, thin strips, approximately 1 inch wide.

Starting at the base of the spear, wrap the pastry strips—prosciutto and cheese side inward—snugly around the asparagus in a spiral, like stripes on a candy cane.

Place the wrapped asparagus spears on ungreased baking sheets. (You'll likely need two baking sheets.)

Bake until pastry is golden brown and the asparagus is tender, roughly 15 minutes.

Serve hot.

Parmesan Crisps

～ From *Agony of the Leaves* by Laura Childs ～

MAKES 16 CRISPS

8 ounces Parmesan cheese, shredded

Preheat the oven to 350° F. Line a baking sheet with parchment paper.

Place 1 tablespoon Parmesan on the baking sheet and gently flatten. Repeat, leaving about 2 inches between each flattened mound. Bake for 4 to 5 minutes, until the edges turn golden brown. Use as toppers for soup or salads.

Cranberry-Pecan Brie en Croûte

∽ From *Affairs of Steak* by Julie Hyzy ∽

MAKES 8 APPETIZER PORTIONS

1 (16- to 20-ounce) package puff pastry, thawed

2 (8-ounce) Brie rounds

8 ounces whole pecans, shelled and picked over to
     remove any shell pieces

4 ounces dried cranberries

¼ cup good maple syrup

1 egg

1 tablespoon water

Preheat oven to 400° F.

Roll out puff pastry. Place an unwrapped round of Brie cheese in the center of each sheet of puff pastry. Top each round with half the pecans, half the dried cranberries, and half the maple syrup. Fold the puff pastry around the Brie, trimming off extra pastry as needed.

Place the egg and water in a bowl and whisk to mix.

Use the egg mixture to cement the pastry folds closed.

Place the pastry-wrapped rounds on an ungreased baking sheet, seam sides down. Brush all over with the egg wash. If desired, use the leftover puff pastry to make decorations for the top of the Brie rounds, and cement them onto the pastry with the egg wash.

Place the prepared rounds in the oven until the pastry is golden brown and cooked through, roughly 25 minutes.

Let cool for 20 minutes before serving to let the cheese inside the pastry equalize in temperature and melt. Cut each round into quarters with a sharp knife, and serve warm.

To Brie or Not to Brie

by Avery Aames

"Charlotte Erin Bessette, you're a goner." A blissful moan escaped my lips. Had I died and gone to heaven? I took another bite of the ciabatta, spinach, and goat cheese crostini—one of many appetizers sitting on the granite counter in the Cheese Shop kitchen—and sighed again. Adding minced sun-dried tomatoes to the recipe had done the trick.

I downed the remainder of the scrumptious morsel and eyed the array that I had started at six A.M. The jalapeños packed with mascarpone and seasoned with Cajun spices had nearly seared the roof of my mouth, but the ricotta-stuffed mushrooms were a good balance. All in all, the experiment was a success. I had at least ten winning choices for the taste-testing.

As I collected cartons of cream to use in the desserts I planned to make, I paused. Did I smell smoke?

I tore out of the walk-in refrigerator. Flames not only licked upward from the sauté pan on the stove, they spiraled from the twenty-five-pound bag of flour beside it.

"Fire!" I yelled to no one. I was alone in the shop. Lured by the ciabatta crostini, I had forgotten that I was frying shallots for one more dish. "Shoot, shoot, shoot." I hadn't patted the shallots dry enough. Water must have boiled a spot of oil out of the pan, which caught fire and nailed the flour bag.

"You dope, Charlotte." I knew what danger lurked in a kitchen. That would teach me to multitask. Why did I always think I could do everything . . . at once? Wonder Woman I was not, though, at the age of seven, I had liked her costume so much that I begged and pleaded to wear it for Halloween. What girl hadn't?

I dumped the cartons of cream on the counter, swooped to the stove, grabbed a lid, and threw it onto the sauté pan to douse the flame. Then I switched off the gas beneath the burner, snatched one of the oven mitts, and batted the bag of flour. I quenched the fire, but smoke coiled toward the ceiling, and the fire alarm began to bleat.

Ricotta-Stuffed Mushrooms

~ From *To Brie or Not to Brie* by Avery Aames ~

MAKES 6 STUFFED MUSHROOMS

2 tablespoons olive oil

6 mushroom caps

4 tablespoons fresh ricotta cheese

2 tablespoons Rice Chex–style cereal, crumbled

1 teaspoon fresh parsley, chopped

1 teaspoon fresh rosemary, chopped

½ teaspoon salt

½ teaspoon ground pepper

3 dashes Worcestershire sauce

Paprika, for garnish

Parsley sprigs, for garnish

Mixed lettuce, for serving

Preheat oven to 400° F. Brush a flat baking pan or cookie sheet with 1 tablespoon olive oil, and set aside.

Wash and scoop out mushroom caps. Drain on paper towels.

Meanwhile, mix ricotta cheese, cereal, parsley, rosemary, salt, pepper, and Worcestershire sauce in a bowl.

Brush mushrooms with remaining olive oil. Spoon a tablespoon-plus of cheese mixture into each mushroom cap. Set the caps on the prepared baking pan or cookie sheet and bake for 15 minutes.

Remove from oven. Sprinkle with paprika. Set a sprig of parsley on each. Place on a serving plate adorned with mixed lettuce.

Serve warm. (Warning: Do not eat right out of the oven or they will burn the inside of your mouth!)

Smoked Salmon Florets

From *The Teaberry Strangler* by Laura Childs

MAKES 6 FLORETS

6 toast rounds
Chive cream cheese
6 strips lox smoked salmon
Fresh chives, for garnish

Spread 6 toast rounds with cream cheese. Cut each piece of smoked salmon lengthwise into 2 strips. Roll 2 strips together, pinching and arranging until it resembles a flower. Perch atop toast round and add a snip or two of fresh chive.

Stuffed Cherry Tomatoes

~ From *Hail to the Chef* by Julie Hyzy ~

SERVES 6 TO 8

1 (8-ounce) block cream cheese, softened
¼ cup sour cream
1 small bunch chives, washed and chopped, about 3 to 4
    tablespoons, 1 tablespoon reserved for garnish
2 cloves garlic, peeled and minced
20 fresh basil leaves, washed and cut into thin strips
Pinch kosher or sea salt, to taste
1 pint cherry tomatoes, washed and dried

Make the filling by combining the first six ingredients in a bowl and stirring well. Place in a pastry bag fitted with a large star point, if desired. Otherwise, the filling can be spooned into the tomatoes. Set filling aside.

Using a sharp paring knife, cut a small slice off the bottom of a cherry tomato so that it will sit firmly on a tray without rolling around. Cut an *X* into the top of the cherry tomato with the same knife. Either use a watermelon baller to remove the pulp from the tomato, or squeeze it gently over a waste bowl to get the pulp out. Repeat with all the cherry tomatoes, laying them out in rows on the serving tray, ready to be filled.

Pipe the cream cheese mixture into the prepared tomatoes, or spoon it, for a more rustic look.

Sprinkle finished dish with reserved chopped chives. Serve chilled.

Main Courses

Beef Wellington...171

Grilled Flank Steak..173

Charmed Meat Pies with Paprika Aioli.......................175

    EXCERPT FROM *MURDER BY MOCHA* BY CLEO COYLE.......177

Roasted Rock Cornish Game Hens with Rosemary and
    Lemon Butter...179

Individual Chicken Pot Pies..181

Clare's Roasted Chicken with Rosemary and Lime
    for Mike..182

    EXCERPT FROM *CRIME RIB* BY LESLIE BUDEWITZ.........184

The World's Best Grilled Chicken Breasts..................186

Clare's Chicken Marsala for Mike................................188

    EXCERPT FROM *IF FRIED CHICKEN COULD FLY* BY
    PAIGE SHELTON..191

Fried Chicken..193

Fake Fried Chicken...195

    EXCERPT FROM *NO MALLETS INTENDED*
    BY VICTORIA HAMILTON..197

Turkey Roulettes..199

Planked Fish... 202

Nantucket Sea Scallops... 203

    EXCERPT FROM *ASSAULT AND PEPPER*
    BY LESLIE BUDEWITZ.. 205

Penne Rigate with Asparagus and Sesame-Chile
    Shrimp... 207

Smoked Salmon and Mascarpone Risotto 209

Pasta with Strawberry, Leek, and Fennel 210

Clare Cosi's Skillet Lasagna (for Mike) 211

Fettucine with Minted Tomato Sauce,
    aka Fettucine a la Fresca 213

Beef Wellington

From Affaifs of Steak by Julie Hyzy

This recipe is actually very easy to make, but you'll need about three hours to get it on the dinner table from start to finish, so plan your schedule accordingly.

SERVES 8

1 (2-pound) beef tenderloin
1 tablespoon steak seasoning
1 egg
1 tablespoon water
2 tablespoons canola or olive oil
1 small onion, peeled and minced
8 ounces fresh mushrooms, cleaned and finely chopped
1 (16- to 20-ounce) package puff pastry, thawed

Preheat oven to 425° F.

Rub the tenderloin with the steak seasoning. Grease a roasting pan, place the meat in it, and place in the oven for 40 minutes. Remove the meat from the oven, and place it in the refrigerator for 1 hour. (This will distribute the meat juices throughout the piece and tenderize it.) Keep oven on.

While the meat is chilling, whisk the egg and the water together in a small bowl and set aside.

Heat the oil in a skillet over medium heat. Stirring often, sauté the onion until it is translucent, then add the mushrooms and sauté until

MAIN COURSES

171

the liquid that comes from the mushrooms has evaporated, leaving the mushrooms and onions cooked through and tender, about 3 minutes.

Roll out the puff pastry sheets. Use the egg wash as a glue to paste the two puff pastry sheets together on their long edges to give you enough pastry to work with. Overlap the sheets together by 1 inch, after painting the joined edges with egg wash to seal the joint. Make sure that after you roll it out, the finished puff pastry sheet is at least 6 inches longer than the tenderloin piece and 5 inches wider than it needs to be to wrap all the way around the tenderloin.

Spoon the mushroom mixture down the center of the puff pastry. Remove the chilled meat from the refrigerator and place it over the mounded mushroom mixture in the middle of the puff pastry. Fold the pastry up and around the tenderloin, sealing the edges with egg wash.

Place the wrapped tenderloin seam side down on a roasting pan or rimmed baking sheet, and brush with egg wash.

Place the wrapped tenderloin in oven. (I cook my side dishes in it during the interval—or you can reheat it, as you prefer.) Bake 25 minutes for medium-rare, or 32 minutes for medium.

Remove from oven. Let rest for 5 minutes to let the juices equalize inside the pastry. Slice and serve warm.

Grilled Flank Steak

∽ From *Crime Rib* by Leslie Budewitz ∽

SERVES 6

MARINADE

2 teaspoons minced garlic

1 tablespoon grated orange rind

½ cup fresh orange juice

2 tablespoons white wine vinegar

½ teaspoon cayenne pepper

1 teaspoon Dijon mustard

1 tablespoon fresh mint, minced

OTHER INGREDIENTS

1½ pounds flank steak, well-trimmed of fat

2 large oranges, peeled, cut in half across the segments, and thinly sliced, for serving

Fresh mint (use whole leaves if small, or cut in ribbons, known as a chiffonade), for garnish

In a shallow glass or ceramic dish, combine ingredients for marinade. Add steak to marinade; turn once to coat. Cover and refrigerate for at least 4 hours, turning steak occasionally. Remove steak. Transfer marinade to a small saucepan and bring to a boil. Remove from heat and set aside.

Heat grill. Sear steak, 1½ minutes per side. Flip to first side, brush with a little marinade, and cook 5 minutes, then turn and continue cooking, brushing occasionally with marinade. Test for doneness.

(Flank steak is best cooked slightly pink; if well-done, it becomes chewy.) Transfer to a carving board and cover with foil or a pot lid and let rest, about 5 to 7 minutes, so juices can return to the meat.

Arrange orange slices on outer edge of platter. Slice steak diagonally across the grain into very thin slices and arrange in center of platter; garnish with mint.

Charmed Meat Pies with Paprika Aioli

~ From Pecan Pies and Homicides by Ellery Adams ~

SERVES 6

DOUGH

2½ cups flour

2 teaspoons salt

½ cup vegetable oil

½ cup ice water

FILLING

2 tablespoons butter

1 pound ground beef chuck

2 large cloves garlic, finely minced

1 onion, finely diced

3 tablespoons tomato paste

¼ teaspoon cayenne pepper

¼ teaspoon ground cloves

¼ teaspoon allspice

½ teaspoon chopped fresh thyme

3 dashes Tabasco sauce, or more, if desired

PAPRIKA AIOLI

¼ cup fresh lemon juice

5 cloves garlic, finely minced

¼ teaspoon cayenne pepper

1½ teaspoons paprika (sweet or Spanish)

2 tablespoons sugar

1½ tablespoons tomato paste

1½ cups mayonnaise

In a large skillet, melt the butter over low to medium-low heat. Add the ground beef and cook until no pink is showing. Add the garlic and onion and cook over medium heat, stirring occasionally, until the onion is translucent, about 8 minutes. Stir in the tomato paste, cayenne, cloves, allspice, and thyme, and cook for 3 minutes. Season with Tabasco and let cool. Transfer the filling to a food processor and pulse until chopped.

Preheat the oven to 350° F. Line a large baking sheet with parchment paper, and set aside.

On a floured work surface, roll out each disk of dough to a 12-inch round. (If you don't want to make the dough by hand, pre-made piecrusts will work just as well.) Using a 4-inch biscuit cutter, stamp out 6 rounds from each piece of dough. Brush the edges of the rounds with some of the egg wash and place 1 rounded tablespoon of filling to one side of each circle. Fold the other half of the dough over the filling and press to seal. Crimp the edges with a fork. Transfer the pies to the prepared baking sheet and brush with the egg wash. Bake for 25 minutes, until golden brown.

While pies are baking, blend together all the ingredients for the paprika aioli. Serve in individual bowls for dipping.

Murder by Mocha

by Cleo Coyle

My grandmother's name was Graziella—Italian for Grace. "God put beauty in everything," she'd say, "if you take the trouble to see it . . ."

Like a vanilla bean in simmering milk, she infused my world with the sweetest essence, showing me the magic of rising yeast breads; the music of snapping green beans; and the gardener's palette of ripe-red tomatoes, dark purple eggplant, yellow-gold zucchini flowers, and pale orange peppers.

Not that my childhood had been a blithely, pain-free play. At seven, I saw no beauty in my mom leaving my pop for a salesman on his way back to Miami. Tears had been the culmination of that act. Tears and fear and confusion. But then Nonna stepped in.

Day in and day out, she'd been there for me, just as she'd been there for the customers of her little grocery—just as I wanted my coffeehouse to be there for my customers when they stopped by for a warm cup of something that would reassure and renew.

That's why time in my kitchen always made me feel closer to Grace—and Joy, because I'd raised my daughter to believe what my grandmother believed: that simply taking, taking, taking made you a sucking void, hollow, "like a dead person." But preparing a meal was an act of giving, and giving was evidence of living. That's why cooking meant so much to the likes of us. It was more than love. It was life.

Roasted Rock Cornish Game Hens with Rosemary and Lemon Butter

~ From *Murder by Mocha* by Cleo Coyle ~

An elegant yet easy entrée, Clare Cosi cooked up four of these Rock Cornish hens in about an hour—all the time she had to prepare that promised "home-cooked dinner" for Sergeant Franco, Joy, and Lieutenant Mike Quinn. This quick-roasting method produces a crispy, buttery skin. The lemon infuses the moist meat with tangy brightness while the herbs tickle the tongue. These elegant little birds usually weigh in around 2½ pounds each, so plan on one bird per person for your service.

SERVES 2

2 Rock Cornish game hens

Sea salt and ground white or freshly ground black pepper

3 tablespoons chopped fresh rosemary, or 3 teaspoons dried rosemary

3 tablespoons chopped fresh thyme, or 3 teaspoons dried thyme

2 medium lemons, quartered

6 tablespoons (¾ stick) butter, softened, for paste, plus 2 tablespoons butter, melted, for basting

4 toothpicks (for closing cavity during roasting)

Step 1—Prep hens: Preheat the oven to 450° F. (Tip: Many ovens need extra time to reach this temperature. Don't trust the preheat beeper. Give your oven a full 30 minutes to properly preheat.) Lightly coat the rack of a roasting pan with nonstick cooking spray. Remove the giblets from each hen's cavity, rinse each hen, and pat dry. Salt and pepper the inside cavity. Stuff each game hen with ½ tablespoon of the fresh rosemary, ½ tablespoon of the fresh thyme (if using dried herbs use ½ teaspoon of each), and 3 lemon quarters. Place the two hens on the rack of the roasting pan.

Step 2—Make butter paste: Place the softened butter in a bowl, and using a fork (or clean fingers) mix in the remaining fresh (or dried) rosemary and thyme until you've made a nice herb-butter paste. Slather each of the game hens all over with the butter mixture. Sprinkle each game hen with additional salt and pepper. To prevent lemons from falling out during roasting, draw together excess skin on either side of the open cavity. Drive toothpicks through the skin to secure (2 tooth-picks per bird should do it).

Step 3—Roast the meat: Place the roasting pan in the oven and roast for 30 minutes. Baste the hens with melted butter and return the hens to the oven for another 10 minutes. (Tip: Encase the wing tips in aluminum foil to prevent scorching.) Baste the hens a second time and return to the oven for the final 8 minutes of cooking. Remove from the oven, tent foil around the birds to keep them warm, and allow them to rest for 10 minutes before serving. If you skip this resting period, when you slice into the meat, the juices will run out and the meat will taste dry. Allowing the meat to rest gives the juices a chance to re-collect and the meat to remain moist.

Individual Chicken Pot Pies

~ From *Affairs of Steak* by Julie Hyzy ~

SERVES 6

4 tablespoons butter

2 tablespoons all-purpose flour

2 cups chicken broth

½ teaspoon salt

Freshly ground pepper, to taste

¼ cup sherry or white wine

½ pound cooked, cubed chicken

8 ounces fresh mushrooms, cleaned and very thinly sliced

1 (10-ounce) bag frozen peas and carrots, thawed

1 (16- to 20-ounce) package puff pastry

Preheat oven to 375° F.

Melt the butter in a large saucepan over medium heat. Whisk in the flour until it forms a smooth paste. Very gradually whisk in the chicken broth until smooth. Bring the sauce slowly to nearly a boil, whisking constantly until it thickens. Reduce heat to a low simmer. Add salt and pepper, to taste. Whisk in the sherry. Add the chicken, mushrooms, and peas and carrots. Stir until the additions are warmed through. Leave the sauce to simmer slowly.

Arrange 6 ovenproof bowls, soufflé dishes, or other individual containers on a baking sheet. Spoon the chicken filling into the containers. Cut puff pastry to fit over each container, and cover.

Place the pies into the oven. Bake until the puff pastry is brown and puffed, about 25 to 30 minutes.

Serve warm.

Clare's Roasted Chicken with Rosemary and Lime for Mike

∼ From *A Brew to a Kill* by Cleo Coyle ∼

Rosemary and lemon may be a classic flavor combo for chicken, but Clare saw a beautiful green mountain of plump, juicy limes at her local market and decided to bring their refreshing summer flavor to a gently roasted bird. Mike Quinn flipped for it, and she made good on her promise, roasting him this chicken the Sunday before he hopped the Acela Express down to Washington. With a side of her Fully-Loaded Colcannon for dessert, Mike swore he'd be back for a visit the very next weekend—and he was.

SERVES 4 TO 6

- 3 tablespoons olive oil, divided
- 1 (4- to 6-pound) whole chicken
- 5 to 6 fresh limes (medium size)
- 1 tablespoon sea salt
- ½ teaspoon white pepper, plus additional for seasoning
- 6 cloves garlic
- 2 tablespoons chopped, fresh rosemary
- 1 teaspoon poultry seasoning

Step 1—Prep meat: Preheat oven to 350° F. Lightly coat the top of a broiler pan or roasting rack with 1 tablespoon of olive oil, and set aside. (For easier cleanup, I also like to cover the bottom portion of my pan with aluminum foil.) Allow the meat to reach room temperature

(20 to 30 minutes outside the refrigerator). Rinse the chicken and pat dry. If your limes were in the refrigerator, warm them to room temperature, as well.

Step 2—Stuff the bird: Quarter one lime and place the sections inside the chicken cavity, along with a dash of sea salt and white pepper. Close the cavity. (I use a simple wooden skewer for this.)

Step 3—Create the rosemary-lime slurry: Place the sea salt into a small bowl and smash the garlic on it. Mix in the freshly squeezed juice of 2 to 3 limes (enough to measure about ¼ cup). Add the chopped rosemary, poultry seasoning, white pepper, and remaining 2 tablespoons of the olive oil. Rub this slurry all over the bird and place breast side up on the prepared rack or pan.

Step 4—Roast: Place your pan in the center of your oven for about 25 minutes per pound, giving a bird of 6 pounds about 2½ hours of cooking time; a bird of 4 pounds about 1 hour and 40 minutes. You're watching for the thickest part of the thigh to reach an internal temperature of 165° F.

To Finish: Once cooked, allow the chicken to stand for 15 minutes before carving. To keep it warm, tent foil over the bird. This resting period is important. If you cut into the bird right out of the oven, the juices will run out and your chicken will be dry instead of succulent, which is almost as bad, in Clare's opinion, as missing a clue.

Crime Rib

by Leslie Budewitz

Kim Caldwell stood on the porch, her expression sober.

"We got him," she said. "What smells so good?"

"Hmm? Oh, that's the grill heating. The chicken will go on in a minute. There's plenty." She followed me inside. I gestured with my glass. "You off duty?"

"And still off the case. Nice roses." She took a sniff. "Secret admirer?"

"Not so admiring, I'm afraid." I handed her a glass of wine. "The other day, at the office, I'm so sorry—"

"Completely my fault," she said. "I've been a clod lately."

Join the club. I picked up the bowl of chicken. "Tell me more. About arresting Gib."

"That's all I know. I am persona non grata. Non everythinga. Exiled from my own office and reassigned to Pondera for the duration. I'm not even supposed to go to the Lodge or talk to my family." She looked miserable.

"Criminy. So Ike's finally convinced the two deaths are related?"

"Maybe convinced, maybe related. And my father and my cousin are witnesses. Not to the homicides, but to Amber Stone's movements. What did you call it?"

"Her whabouts." I forked the chicken breasts onto the grill, poured the marinade into a small saucepan, and set it on the flame to reduce. Kim and I sat at the café table, our chairs angled toward the lake view. In a cloudless sky blessedly free of smoke from forest fires, the sun looked almost white as it hung above the horizon. The closer it got, the deeper it would glow.

The World's Best Grilled Chicken Breasts

~ From *Crime Rib* by Leslie Budewitz ~

The flavorful marinade makes this chicken incredibly moist. And since you've got the grill hot, serve with grilled naan. Brush olive oil on both sides of naan and grill 3 to 4 minutes a side. The grilling brings out the natural sweetness of the bread and is a great complement to a salad and chicken.

SERVES 4

4 boneless, skinless chicken
    breast halves, well-trimmed
1 tablespoon Dijon mustard
⅓ cup white wine vinegar
1 tablespoon minced garlic
1 tablespoon honey
2 tablespoons minced fresh thyme, or
    2 teaspoons dried thyme
½ teaspoon red pepper flakes
½ teaspoon coarse sea salt
1½ tablespoons olive oil
Thyme sprigs, for garnish

Cover the chicken breasts with plastic wrap and flatten slightly with the palm of your hand or the flat of a chef's knife, to promote even grilling. Place in a shallow glass dish.

For marinade: Put mustard, vinegar, garlic, and honey in a small bowl. Crumble in the thyme and pepper flakes and add the salt; stir to combine. Whisk in the olive oil. Pour marinade over the chicken, cover, and marinate; 2 hours is optimal, but even 20 minutes will make for a moist chicken. Pour marinade into a small saucepan and bring to a boil, to kill off any bacteria from the raw chicken.

To grill: Erin uses a gas grill, preheating to medium. For a charcoal grill, heat until coals are gray. Lightly coat your grill rack with a cooking spray, if needed. Place chicken on grill, basting frequently with the cooked marinade, about 6 minutes on each side. And don't flip the darned things back and forth—leave them put! Check for doneness, then transfer to serving plate and garnish with thyme sprigs.

Clare's Chicken Marsala for Mike

~ From *Holiday Buzz* by Cleo Coyle ~

Chicken Marsala is one of the most popular dishes in Italian restaurants worldwide. The chicken melts like butter, the mushrooms provide an earthy richness, but the key ingredient (and the secret to this dish's charm) is dry Marsala, a fortified wine from Sicily similar to sherry or port.

Clare adds an extra step to this one-skillet recipe—an easy marinade. Do not skip this step. The marinade truly heightens the flavor, bringing this dish to a whole new level.

Though Chicken Marsala is traditionally dished over pasta or presented with potatoes, Clare served Mike Quinn her Marsala the way many Italian eateries in New York City do—on a crispy, fresh Italian roll, the perfect late-night sandwich for Quinn after a day of holiday sightseeing with his children.

SERVES 4

1 to 1½ pounds boneless, skinless chicken breasts

1¾ cups dry Marsala, divided

4 tablespoons olive oil, divided

6 cloves garlic, smashed

¼ teaspoon kosher salt or ground sea salt, divided

¼ teaspoon freshly ground black pepper, divided

½ cup all-purpose flour

3 tablespoons butter, divided

1 large onion, diced

3 cups sliced mushrooms (baby bellas, cremini,
      button, or a mix)

1 cup chicken stock

Step 1—Prep the chicken and marinate: Wash chicken breasts and slice in half. On a cutting board, use a meat hammer to pound breasts thin. (Or you can buy pre-filleted breasts, but because the goal is tenderness, you still *must pound* the chicken.) In a covered bowl, mix ¾ cup of Marsala with 1 tablespoon olive oil, the garlic, ⅛ teaspoon salt, and ⅛ teaspoon pepper. Place the chicken in the marinade and refrigerate for 30 minutes, or up to 3 hours.

Step 2—Dredge marinated chicken and sauté: Remove chicken from marinade, do not rinse. (Discard the liquid.) Dredge in ½ cup all-purpose flour. Heat 3 tablespoons olive oil in a large skillet over low heat. Add 1 tablespoon of butter to the hot oil, then gently sauté the coated chicken until golden brown (3 minutes per side should do it, turning once). When the chicken is cooked through, remove from the pan and set aside.

Step 3—Sauté the aromatics: Add the diced onion to the oil, and cook over medium heat until the onions are clear and tender (about 5 minutes). Add 1 tablespoon of butter to the skillet. When melted, throw in your sliced mushrooms and sauté. The mushrooms will quickly absorb the oil, but keep cooking until the edges are brown and they begin to release their juices again.

Step 4—Add wine, reduce: Now pour into the pan your remaining 1 cup of Marsala. Increase the heat and bring to a low boil. Simmer until the liquid has been reduced by half, 5 to 6 minutes. Add the chicken stock and simmer for another 3 minutes.

Step 5—Sauce the chicken: Return the chicken breasts to the pan along with any juices that might have accumulated in the holding dish. Lower the heat, and cook until the chicken is heated through and the sauce thickens, about 5 to 7 minutes. Toss in that final 1 tablespoon of butter, ⅛ teaspoon salt, and ⅛ teaspoon black pepper. Serve hot.

If Fried Chicken Could Fly

by Paige Shelton

Gram knew how to cook food that she and her parents and her parents' parents fixed and ate. Gram made food with butter and cheese and flour coatings. Her food wasn't light on calories or light on flavor. It was full and hearty and made taste buds stand up and pay attention and then swoon with delight. And when her students presented a certificate from her program, restaurant owners knew that they were hiring someone who'd learned the ins and outs of amazing fried chicken, creamy sauces and soups, potato dishes of all kinds, breads, and desserts that kept customers coming back for more.

In the real world, Gram's skills and methods were almost becoming things of the past, of a time when people didn't write down recipes but just added some of this and some of that, a time when cooking secrets were passed down through generations—passed down verbally and in the kitchens of country homes, kitchens that didn't have electricity or natural gas. So in the restaurant world, Gram's skills were fast becoming a lost art.

She was the first one to say that eating food cooked in lard wasn't smart to do every day, but every once in a while eating should be all about flavor and comfort. That's what we did: flavor and comfort, with a little lard added for good measure.

Fried Chicken

⌐ From *If Fried Chicken Could Fly* by Paige Shelton ⌐

My dad has often told me about how, when he was dating my mother, her mother would fry up some chicken and leave it warming in the oven just for him. He claims it was the best fried chicken he's ever eaten. Of course, I remember my grandmother's delicious chocolate chip cookies and her delicious Thanksgiving dinners. Sadly, those were the days when things like amazing fried chicken and chocolate chip cookie recipes didn't get written down. My grandmother cooked and baked by adding a little of this and a little of that. My mother had no interest in such things so she never paid attention, and my grandmother died when I was nine, long before I had any cooking or baking interest myself.

I would love to have her fried chicken recipe, all of her recipes. I would love to share it with the world. But I don't. And it seems no one else does either. So I went in search of the "best fried chicken recipe ever" to include in this book. What I found was something beyond ingredients and directions; I found tradition, family, and lots of love. A fried chicken recipe is one of those things that brings families together, puts future generations in touch with something that was theirs even before their time. I think the following recipe is pretty darn good. I'm not done searching, though. Maybe I'll find something better, maybe I won't. If you have a fried chicken recipe in your family, I'll bet you think it's the best—and it is. And if you're lucky enough to have someone in your family who knows the recipe well, do me a favor: write it down and keep it close.

3 cups all-purpose flour

2 teaspoons salt

2 teaspoons freshly ground black pepper

1 teaspoon paprika

1 whole chicken cut into pieces, skin left on

Milk (I use whole)

Vegetable oil, for frying

In a large shallow bowl or pie plate, mix together the flour, salt, pepper, and paprika. Rinse the chicken pieces, and pat them dry with a paper towel. Dip the chicken pieces in milk, and then dredge through your flour mixture. Let the chicken stand for 20 minutes, and then dredge again.

Fill a cast-iron skillet with about ½ inch vegetable oil, and heat it on medium-high heat. Maintain this temperature throughout this first frying process. This will ensure that the skin browns, not burns.

Dip the chicken pieces, 1 or 2 pieces at a time, into the oil. Brown both sides. Remove to a platter until all the pieces have been browned. Return all of the chicken pieces to the skillet. Reduce heat to low or medium-low, and cover. Cook slowly and gently for about 20 minutes, or until the chicken is done all the way through and is fork-tender. Remove the cover. Turn up the heat to medium-high, and recrisp the chicken, about 5 minutes, turning once after the skillet is hot again. Serve!

Fake Fried Chicken

I can't say the following recipe is healthy—flour is involved. It isn't fried but tastes almost like it is. This has turned into one of my son's favorite dishes. When I first made it, he couldn't get enough so I doubled it. This is the doubled version. It'll work if you have a large group or a teenage son or two. Not only does this make a satisfying dish for a meal, it's also a great appetizer to serve for a TV sporting event.

MAKES 10 TO 12 STRIPS

2 pounds skinless chicken strips
2 cups low-fat milk
1 tablespoon vegetable oil
2 cups all-purpose flour
2 teaspoons salt
2 teaspoons freshly ground black pepper
Vegetable spray

Rinse and dry chicken.

Place chicken and milk in a gallon-size storage bag. Refrigerate for 30 minutes.

Preheat oven to 400° F.

Spread the vegetable oil on the bottom of a 13 × 9-inch baking dish until coated, and set aside.

Place flour, salt, and pepper in another gallon-size storage bag, seal, and shake until all ingredients are blended.

Remove the chicken from first storage bag, drain, and then place it into the bag filled with the seasoned flour. I put in a few strips at a time. Shake to coat the chicken well.

Place chicken in the prepared baking dish.

Coat the top of the chicken with a generous coat of vegetable spray—this is pretty important. Try to get a little spray on all exposed parts of the chicken. This gives it a great texture.

Bake on center rack in oven for 20 to 25 minutes, or until chicken is browned on the outside and cooked through on the inside.

No Mallets Intended

by Victoria Hamilton

She was making turkey roulettes from an old Betty Crocker recipe, but she thought instead of using minced raw onion and peppers, she'd sauté them before adding them. Also, she'd improve the dish by adding some cranberry sauce and a hint of poultry seasoning. She made the dough, rolled it out, chopped the leftover turkey from a breast she had roasted and sprinkled it thickly over the square of rolled dough. She then added some cranberry sauce, the sautéed onions and peppers, and lightly sprinkled it with poultry seasoning. She curled the sheet of dough into a long roll, cut it crosswise into thick slices and arranged them on a baking sheet, giving each a little space so they would brown on the sides. She decided she didn't want them softer, or she would have crowded them on the sheet to keep them together.

She looked at the clock. Valetta would be there soon, so she popped the roulettes in the oven and made a salad and some turkey gravy. By the time her friend tapped on the back door the whole kitchen smelled like Thanksgiving. If it tasted as good as it smelled, it was going to be the perfect recipe to use in her Vintage Eats pre-Thanksgiving column for the Howler! Ways to use up turkey were always favorites with thrifty cooks.

Turkey Roulettes

~ From *No Mallets Intended* by Victoria Hamilton ~

Adapted from a Betty Crocker recipe from the 1950s.

MAKES 12 ROULETTES

DOUGH

2 cups sifted all-purpose flour

3 teaspoons double-acting baking powder (Note from
    Jaymie: I made twice, using regular baking powder
    once, and then double-acting. I didn't notice much
    difference, though the double-acting baking powder
    may have made the roulettes a little more tender.)

¾ teaspoon salt

4 tablespoons shortening

⅔ to ¾ cup milk (enough to make soft dough)

FILLING

1½ to 2 cups leftover turkey (or chicken), chopped into
    bite-size pieces

2 to 3 tablespoons gravy

You could also use in the filling:

Poultry seasoning, aka stuffing seasoning, or rubbed sage

Some leftover cranberry sauce, if desired, thinned

Leftover vegetables, like corn or diced carrots, or some
    sautéed diced onions

1—Preheat oven to 425° F. Grease a baking pan, and set aside.

2—Sift together flour, baking powder, and salt.

3—Cut in shortening using pastry blender or two knives until mixture looks like dry oatmeal.

4—Stir in milk until dough holds together, then knead very lightly on floured surface.

5—Roll the dough out until it makes a 9 × 18-inch rectangle.

6—Mix together turkey and gravy, then spread uniformly on the dough. If you want, you can drizzle some thinned cranberry sauce over it, or sprinkle some corn or other veggies, or lightly sprinkle the whole with poultry seasoning. I'm not sure I'd do all of those things, but go for it if you want!

7—Roll up tightly, beginning at wide side. Seal well by pinching edge of dough into roll.

8—Cut into 12 slices, about 1½ inches thick, then arrange, cut side up, in well-greased pan, close together for roulettes with soft sides, or with spaces in between for roulettes with crusty sides.

Note: Mine didn't spread as much as the photo from the recipe I used shows, so next time I think I will smoosh the rolls down in the pan a little before baking, just to make them spread out a little. I baked them apart, and the crust was a lovely golden brown.

9—Bake for 15 to 20 minutes. Serve with hot gravy, allowing at least 2 roulettes per serving.

Note: This is essentially a tea biscuit or baking powder biscuit crust, so be sure the folks you are feeding like tea biscuits! I don't really think of this as a dinner item, but I do think it is ideal for a luncheon with friends, or an afternoon get-together near Thanksgiving or Christmas. It would be awesome for a holiday potluck. Denver the Crabby Tabby told me that the filling was yummy, but asked why I wasted perfectly good turkey by putting it in something! Next time I'll just give him some of the filling in a dish. Hope you enjoy it!

Planked Fish

From The English Breakfast Murder by Laura Childs

SERVES 6

1 (3-pound) salmon filet

Sea salt and freshly ground black pepper, to taste

2 small Vidalia onions, thinly sliced

3 cloves garlic, minced

2 green onions, finely chopped

2 tablespoons fresh rosemary, chopped

2 tablespoons rice wine vinegar

2 tablespoons olive oil

Drill several holes in a 1-inch thick cedar plank or purchase a "grilling plank" from a gourmet shop. Allow plank to soak in water for 1 hour.

Preheat grill to medium-high heat.

Season salmon with salt and pepper. Place on prepared plank.

Combine onion, garlic, green onions, rosemary, vinegar, and olive oil in a small bowl. Spoon mixture over fish and place plank on grill. Cover and cook over medium-high heat until fish flakes with a fork, about 20 minutes. Garnish with lemon wedges.

Nantucket Sea Scallops

~ From *Buffalo West Wing* by Julie Hyzy ~

Cooking scallops is easy. Cleaning them is hard. And finding good, fresh scallops is the real secret for making this into a food fit for feasting.

In most cases, you can get your supplier to clean the scallops for you. If you can, go for it. But, just in case you can't, here are the instructions for dealing with live scallops and getting them ready to eat.

Place the scallops on ice. This makes the animal inside relax and open up its shell.

Hold the scallop firmly in your palm, with its hinge side toward your fingertips and its rounded side toward your palm.

Place a sturdy paring knife in between the two halves of the shell. Twist and cut against the top of the shell, opening the scallop up and severing the muscle from the top shell half. Discard the top shell. Scrape the dark meat away from the scallop by running a spoon over the bottom scallop shell from the hinge toward your palm. Discard the dark stuff. You should be left with a gorgeous, pearly-white scallop muscle on the bottom shell. Cut beneath the muscle to release it from the shell. Remove any tough tendon from the outside edge of the scallop. Your scallop is now cleaned and ready to cook.

SERVES 3 TO 6

2 tablespoons canola oil
4 tablespoons butter
1 clove garlic, smashed, cleaned, and finely minced

3 cleaned scallops per person for an appetizer portion;
6 cleaned scallops per person for a main course
Salt and pepper, to taste

You will need a sturdy cast-iron skillet or equivalent. I am particularly fond of enameled cast-iron cookware. You want something with a heavy bottom that will evenly distribute the heat from your cooktop, and not have hot spots that might burn the scallops. Place the pan on a burner set on medium-high heat. Place the canola oil in the bottom of the pan with the butter. Mix together as the butter melts. Toss in the minced garlic and give the pan a stir. Let the oil heat up until it is hot, but not smoking. You can test the surface to see if it's hot enough by carefully dropping a drop of water into the pan. If it sizzles and dances across the surface, the oil's hot enough.

Using tongs, transfer the scallops to the prepared hot oil. Let brown for roughly 2 minutes, then turn to brown the other side. Remove cooked scallops from skillet onto warmed plates. Season with salt and pepper, to taste. Serve on a bed of Creamed Spinach with Olive Oil and Shallots (page 220).

Assault and Pepper

by Leslie Budewitz

The ice bag slid off my foot and I wriggled it back in place. The loft door opened and Reed walked in, followed by his father, carrying a worn black medical bag. Behind him came Laurel and Tag, lugging a basket of familiar white take-out bags.

"Am I throwing a party and didn't know it?" I asked.

Bags were set down, kisses exchanged, inquiries made.

"My son said you needed help." Ron Locke gestured toward my ankle. He had the same unruly black hair as his son.

Reed shrugged. "Can't have you on the sick list. Not while there's a killer on the loose."

Five minutes later, I was pinned down good, acupuncture needles ringing my ankle. In the kitchen, Tag and Laurel unpacked her bags and opened wine. A tossed salad and penne rigate with shrimp, asparagus, and a sesame-chile sauce. Warm, herby aromas drifted through the loft.

Laurel took pity on me and brought me a salty, crusty Parmesan breadstick, one of my very favorite foods, and a glass of white wine.

"And salty oat cookies for dessert?" I said, hopeful.

Tag made a noise like a seagull when it finds a cache of abandoned french fries.

"Sorry," she said. "Sold out."

The seagull squawked pitifully.

Tag and Laurel don't exactly hate each other. It's more like disdain. She considers him a two-timing, self-indulgent playboy who thinks he's God's gift to women.

And he sees her as an interfering, self-righteous snob.

They've each got a point. And yet he'd called her, and she'd come.

"Brother Cadfael," Ron Locke said a few minutes later, when we all had full plates and drinks. "Love those books."

"What's in the salad dressing?" Reed asked Laurel.

"My secret blend." She winked at me. One of our new blends.

They'd all come here to take care of me. Reed and Laurel wanted me to keep helping Tory, Tag didn't, and Ron Locke had no dog in the fight. But they all wanted me back on my feet—no pun intended—safe and sound.

It's enough to make a grown woman's eyes sting.

And it did.

Penne Rigate with Asparagus and Sesame-Chile Shrimp

~ From *Assault and Pepper* by Leslie Budewitz ~

No caterer on call? No matter! At Ripe, Laurel makes this with penne rigate, the short, ridged tubes, but the thicker-ridged rigatoni or far-falle, better known as bow ties, also work well.

This is an easy salad to serve warm or at room temperature, and requires very little shopping. Pepper keeps a small jar of minced ginger in her fridge for emergency cravings. If you like a little more heat, use hot sesame chili oil.

SERVES 6 TO 8

¼ cup white or brown sesame seeds

1 pound penne rigate

1 pound asparagus, trimmed and cut in ½-inch pieces (depending
    on what's available, substitute green beans or broccolini)

¼ cup peanut butter (chunky or fresh-ground)

¼ cup rice wine vinegar

¼ cup soy sauce

2 tablespoons sesame oil

2 tablespoons brown sugar

2 cloves garlic, pressed

1 tablespoon minced fresh ginger

½ teaspoon red pepper flakes

¼ cup hot water

1 pound medium shrimp, tails off, cooked

1 red bell pepper, seeded and cut into thin strips ("julienne")

4 green onions, thinly sliced and cut into 3- to 4-inch-long pieces

½ cup chopped fresh cilantro, divided

Preheat oven to 300° F. Spread the sesame seeds on a baking sheet and toast about 10 minutes. Don't overbake; they will continue to brown a bit as they cool.

Bring a large pot of water to boil. Cook pasta. During the last minute of cooking time, add the asparagus. Drain in a colander and rinse with cool water to stop the cooking.

While the pasta is cooking, make the sauce: Combine the peanut butter, vinegar, soy sauce, sesame oil, brown sugar, garlic, ginger, and red pepper flakes. Add the hot water and stir—a fork or small whisk works best—until sauce is smooth, breaking up any chunks.

Pour the pasta into a large bowl for serving. Add the shrimp, red bell pepper, green onions, and ¼ cup of the cilantro. Add the sauce and mix to combine all the ingredients. Top with the remaining ¼ cup cilantro and toasted sesame seeds.

Smoked Salmon and Mascarpone Risotto

~ From *The Long Quiche Goodbye* by Avery Aames ~

SERVES 4 TO 6

2 tablespoons unsalted butter
1 medium shallot, chopped
¼ cup yellow onion, chopped
1½ cups Arborio rice
1 cup dry white wine
2¾ cups chicken stock
1½ cups spinach, julienned
¼ cup fresh chives, minced, plus additional for garnish
4 ounces smoked salmon, chopped into bites
1 cup mascarpone cheese
Salt and pepper to taste

Heat 1 tablespoon of butter in 6-quart saucepan over medium heat. Add shallot and onion and cook until limp, approximately 3 minutes. Add rice and stir for 30 seconds. Add wine; stir to sizzling. Add 1 cup stock and bring to boil.

Turn heat down immediately and simmer. When rice absorbs liquid, add 1 more cup stock. Repeat until all stock is absorbed, approximately 10 minutes. Add water if needed (up to ½ cup) to keep rice moist.

Add spinach, chives, and salmon. Mix and cook 3 to 4 minutes. Remove from heat. Add cheese and rest of butter. Set on warm plates, garnished with chives.

Serve immediately.

Pasta with Strawberry, Leek, and Fennel

~ From *Town in a Strawberry Swirl* by B. B. Haywood ~

SERVES 4

2 tablespoons olive oil

2 tablespoons butter

½ fennel bulb, cut into small pieces (about 1 cup)

1 leek, cut into small cubes or strips

1 dozen strawberries, hulled and chopped

8 ounces angel hair pasta

½ cup grated Parmesan cheese

In a skillet, melt the olive oil and the butter over medium heat. Sauté the fennel and leek for 10 minutes.

Add the strawberries to the pan, sauté for an additional 2 to 3 minutes, or until they are soft.

While the leek and fennel are in the pan, bring a large pot of water to boil. Add the pasta and cook according to package directions. Drain and return pasta to cooking pot.

Add the leek, fennel, and strawberry to the pasta and mix.

Serve with grated Parmesan cheese sprinkled on the top.

This is a favorite dish at the Lightkeeper's Inn!

Clare Cosi's Skillet Lasagna (for Mike)

~ From *Billionaire Blend* by Cleo Coyle ~

On the night of the explosion, Clare was craving the comfort food of her childhood, namely her nonna's hearty lasagna. Without the time (or energy) to make her grandmother's many-layered casserole, she whipped up this quickie skillet version for herself and Detective Mike Quinn.

Given Quinn's interest in other kinds of comfort that night, they didn't actually eat this meal for many hours after it was cooked. No worries. Clare Cosi's Skillet Lasagna tastes even better as a leftover dish. "Heat and reheat"—good advice for this dinner, as well as Clare and Mike's weekend-to-weekend relationship.

SERVES 4

6 ounces curly lasagna noodles

Olive oil, for sautéing

1 yellow onion, finely chopped

1 cup baby bella mushrooms (optional), chopped

2 cloves garlic, minced

½ pound lean ground beef

½ pound ground pork or chicken

1 (28-ounce) can whole peeled tomatoes, drained and chopped
    (you can use a food processor for this)

¼ cup tomato paste

1 tablespoon Italian seasoning or a mix of dried rosemary, basil,
    and oregano

Handful of fresh, Italian (flat-leaf) parsley, chopped

¾ cup ricotta cheese (whole milk will give the best flavor)

½ cup mozzarella cheese, shredded (whole milk will give
the best flavor)

Sprinkling of grated Romano or Parmesan cheese, to taste

Step 1—Boil lasagna noodles: Bring a large pot of water to a boil. Break lasagna noodles into 3-inch pieces and cook according to the package directions. Drain well and set aside.

Step 2—Meat and veg: Lightly coat a large skillet with olive oil and set over medium heat. Add chopped onion. Cook and stir for 5 minutes, until translucent. Add the mushrooms and garlic and cook another 2 minutes. Stir in ground beef and pork, breaking up and cooking until meat is browned and no longer pink, about 5 to 7 minutes. When the meat is cooked, add chopped tomatoes, tomato paste, and Italian seasoning, stirring frequently, until thickened, about 6 minutes. Stir in parsley.

Step 3—Finish with noodles and cheese: Add in the cooked lasagna noodles and gently stir until heated through, about 5 minutes. Use a spoon to evenly top the mixture with big dollops of ricotta. Sprinkle the shredded mozzarella on top. Cover and cook a few more minutes, until everything is heated through. Dish out helpings and garnish with a sprinkling of grated Romano or Parmesan cheese and a bit of parsley on the side. To reheat, add more mozzarella, cover, and melt. *Molto bene!*

Fettucine with Minted Tomato Sauce, aka Fettucine a la Fresca

∽ From *Death al Dente* by Leslie Budewitz ∽

Francesca's nickname, Fresca, means "fresh" in Italian.

A great vegetarian option—something Erin and Fresca like to include in dinners for large groups.

SERVES 4 TO 6

½ cup walnuts, coarsely chopped

2 large ripe tomatoes or 1 (15-ounce) can chopped tomatoes
    (not a seasoned variety)

¼ cup dry white wine

1 tablespoon fresh basil leaves, chopped

¼ cup fresh mint leaves, chopped

¼ teaspoon salt

¼ teaspoon pepper

⅓ cup olive oil

1 small onion, finely chopped

1 clove garlic, minced or pressed

8 ounces fettucine

Additional grated Parmesan, for serving

Preheat oven to 350° F. Toast walnuts in a shallow pan for about 10 to 12 minutes. (Don't wait until they look dark, as they will continue cooking after being removed from the oven.)

If you're using fresh tomatoes, peel, seed, and chop them. In a medium bowl, mix the tomatoes with the wine, basil, mint, salt, and pepper.

Heat oil in a medium sauté pan over medium heat. Sauté onion until soft and just starting to brown; stir in garlic and cook briefly. Add tomato mixture and cook at a gentle boil, uncovered, about 5 minutes. Stir occasionally.

Meanwhile, bring a large pot of water to boil. Cook the pasta and drain well. Place in a warm serving bowl and spoon in the sauce, lifting to mix. Alternatively, make nests of spaghetti in individual bowls and spoon sauce into the middle of each nest. Sprinkle with toasted walnuts, and serve with a bowl of Parmesan. If you like bread with pasta, go ahead! Erin and Fresca readily mix homemade dishes with tasty commercial products. Ciabatta, baguettes, and French country bread complement these pastas beautifully.

Side Dishes

EXCERPT FROM *HOME OF THE BRAISED* BY JULIE HYZY......................217

Creamed Spinach with Olive Oil and Shallots.......................................220

Mashed Potatoes...221

Clare's Fully Loaded Colcannon for Mike 222

Funeral Potatoes..224

EXCERPT FROM *BOWLED OVER* BY VICTORIA HAMILTON 226

Jaymie's Fourth of July Potato Salad...227

Twice-Baked Potatoes..229

Molasses Whipped Sweet Potatoes 231

EXCERPT FROM *TOWN IN A PUMPKIN BASH*
BY B. B. HAYWOOD...232

Wild Rice and Pumpkin Pilaf 234

EXCERPT FROM *THE LONG QUICHE GOODBYE*
BY AVERY AAMES..235

Polenta with Taleggio and Basil...237

Home of the Braised

by Julie Hyzy

"What is with the two of you today?" I asked Cyan the next afternoon.

She dropped an armload of shallots onto the workspace before her. "What are you talking about?"

Standing at the long stovetop, I raised the spoon I'd been using to check on the simmering chicken stock and gestured vaguely out the door. "You and Bucky have been the disappearing twins." I pointed the spoon at the shallots. "How long ago did you leave to get those?" I asked. "It should have taken you five minutes, tops. You were gone for at least a half hour."

Virgil leaned against the giant mixer, watching as its beater smoothed lumps from sweet potatoes. "About time you call the two of them out for slacking instead of always finding fault with me." He flashed an unpleasant smile. "Gets boring with only one whipping boy, you know."

I'd confronted Virgil this morning about his abrupt departure after the tasting, reminding him that I'd wanted to talk with him, and reprimanding him for taking off without telling me. He'd reacted with dismissive anger, claiming that I singled him out for censure. I was getting tired of his antics and attitude.

Cyan looked up at the clock. "Has it been that long?" She began sorting the shallots, examining the rose-colored bulbs one at a time, wrinkling her nose when she encountered the occasional moldy one and pushing those off to the side. "You sure?"

I was about to answer when Bucky returned, whistling. He gave me a grin as he pulled a fresh apron from the pile.

"You both remember that we have a state dinner in three days," I said. "It could be the most important state dinner President Hyden has ever hosted."

"I don't think anyone has forgotten that," Bucky said. He crossed the kitchen to peer over Virgil's shoulder. "The kitchen is running at full efficiency, isn't it?"

"Personal space, man. Personal space," Virgil said. "Back off."

Unruffled, Bucky gave a crooked grin. "Yep," he said. "Full efficiency given our"—he rolled his eyes, indicating Virgil—"current resources."

"Hey," Virgil said, turning. "Ever since I agreed to help with this dinner, you and Miss Chameleon Eyes have been pretty scarce. All your work is falling on me."

That was an exaggeration if I'd ever heard one. Even though Bucky and Cyan had been out of the kitchen more often than usual, their work hadn't suffered because of it. I wondered if my including Virgil in the plans had upset them so much they couldn't stand to be in the same room with him anymore? Regret over my hasty decision was growing.

"Give me a break," Bucky said. "Except for the First Lady's tasting, which I heard was the worst-run one in the history of this kitchen, you haven't done anything to move this state dinner further along."

"Oh yeah?" Virgil pointed. "I'm making these potatoes. Again." He pointed at me. "This time with the lame recipe she's making me use instead of with the special touch that made them interesting."

"Whoa! Be still my heart," Bucky said, grasping at his chest. "You're following directions? I don't know if I can handle the shock."

Virgil turned his back on the potatoes to face Bucky. "You're just afraid of me. Admit it. You know that the minute I take over the state dinners, you're on your way out."

The last thing I needed was for this to erupt into a brawl.

I was about to step in, but Bucky surprised me by saying. "You know what, Virgil, you have a point. Seems to me you're moving up so quickly here that Ollie's not going to need me anymore." He turned to me and winked. "Think I should update my resume?"

He had to be joking. "Bucky," I said. "Don't tease."

Virgil scowled. "I wouldn't want to get my hopes up."

"Stop this right now," I said. "We get far more accomplished when we work together. Agreed?"

Bucky was still grinning, which always had the capacity to unnerve me. Although he'd proven to be a trustworthy ally, he was crusty and blunt. Smiling was not his face's natural state. Something was up. Something big. Virgil ignored me. Cyan was the only one to show solidarity when she said, "That's absolutely right."

Creamed Spinach
with Olive Oil and Shallots

~ From *Buffalo West Wing* by Julie Hyzy ~

SERVES 6

2 tablespoons olive oil

¼ cup shallots, finely minced

10 to 12 ounces fresh spinach, washed, dried,
    and trimmed to remove tough stems

2 tablespoons butter

1 tablespoon flour

½ cup liquid—milk, chicken broth, or white wine,
    depending on personal taste

1 pinch freshly ground nutmeg

¼ to ½ tablespoon salt, or to taste

Freshly cracked black pepper, to taste

¼ cup grated Parmesan cheese

Put olive oil in a sturdy cast-iron skillet or equivalent over medium-high heat. When oil is hot, add shallots, stirring until they are translucent, about 1 minute. Add spinach, and continue stirring until mixture is heated through and reduced and wilted, about 2 to 3 minutes.

Remove from heat. In a large skillet, melt the butter over medium heat. Add flour and whisk vigorously until a smooth bubbling paste forms, about 1 minute. Slowly whisk in the liquid. Keep stirring until you have a thickened sauce. Add the nutmeg and salt and pepper, to taste. Whisk. Add in the spinach mixture. Stir to coat. Plate. Top with grated cheese. Serve.

Mashed Potatoes

~ From *If Mashed Potatoes Could Dance* by Paige Shelton ~

Long before I even knew nonmechanical potato mashers existed, I'd watch my own grandmother whip up her mashed potatoes—and that's what it seems they're called these days: whipped. But to me, this will always be the best version of mashed.

SERVES 7 TO 12

5 pounds baking potatoes, peeled and cut into chunks
1½ cups (2½ sticks) salted butter, softened
Splash of milk
Salt and pepper, to taste

In a large pot of boiling water, cook the potatoes until they are soft enough that a fork moves easily through them, about 30 to 40 minutes. Drain the potatoes and either return them to the pot or put them in a mixing bowl. (I prefer the pot, as the residual heat helps melt the butter.) Add the butter and a splash of milk and mix with an electric mixer until all the ingredients are blended together and the potatoes aren't too lumpy (I like a few lumps). Add salt and pepper, to taste, and give the potatoes one more mix.

This is a huge amount of mashed potatoes. I've fed as many as 12 people with this recipe, but if you have big potato fans, this will serve 7 or 8. The leftovers reheat well, too.

Clare's Fully Loaded Colcannon for Mike

~ From *A Brew to a Kill* by Cleo Coyle ~

Growing up in a big, Irish-American family, Mike Quinn ate colcannon on a regular basis. The dish takes its name from the Gaelic word cál ceannann, meaning "white-headed cabbage"—and kale or cabbage is in the traditional recipe, along with potatoes, onions (or scallions, chives, or leeks), and cream and/or butter.

Clare often made the traditional version for Mike, but for this recipe, she decided to give it an Italian kiss of olive oil; a warm, sweet hug of garlic; and a big old American-style finish of gooey melted Cheddar and smoky crumbled bacon. Like a "fully loaded" baked potato, she's loaded Mike's colcannon with comfort-food flavor.

MAKES ABOUT 6 CUPS

1 pound red potatoes, cut into uniform pieces

2 slices thick-cut bacon (or 4 regular bacon slices)

1 tablespoon olive oil

2 cloves garlic, chopped

1 large onion, chopped

½ head cabbage, sliced thin (approximately 6 cups)

1 cup milk

1 tablespoon butter

½ teaspoon salt

¼ teaspoon white pepper

⅔ cup Cheddar cheese, shredded

Step 1—Cook the potatoes: Clare uses a simple collapsible steamer basket in a deep pot. Steam the halved red potatoes until cooked through, about 15 to 20 minutes. Remove the pot from heat, drain any extra water, and cover to keep the potatoes warm.

Step 2—Render bacon and sauté veggies: While potatoes are steaming, chop bacon into ½-inch pieces and cook over very low heat to render the fat. When bacon is brown, remove from pan and set aside. Turn the heat to medium, and add the olive oil to the drippings in the pan. Then add the garlic and onion and cook until the onions are translucent, about 3 minutes. Add cabbage and continue cooking another 5 minutes, stirring often.

Step 3—Reduce heat to low. Stir in milk, butter, salt, and white pepper; cover and cook until the cabbage is tender, about 8 minutes.

Step 4—Add the hot cabbage mixture to the potatoes. Mash with a metal potato masher or large fork until the ingredients are blended. Fold in the cheese and cover the pot until the cheese is melted. Serve topped with crumbled bacon bits.

Funeral Potatoes

~ From *If Mashed Potatoes Could Dance* by Paige Shelton ~

When I first moved to Utah, I heard someone talking about funeral potatoes. My first reaction was one of distaste for the name—how horrible!—but its origin was soon explained. Frequently, funeral potatoes are served as part of a dinner for a grieving family. Upon hearing this explanation, I said, "Oh, so they're like casserole potatoes?" The person I was talking to was none too pleased to have the name messed with. I learned quickly, and once I tasted them for myself, I grew to respect their well-known moniker. They are delicious and, I've discovered as time has gone on, not served only at funerals.

SERVES 10, BUT I DOUBLE THE RECIPE IF I EXPECT
THERE WILL BE MORE THAN 8 PEOPLE ENJOYING IT

1 (32-ounce) bag frozen shredded hash browns
　　(I use Simply Shred brand)
2 (10¾-ounce) cans condensed cream of chicken soup
2 cups sour cream
1½ cups grated Cheddar cheese (I use sharp,
　　but any kind is fine)
½ cup (1 stick) salted butter, melted, plus
　　1 to 2 tablespoons for sautéing onions
½ cup chopped onion, sautéed in butter until translucent

TOPPING
2 cups finely crushed cornflakes
2 tablespoons butter, melted

Preheat the oven to 350° F. Grease the bottom and sides of a 9 × 13-inch baking dish.

In a large bowl, combine the hash browns, soup, sour cream, cheese, ½ cup of melted butter, and sautéed onion, and pour into the baking dish.

In a small bowl, combine the cornflakes and 2 tablespoons of melted butter, and sprinkle over the top of the potato mixture. Bake 30 minutes.

A special thanks to my hairdresser, Matt Barney, for his invaluable contributions to this recipe, and for all the others we discuss and ponder. You're the best, Matt!

Bowled Over

by Victoria Hamilton

In the kitchen, boiled potatoes and bowls of pasta were cooling to be made into salads. Jaymie had intended to try a recipe from one of the vintage cookbooks from the box Becca had brought home, *The Lilly Wallace New American Cook Book*, from 1943. But looking at it again, it appeared too complicated; she'd have to make not just one but two dressings, homemade French and homemade mayonnaise. Instead, she rifled through her grandmother's well-worn handwritten recipe book and found Grandma Leighton's classic potato salad. Much better!

She also couldn't resist making something quite different: A weird-looking lime jelly mold was chilling in the fridge. Jaymie was fascinated by the recipe's description of it as "elegant enough for guests, nutritious enough for the children, and sure to be the belle of your buffet ball!" There were always lots of exclamation points after such dubious claims. Shredded cabbage and carrot, along with frozen peas, peered mysteriously through the brilliant green miasma of lime gelatin. If she put wobbly eyes on it, it could pass for an alien life-form. Like fruitcake, it was doomed to be an inedible conversation piece, but if it got a few laughs, it would serve its purpose.

Jaymie's Fourth of July Potato Salad

~ From *Bowled Over* by Victoria Hamilton ~

SERVES 6 TO 8

8 medium potatoes (leave the peel on
    for best nutrition)
1½ cups mayonnaise
2 tablespoons cider vinegar, or substitute
    dill pickle juice, as you like
1 tablespoon yellow mustard
1 teaspoon garlic powder
1 teaspoon celery salt
½ teaspoon pepper
1 to 2 celery ribs, diced
1 carrot, grated coarsely
2 green onions, chopped
5 hard-boiled eggs, coarsely chopped
Paprika, for garnish
Chives, for garnish

1—Boil peeled potatoes in salted water until just tender. Cool to room temperature. Dice however small you want the chunks, and place in a large bowl.

2—Mix mayonnaise, cider vinegar, mustard, garlic powder, celery salt, and pepper in another bowl.

3—Pour over potatoes. Add celery, grated carrot, and onions, and mix well. Stir in chopped eggs.

4—Turn in to a pretty bowl, and sprinkle a little paprika and chopped chives on top.

Best done the night before for the flavors to meld and develop. Do not let this potato salad stay at room temperature for long! Mayonnaise spoils quickly in the heat.

Twice-Baked Potatoes

~ From *If Mashed Potatoes Could Dance* by Paige Shelton ~

Twice-baked potatoes aren't very difficult, but I've sometimes found that too many ingredients are added. I love this full recipe, with the bacon, but occasionally I make these potatoes just with cheese. And don't be afraid to experiment with the type of cheese. My sister-in-law made twice-baked potatoes last year with an Irish Cheddar, and they were delicious. Other variations include adding garlic and herbs like rosemary, but I still like to stick with the original recipe.

SERVES 4

4 large baking potatoes
8 slices bacon (optional)
1 cup sour cream
½ cup milk
¼ cup (½ stick) salted butter, softened
½ teaspoon salt
½ teaspoon pepper
1 cup shredded Cheddar cheese (again, I like sharp,
    but use whatever kind you prefer)

Preheat the oven to 350° F.

Scrub the potatoes, pat dry, and poke each one several times with a fork. Wrap the potatoes individually in foil and bake them in the oven for 1 hour. Meanwhile, place the bacon in a skillet over medium-high heat and cook until crispy. When done, remove the bacon from the pan, drain it on some paper towel, then crumble it and set it aside. Skip this part if you don't want to include bacon.

When the potatoes are done, remove from the oven and let them cool for about 10 minutes, then slice them in half lengthwise and scoop out the innards into a bowl. Reserve skins and set them aside.

To the potatoes, add the sour cream, milk, butter, salt, pepper, and half of the cheese. Mix with an electric hand mixer until creamy.

Spoon some of the potato mixture into each of the potato skins. Top each with some of the remaining cheese and crumbled bacon. Bake for another 15 minutes. Serve!

Molasses Whipped Sweet Potatoes

~ From *Home of the Braised* by Julie Hyzy ~

Served at the Inaugural Luncheon, 2009.

MAKES 2 QUARTS

3 large sweet potatoes (about 3 pounds)

2 tablespoons unsalted butter

1 teaspoon kosher salt

¼ cup orange juice

½ tablespoon brown sugar

1 teaspoon ground cumin

1 tablespoon molasses

2 tablespoons maple syrup

Preheat oven to 400° F.

Place sweet potatoes on a baking sheet and roast until easily pierced with a fork, about 1 hour.

Peel the skin off of the sweet potatoes while still hot. By hand or mixer, smash potatoes until all large chunks are gone. Combine the potatoes, butter, salt, orange juice, brown sugar, ground cumin, molasses, and maple syrup in a large bowl. Continue to mix all together until all lumps are gone. Adjust any of the seasonings to your specific tastes.

Note: Can be made 1 day before; keep refrigerated and reheat just before serving.

Town in a Pumpkin Bash

by B. B. Haywood

The Lightkeeper's Inn was crowded and the parking lot was full, but Tristan Pruitt dropped the car with a valet, and they were promptly seated at one of the best tables in the dining room, in a softly lit alcove with a bay window overlooking the front of the inn toward the sea.

A waitress came by, took their drink orders, and chatted briefly with Tristan before heading off toward the bar. Tristan waved a friendly greeting to the bartender, and both Oliver LaForce, the head innkeeper, and Alben "Alby" Alcott, the assistant innkeeper, stopped by to say a quick hello. Mason Flint, the chairman of the town council, also paid his respects.

"My," Candy said, "you're certainly a popular person tonight. When I agreed to have dinner with you, I didn't know I'd be sitting at a table with a celebrity."

Their drinks arrived, with an appetizer. It was one of Chef Colin's seasonal creations—lobster dumplings with goat cheese, accompanied by a spicy apple dipping sauce, and on another warmed plate, roasted butternut-squash bruschetta sprinkled with olive oil and aromatic herb seasoning. They were also treated to glasses of authentic Colonial cider, prepared especially for Chef Colin's kitchen.

As they dipped, munched, and drank, they talked about Pruitt Manor and Tristan's family, the wealthy Pruitts, until the waitress returned and took their dinner orders. Tristan watched Candy the entire time as she chose blackened tilapia with rice pilaf and a fall vegetable medley, and then she watched with interest as he scanned the menu, flipped it closed, and crisply handed it back to the waitress. "I'll have the usual."

"And what's that?" Candy asked curiously.

He shrugged. "Their prime rib here is excellent. Chef Colin uses this amazing bourbon glaze."

"What, you're not ordering a cigar too?" she asked, amused by his order.

"That comes later."

Wild Rice and Pumpkin Pilaf

~ From *Town in a Pumpkin Bash* by B. B. Haywood ~

SERVES 4 TO 6

2 tablespoons butter

1 large onion or 2 shallots, chopped

2 cups wild rice or wild rice blend (usually with brown rice)

4 cups vegetable broth

1 cup cubed fresh pumpkin or squash

2 tablespoons olive oil

½ cup chopped mushrooms

In a large saucepan over medium heat, melt butter. Add the onion and sauté until soft, about 5 minutes.

Add the dry rice and mix with the onions.

Add the vegetable broth, making sure the rice/broth ratio is correct, according to package directions.

Cook the rice 50 minutes, or according to package directions.

While the rice is cooking, cube the pumpkin or squash.

Heat the olive oil in a large skillet over medium heat.

Add the mushrooms and pumpkin cubes.

Cook, stirring until browned.

When the rice is cooked, stir in the pumpkin and mushrooms.

This recipe is a favorite of Doc's. Enjoy!

The Long Quiche Goodbye

by Avery Aames

"I'm not dead, Charlotte," Grandpère Etienne said.

"But you are retired, Pépère." I tweaked his rosy cheek and skirted around him to throw a drop cloth over the rustic wooden table that usually held wheels of cheese, like Abbaye de Belloc, Manchego, and Humboldt Fog, the latter cheese a great pairing with chardonnay. Dust billowed up as the edges of the drop cloth hit the shop floor.

"A retired person may have an opinion."

"Yes, he can." I smiled. "But you put me in charge."

"You and Matthew."

My adorable cousin. If I had a brother, he would be just like Matthew. Bright, funny, and invaluable as an ally against my grandfather when he was being stubborn.

"What does Matthew say about all this?" Pépère folded his arms around his bulging girth. The buttons on his blue-striped shirt looked ready to pop. The doctor said Pépère needed to watch his weight and cholesterol, and I had been trying to get him to eat more of the hard cheeses that contained a lower fat content than the creamy cheeses he loved so much, but he had perfected the art of sneaking little bites. What was I to do?

I gave my grandfather's shoulder a gentle squeeze. "Pépère, I love this place. So does Matthew. We only want the best for it. Trust us. That's why you made us partners."

"Bah! So many changes. Why fix something that isn't broken? The shop made a good profit last year."

"Because life is all about change. Man does not live by cheese alone," I joked.

Polenta with Taleggio and Basil

∽ From *The Long Quiche Goodbye* by Avery Aames ∽

SERVES 6 TO 8

4 cups water

1 teaspoon salt

1 cup polenta cornmeal

2 to 4 tablespoons extra-virgin olive oil

1 cup fresh basil leaves, separated

8 ounces Taleggio cheese, thinly sliced

Bring water and salt to a boil. Add polenta cornmeal in a thin stream. Keep stirring until cornmeal pulls away from sides of pan (no lumps). Turn down heat to simmer for 25 minutes, stirring every 5 minutes or so.

While the cornmeal is cooking, in a separate pan over medium heat, stir-fry the basil in olive oil until crispy, then drain on paper towels. Spoon hot polenta onto each plate. Lay a couple of slices of Taleggio cheese on each portion, and finish with the fried basil.

Desserts

EXCERPT FROM READ IT AND WEEP BY JENN MCKINLAY 243

Nancy's Raspberry Petit Fours 245

Blueberry-Lemon Shortbread 247

Champagne Cookies 248

Anginetti (Glazed Lemon Cookies) 250

EXCERPT FROM FINAL SENTENCE BY DARYL WOOD GERBER 253

Aunt Vera's Gluten-Free Orange-Chocolate Biscotti 255

Chocolate Zombie Clusters 258

Sandy's Favorite Whoopie Pies 260

Aphrodisiac Brownies 262

Nanna Tibbetts's Moose Mincemeat (and Moose
    Mincemeat Cookies) 265

Chocolate Soufflé 267

Melody's Chocolate Mousse 269

Lemon Steamed Pudding 270

Granny Sebastian's Bread Pudding 271

Candy Holliday's Blueberry Whipped Cream 273

Brie-Blueberry Ice Cream (and Blueberry Sauce) 274

Theodosia's Earl Grey Sorbet 276

Jenna's Caramel Macchiato Ice Cream (and Sauce) 277

Baileys Irish Cream and Caramel-Nut Fudge 280

Jasmine Tea Truffles 282

Cake Pops 283

EXCERPT FROM A DEADLY GRIND BY VICTORIA HAMILTON 285

Queen Elizabeth Cake 287

Death by Chocolate Cupcakes 290

    EXCERPT FROM *IF FRIED CHICKEN COULD FLY*
    BY PAIGE SHELTON 292

Red Velvet Cake/Cupcakes 294

Orange Dreamsicle Cupcakes 296

Moonlight Madness 298

    EXCERPT FROM *SPRINKLE WITH MURDER* BY JENN MCKINLAY 300

Mojito Cupcakes 301

Tinkerbells 302

Gluten-Free Chocolate Cupcakes with Ganache Frosting 304

Vegan Vanilla Cupcakes 306

Pumpkin Cupcakes with Whipped Cream Frosting 308

Candy Holliday's Pumpkin Cheesecake Swirl 310

    EXCERPT FROM *PIES AND PREJUDICE* BY ELLERY ADAMS 312

Charmed Shoofly Pie 314

Charmed Piecrust and Egg Wash 315

    EXCERPT FROM *PEACH PIES AND ALIBIS* BY ELLERY ADAMS 317

Charmed Georgia Peach Pie 319

Charmed Banana Puddin' Pie 321

Charmed Chocolate-Bourbon Pecan Pie 323

Charmed Red Hot–Apple Pie 324

Charmed Mini Maple-Pecan Pies with Maple
    Whipped Cream 326

Charmed Heart-Shaped White Chocolate–Raspberry
    Cream Two-Bite Pies 328

    EXCERPT FROM *IF MASHED POTATOES COULD DANCE*
    BY PAIGE SHELTON 330

Sweet Potato Pie with Marshmallow Meringue 331

Key Lime–Strawberry Whipped Topping Pie 334

Sandra Gregoire's Charmed "Customer of the Week"
Lime Pie...336

EXCERPT FROM TOWN IN A STRAWBERRY SWIRL
BY B. B. HAYWOOD...338

Herr Georg's *Obstkuchen*: German Strawberry Torte.............341

Chocolate Stout Brownie Torte...343

Deep-Fried Bananas with Baked Plantains.............................345

Charmed Apple, Pear, and Cherry Crisp................................347

Read It and Weep

by Jenn McKinlay

"So, what did I miss?" she asked. "Have we gotten to the part where we all agree that Colin Firth was the best Darcy ever?"

"We just started, and I thought we were discussing the book not the film," Lindsey said.

She reached over the card she was working on and took a finger sandwich off of the tray Nancy had brought since it was her turn to bring the food. She had run with the tea idea, so it was finger sandwiches, hot tea and petit fours.

"Who do you think would make a better Darcy?" Charlene asked. "Sully or Robbie?"

She caught Lindsey on an inhale and she began to hack and choke. Violet pounded her on the back while the others watched anxiously.

"Neither," Lindsey said. "If one is Darcy than the other would be Wickham and I don't think that either of them could be—Ugh, did you know that Mark Twain is said to have felt an 'animal repugnance' toward Austen's writing?"

They all looked at her.

"What?" she asked.

"That wasn't even an attempt at a smooth transition," Mary said with a sad shake of her head. "It was pathetic."

"Do you think we'll ever have a book club meeting where my personal life is not a part of the discussion?" Lindsey asked.

The others all exchanged a look and as one they turned back and said, "No."

Nancy's Raspberry Petit Fours

～ From *Read It and Weep* by Jenn McKinlay ～

MAKES 3 DOZEN

½ cup (1 stick) salted butter, softened

1 cup sugar

1 teaspoon vanilla extract

1⅓ cups all-purpose flour

2 teaspoons baking powder

½ teaspoon salt

⅔ cup milk

3 egg whites

Seedless raspberry jam

GLAZE

32 ounces (4 cups) confectioners' sugar

⅔ cup water

2 teaspoons orange extract

Candy beads or frosting rosebuds, for garnish

Preheat oven to 350° F. Grease a 9-inch-square baking dish and set aside.

In a large bowl, mix together the butter, sugar, and extract until fluffy. In a medium bowl, whisk together the flour, baking powder, and salt. Slowly add to the wet mixture, alternately adding with the milk until well blended. In a small bowl, beat the egg whites until they form soft peaks, then gently fold into the batter. Pour batter into the baking dish and bake for 20 to 25 minutes until a toothpick inserted near the center comes out clean. Once cake is completely cooled, cut into 1½-inch squares. Remove the squares from the baking dish and set on a large cookie sheet about two inches apart. Once on the cookie sheet, slice each square into two layers and put a teaspoon of raspberry jam between the two layers.

In a large bowl, combine the glaze ingredients and beat until glaze is a smooth consistency. Now pour the glaze evenly over the tops and sides of each cake square. Make sure they are coated completely. Garnish the top with candy beads or frosting rosebuds or the garnish of your choice. Allow to dry.

Blueberry-Lemon Shortbread

~ From *Town in a Blueberry Jam* by B. B. Haywood ~

MAKES ABOUT 2 DOZEN

2 cups all-purpose or white whole wheat flour

⅛ teaspoon salt

½ cup dark brown sugar

½ tablespoon grated lemon zest

¾ cup dried Maine wild blueberries

1 cup (2 sticks) butter, softened

Preheat oven to 350° F.

In a large bowl, combine flour, salt, sugar, lemon zest, and dried blueberries.

Cut in the butter and mix until crumbly.

Continue mixing until a smooth dough forms.

Chill for 30 minutes.

Roll out the cold dough to ½-inch thickness between two sheets of wax paper.

Cut out with cookie cutters or score and cut into squares.

Place 1 inch apart on an ungreased cookie sheet.

Bake for 15 to 18 minutes, or until lightly browned.

Champagne Cookies

~ From *If Fried Chicken Could Fly* by Paige Shelton ~

To this day, I crave Barbara's Bake Shop champagne cake. I lived in Des Moines, Iowa, for a number of years when I was a kid. Barbara's was only a few blocks from our house, but once I discovered the shop's champagne cake, I was a convert. When I got to choose the cake, it was always champagne and it was always from Barbara's. Sadly, Barbara's closed a number of years ago.

I created this recipe with the champagne cake flavor in mind. I had some help with the frosting. Thank you, Heidi Baschnagel!

MAKES ABOUT 2 DOZEN (2-INCH-WIDE) COOKIES

3½ cups all-purpose flour

½ tablespoon baking powder

½ teaspoon baking soda

½ teaspoon salt

½ cup (1 stick) unsalted butter, softened

1 cup sugar

4 ounces cream cheese, softened

2 eggs

½ tablespoon vanilla extract

5 drops red food coloring

½ cup champagne (I use an affordable pink variety.)

FROSTING

4½ cups confectioners' sugar

¾ pound (3 sticks) salted butter, softened

2 tablespoons pink champagne

A few drops red food coloring

Up to 4 tablespoons water, for consistency

Edible silver glitter (optional)

Preheat oven to 350° F.

In large bowl mix together the flour, baking powder, baking soda, and salt.

In another large bowl, cream together the butter, sugar, and cream cheese.

Add the eggs, vanilla, red food coloring, and champagne. Blend to incorporate.

Add flour mixture and mix until combined.

Chill in refrigerator for at least 2 hours.

On floured surface, roll out the dough to ¼ to ½ inch thick.

Cut into desired shapes, and place shapes about two inches apart on an ungreased cookie sheet.

Bake for about 12 minutes, or until edges are slightly browned. Let the cookies cool on the cookie sheet for about 1 minute and then remove them to a cooling rack. While the cookies cool, make the frosting.

MAKE FROSTING

In a large bowl, mix the sugar, butter, champagne, and food coloring. Add a little bit of water at a time to achieve the desired frosting consistency—I think thicker is better.

Spread the frosting over the cooled cookies, and, if desired, sprinkle with edible glitter.

Anginetti
(Glazed Lemon Cookies)

~ From *Espresso Shot* by Cleo Coyle ~

The anginetti *are a satisfying treat to have with coffee. Light and buttery with a sweet lemon glaze, they often make their appearance during the holidays, and the sprinkle of nonpareils (confetti in Italian) over the glaze makes them an excellent wedding cookie, too, since the colorful sugar balls call to mind the longstanding wedding tradition of giving guests almonds coated with hard-sugar shells as favors. (The bitterness of the almonds and the sweetness of the sugar represent the bittersweet truths of married life.) While recipes for* anginetti *vary—some bakers shape figure-eights or knots from a rope of dough, others simply create lemon drops—my version uses the ring shape in honor of Nunzio's wedding rings. My version is also a bit sweeter than more traditional recipes.*

MAKES 3 TO 4 DOZEN COOKIES, DEPENDING
ON SIZE AND SHAPE OF COOKIE

6 tablespoons unsalted butter, softened

¾ cup granulated sugar

1½ teaspoons pure vanilla extract

½ teaspoon lemon extract

1 teaspoon fresh lemon zest (grated from rind)

⅛ teaspoon salt (pinch or two)

3 large eggs

¼ cup whole milk

2½ cups all-purpose flour (sifted)

4 teaspoons baking powder

LEMON GLAZE

2 tablespoons unsalted butter

4 tablespoons water

2 teaspoons lemon extract

2 cups confectioners' sugar (sifted)

With an electric mixer, cream the butter and sugar together with vanilla and lemon extract, lemon zest, and salt. Add eggs and beat for a minute or two until light and fluffy. Add in flour and baking powder, blending well with mixer until you have a dough (be careful not to overmix the dough or cookies will be tough). Dough should be soft and sticky. Chill for at least 1 hour—cold dough is easier to work with.

Preheat the oven to 350° F. Line baking sheet with parchment paper or silicone sheets or spray surface with cooking spray. With well-greased hands, shape bits of dough into small ropes (about the thickness of a woman's wedding ring finger), make a ring with the rope of dough about 2 inches in diameter, and press the ends together on the baking sheet. Or for lemon drops, simply roll pieces of dough about 1 inch in size and place on baking sheet. (If you want to go really rustic, then don't even bother chilling the dough. Simply drop teaspoonfuls of the sticky dough onto the baking sheet.) Bake about 10 to 15 minutes. Don't overcook. Baking time may vary, depending on your oven. Let the cookies cool before glazing and decorating.

MAKE GLAZE

In a nonstick saucepan, place the butter, water, and lemon extract over low heat. Stir slowly until butter melts. Add confectioners' sugar, a little at a time, stirring constantly. Wait until sugar dissolves before adding more. Continue until all sugar has been added. Stir or whisk until your glaze is smooth. Use a pastry brush to glaze your cooled cookies. (Optional: If you wish to add decorations to your cookies, such as nonpareils or colored sugar, be sure to sprinkle while glaze is still warm. I actually prefer the cookies without any decorations, just the lemon glaze.)

Final Sentence

by Daryl Wood Gerber

I found myself back in the kitchen facing the recipe and the bag of ingredients. Would baking truly help me calm down?

Following Katie's suggestion, I switched on the television and located the Food Network. I couldn't believe it. Though I rarely watched TV, I had landed on a repeat of the *Radical Cake Battle* show that Desiree had judged. Contestants and their assistants raced around their individual kitchens. Dora the Lady in Red wielded a chainsaw; Leo the Latin Lover brandished a blowtorch; Macbeth the Gay Blade hacked with an axe. Like I told Katie, not quite my cup of tea, even with Desiree's appearance. I clicked the dial until I found the Travel Channel and Anthony Bourdain's *No Reservations.* Bourdain was on a food tour of Greece. While he educated his audience about the wild foods found on the islands, I fetched a mixing bowl, measuring cup, and spoon. Next, I pulled a cube of butter from the refrigerator. Katie had reminded me not to cheat on the recipe; I had to use butter, not oil or lard. As the oven preheated, I measured oats and flour, sugar and butter. I cracked eggs. I added vanilla, chocolate chips, and nuts. By the time I had put all the ingredients into the bowl, I was salivating but my palms were clammy. Not from fear. I had put the killer from my mind. No, I was worried that my cookies would stink. I questioned whether I had added baking soda or baking powder. I tasted the raw batter. Not bad. Memories of myself, as a kid, sneaking tablespoons of batter and my mother rapping my knuckles with a wooden spoon, rushed through me.

Fifteen minutes later, I pulled my first batch of chocolate chip cookies from the oven. Obeying the recipe's directions to the letter, I let them rest on the cookie sheet for two minutes. Next, I transferred them, using a spatula, to paper towels to cool. Unable to restrain myself, I snatched two. *Hot, hot, hot.* I juggled them between hands, fetched some kibble for Tigger, and retreated to the comfort of my sofa. The kitty sprang into my lap and snuggled into a ball. By this time, Bourdain—Tony to his friends—was sipping ouzo, a licorice-tasting liqueur David used to enjoy. As the show shifted to commercial, I heard a thud.

Aunt Vera's Gluten-Free Orange-Chocolate Biscotti

∽ From *Final Sentence* by Daryl Wood Gerber ∽

Oh, how I adore making cookies. I love time-intensive cookies, the kind I can sink my hands into. Hands, as you might have figured out, have great meaning to me. They are the symbolic equivalent of power and balance. With your hands, you can make delicious foods as well as bring comfort. These biscotti, which I have chosen to make gluten-free because one of my dearest friends cannot eat wheat, are a wonderful combination of textures and the perfect accompaniment to a good cup of coffee or tea. (I have made these same cookies using regular flour. Just substitute regular flour for the sweet rice flour and tapioca starch. You won't need the xanthan gum, a magical ingredient for gluten-free bakers.)

Note: This recipe takes no time to put together, but the dough takes a long time to bake.

MAKES 30 TO 36 BISCOTTI

1 cup sweet rice flour
¾ cup tapioca starch
½ teaspoon xanthan gum
¼ teaspoon salt
½ teaspoon baking soda
2 eggs

¾ cup sugar

1 teaspoon vanilla extract

¼ teaspoon orange extract

Grated zest of ½ orange

2 tablespoons fresh orange juice

1 cup semisweet chocolate chips

Preheat the oven to 300° F. Place racks in the upper and lower thirds of the oven.

Line a cookie sheet with foil or parchment paper, or grease the cookie sheet.

In a small bowl, mix sweet rice flour, tapioca starch (do not tamp down), xanthan gum, salt, and baking soda. Set aside.

In another bowl, mix the eggs, sugar, vanilla, and orange extract. Over the top of the bowl, grate the orange zest. Add the orange juice. Mix in the gluten-free flour mixture. Then stir in the chocolate chips. The mixture will be cookie-dough consistency—gooey.

Scrape the batter, in 2 skinny lines, the full length of the cookie sheet, leaving 3 inches between lines. Use a spatula to clean up the strips. If necessary, rinse the spatula with hot water.

Put the cookie sheet on the lower rack and bake for 15 minutes. Turn the pan front to back and bake another 20 minutes until golden brown. Remove the pan and cool on a rack for 15 minutes. Leave the oven on.

Using a spatula, transfer the baked strips to a cutting board. Using a serrated knife, slice the loaves on a diagonal into ½-inch-wide slices. Place the cookies on their narrow sides to "stand," this time on an unlined cookie sheet, at least ½ inch apart. Bake for 20 to 25 minutes, until golden brown. If necessary, rotate the pans halfway through the baking process so the cookies are evenly baked.

Cool the biscotti completely before storing. These may be kept in an airtight container for a few weeks. They are fabulous dipped into a cup of coffee.

Chocolate Zombie Clusters

~ From *Murder by Mocha* by Cleo Coyle ~

When Clare Cosi isn't dreaming of Mike, she's dreaming up recipes. From the moment Detective Sue Ellen Bass mentioned zombies on Eighth Avenue, Clare couldn't stop thinking about the challenge of creating a chocolate recipe that was so easy a zombie could make it (no-bake, natch!) and so delicious it would send the eater into a food-bliss trance. Maybe a cross between a cookie and a candy, hmm . . .

For inspiration, she did a little research into real zombies. Historically, the most famous "zombie" case was discovered in Haiti. A man was made into a zombie with a "zombie powder" that contained plants with spines and toxic resins, puffer fish, and ground bones.

Ground bones! she thought. That's it! Her cookies needed to have a satisfying zombie-bones crunch to them. Spying the Nutella chocolate hazelnut spread on her counter next to a container of nuts, she snapped her fingers, pulled out her saucepan, and Chocolate Zombie Clusters were born.

MAKES ABOUT 3 DOZEN COOKIES

2 cups coarsely chopped nuts, toasted (walnuts, pecans, hazelnuts, peanuts, or any combination)

¾ cup Nutella

2 teaspoons vanilla extract

½ cup (1 stick) butter

2 cups sugar

¼ teaspoon salt

½ cup whole or low-fat milk

¼ cup cocoa powder

Step 1—Prep: Later in this recipe, you will need to add the following ingredients very quickly, so get them ready now. Measure out the roughly chopped nuts (toast them first for better flavor, see how at the end of this recipe). Set nuts aside. In a small bowl, mix the Nutella and vanilla and set aside. Line two large baking sheets with parchment or wax paper. This is where you will drop the hot, no-bake cookie dough.

Step 2—Cook up the batter: Place the butter, sugar, salt, milk, and cocoa powder in a nonstick saucepan. Bring this mixture to a boil while frequently stirring to prevent scorching. Boil for 2 minutes. (Be sure to boil for the full 2 minutes to get the best result.)

Step 3—Remove from heat and finish: Remove the pan from the heat. Wait 2 full minutes for the boiling to subside and the mixture to cool off a bit. Stir in the Nutella mixture and the chopped nuts.

Step 4—Drop and cool: Drop the cookies by the tablespoon onto the lined baking sheets. As they cool, they'll harden. To speed up the hardening process, slip the pan into the refrigerator. Then pick one up, take a bite, and become a chocolate zombie!

HOW TO TOAST NUTS

Toasting nuts brings incredible flavor out of them and the process is so easy it's truly worth that extra step. Preheat the oven to 350° F. Spread the nuts in a single layer on a cookie sheet and bake for 8 to 10 minutes. Stir once or twice to prevent scorching. You'll know they're done when your kitchen air become absolutely redolent with the flavor of warm nuts.

Sandy's Favorite Whoopie Pies

~ From *Town in a Wild Moose Chase* by B. B. Haywood ~

Whoopie pies are now the official Maine treat. These are small whoopie pies, about four bites per pie, and not as sweet as most. You'll want to make a double batch—they're that good!

SERVES 8 TO 12

5 tablespoons cocoa powder

6 tablespoons Crisco or other shortening

1 cup sugar

1 egg

1 teaspoon vanilla extract

2 cups flour

1 teaspoon salt

1 cup milk

1¼ teaspoons baking soda

FILLING

½ cup milk

2 tablespoons flour

¼ cup Crisco or other shortening

½ cup (1 stick) salted butter (substitute unsalted butter if desired)

½ cup sugar

1 teaspoon vanilla extract

Preheat oven to 350° F.

Mix together cocoa powder, shortening, sugar, egg, and vanilla. Add in flour, salt, milk, and baking soda.

Drop by tablespoonfuls onto an ungreased cookie sheet.

Bake for 10 minutes. Place cookie sheet on wire rack and let cakes cool completely.

MAKE FILLING

In a medium saucepan, combine milk and flour and place over medium heat, stirring constantly until mixture reaches a paste consistency.

Add shortening, butter, sugar, and vanilla.

Beat until smooth with an electric mixer or by hand until creamy.

Refrigerate the filling until cool.

Spread the filling on half of the cakes. Top with the remaining cakes.

Wrap individually with waxed paper and keep refrigerated.

Don't worry about how long they keep, because after a couple of days there won't be any left!

Aphrodisiac Brownies

~ From *Murder by Mocha* by Cleo Coyle ~

With Alicia's Mocha Magic off the market, Clare Cosi developed this recipe for her coffeehouse customers. As usual, NYPD Detective Mike Quinn was her first taste tester. "These should hit the spot," she told him. "Possibly more than one." The reason? Three of Clare's ingredients have long been considered aphrodisiacs. . . .

Chocolate, of course, is the classic Cupid consumable. The Aztecs were probably the first to make the connection between amorous feelings and the cocoa bean. The emperor Montezuma was said to have fueled his romantic trysts by ingesting large amounts of the bean.

Coffee contains caffeine, a stimulant that is also considered a perk in the department of amorous desires. Historically, when coffee was first introduced to the Turkish culture, husbands were expected to keep their wives well supplied. If the husband could not provide daily coffee for his wife, it was a legitimate cause for her to divorce him. Even if you don't care for coffee, don't skip this ingredient. It enhances and deepens the chocolate flavor in the brownies.

Cinnamon is a fragrant and stimulating spice. The Romans believed cinnamon was an aphrodisiac. Cleopatra famously used it to arouse her many lovers. In these brownies, the cinnamon works hand in hand with the brown sugar to layer in depth of flavor that's subtle yet spicy—sure, it may drive your lover crazy, but as Mike said, "A little bit o' crazy flavors the stew."

¾ cup (1½ sticks) unsalted butter

4 ounces unsweetened chocolate, chopped

1 teaspoon ground cinnamon

1 teaspoon espresso powder

2 large eggs

1 egg yolk

1 cup sugar

½ cup light brown sugar, packed

½ teaspoon salt

¾ cup all-purpose flour

½ teaspoon baking powder

¾ cup semisweet chocolate chips (about 5 ounces)

Step 1—Prep the oven and pan: Preheat the oven to 350° F. Line bottom of 8- or 9-inch-square pan with parchment paper or aluminum foil, extending the paper or foil beyond the pan to make handles (this will allow you to lift the brownies out of the pan while still warm). Lightly coat the paper or foil with nonstick cooking spray. Set pan aside.

Step 2—Make the chocolate mixture: Place the butter and unsweetened chocolate in a microwave-safe container and heat in 30-second increments, stirring between each session, until the mixture has melted. (Or warm the butter and chocolate in a small saucepan over very low heat. Be sure to stir continually to prevent scorching.) After the chocolate mixture is melted and smooth, stir in the cinnamon and espresso powder. Set aside.

Step 3—Create batter and bake: In a large mixing bowl, whisk the eggs and egg yolk. Whisk in the sugars and the salt. Whisk in the chocolate mixture from Step 2. Switching to a spoon or spatula, stir in the flour, baking powder, and semisweet chocolate chips. Blend enough for a smooth batter, but do not overmix or you'll produce gluten in the flour and toughen the brownies. Pour the batter into the pan and bake about 30 minutes. Underbaking is smarter than overbaking. The brownies are done when the top surface has become solid and displays small cracks. Remove from oven and allow to cool in pan no more than 5 minutes. Using the parchment paper (or foil) handles that you made in Step 1, carefully lift the entire brownie cake out of the hot pan and allow to finish cooling on a rack. Cut into small or large squares and eat with joy!

Nanna Tibbetts's
Moose Mincemeat

∽ From *Town in a Wild Moose Chase* by B. B. Haywood ∾

Use given amounts if making mincemeat preserves. Halve the amounts if using for pie filling.

Great for a large family gathering or a pot luck supper.

3 to 4 pounds moose meat (you can substitute venison or beef)
3 to 4 pounds apples, cored, peeled, and chopped
1 pound of suet (you can substitute Crisco)
2½ cups sugar
1½ pounds raisins
2½ cups strong coffee
2 teaspoons nutmeg
1 teaspoon cinnamon
1 teaspoon cloves

Roast moose meat and chop after cooking.

In a large Dutch oven, combine the meat, chopped apples, and suet (or Crisco).

Stir in remaining ingredients.

Simmer for 1 hour, stirring occasionally.

For moose mincemeat pie, use as a filling in any piecrust.

To preserve, pack hot into pint-size canning jars. Process pints for 20 minutes at 10 pounds pressure in a pressure cooker or for 1½ hours in a boiling water–bath canner.

Nanna Tibbetts's Moose Mincemeat Cookies

1 cup shortening

½ teaspoon vanilla extract

1 cup honey

3 eggs, well beaten

3¼ cups flour

1 teaspoon salt

1 teaspoon baking soda

1 cup chopped nuts

1 cup moose mincemeat, drained (page 265)

Preheat oven to 350° F. Grease a cookie sheet, and set aside.

In a large bowl, cream the shortening.

Beat in the vanilla, honey, and eggs.

In a separate bowl, sift together flour, salt, and baking soda.

Add dry ingredients to the egg mixture.

Fold in nuts and mincemeat.

Drop by teaspoonfuls on a buttered cookie sheet.

Bake for 15 minutes or until delicately browned.

Note: These authentic Maine moose recipes, from the collection of Nanna Tibbetts of Denmark, Maine, were generously provided in her loving memory by her children, grandchildren, great-grandchildren, and all the children she loved.

Chocolate Soufflé

~ From *Eggsecutive Orders* by Julie Hyzy ~

Soufflés, by definition, are temperamental. If something goes odd, or somebody bumps the oven wrong, or the phone rings at the wrong time, the thing can deflate like a kid's balloon. So go into this knowing that it will taste good, even if it doesn't look good. But it's actually pretty easy to make—it just isn't always goof-proof.

But it will usually look fantastic, and it will impress your guests like almost nothing else will.

SERVES 8

3 tablespoons unsalted butter, softened
½ cup sugar, divided
6 egg whites
4 ounces best-quality dark chocolate, chopped
½ cup very cold water
⅓ cup cocoa powder
Confectioners' sugar, for garnish (optional)
Berries, for garnish (optional)

Preheat oven to 350° F.

Coat the insides of 6 individual soufflé dishes completely with ½ tablespoon butter. Refrigerate until the butter is set, about 3 minutes. Place 1 teaspoon of sugar into each dish. Shake and turn the dishes until sugar completely coats the butter. Tip out any excess. Add more sugar if needed.

Place prepared dishes on a baking sheet and set aside. In a very clean mixing bowl (any fat will keep the eggs from whipping well), beat the egg whites on medium to high speed until foamy. Gradually add the remaining sugar, a little at a time, and beat until eggs are glossy and soft peaks form when beaters are lifted. Set aside.

Place a large metal mixing bowl over a pan of simmering water. Place the chocolate into the bowl, and stir until melted, glossy, and smooth. Remove from heat. Add the water and the cocoa powder. Stir until smooth. Let cool 1 minute.

Add about ⅓ of the egg-white mixture to the cooled chocolate mixture, folding together gently. Add the folded mixture to the remaining egg whites. Fold together gently.

Spoon into prepared dishes. Using a straight-edged knife, level the egg mixture in the dishes even with the top of the dishes. Wipe the edges of the dishes with a dampened towel to clean them.

Bake until soufflés puff up and are cooked through but still moist in the center, 12 to 14 minutes. Sprinkle with confectioners' sugar and garnish with berries, if using, and serve immediately.

Melody's Chocolate Mousse

⌁ From Town in a Wild Moose Chase *by B. B. Haywood ⌁*

SERVES 2 TO 4

6 ounces semisweet chocolate, chopped, or chocolate chips

1 ounce unsweetened chocolate, chopped

½ cup milk

1 teaspoon vanilla extract

1 cup heavy cream

¼ cup confectioners' sugar

In a small saucepan, combine the semisweet and unsweetened chocolates with the milk. Stir over low heat until melted. Add the vanilla.

Turn off the heat and let stand until cool to the touch.

In bowl, beat the cream and the sugar with a mixer until stiff peaks form.

Add some of the chocolate mixture to the cream mixture and fold together using a wire whisk.

Add the remaining chocolate and fold in until it is all combined.

Spoon the mousse into 6 serving dishes and refrigerate until ready to serve.

This delectable dessert is served daily at Melody's Café!

Lemon Steamed Pudding

∾ From *Home of the Braised* by Julie Hyzy ∾

Served at the Inaugural Luncheon, 2005.

SERVES 8 TO 10

7½ ounces patent flour
½ ounce baking powder
Salt
1 lemon, zested
9 ounces butter
9 ounces sugar
4 whole eggs
1 egg yolk
2½ ounces lemon juice
Timbale pans

Sift dry ingredients together.

Cream butter and sugar until fluffy. Add eggs and a little flour to keep mix from splitting. Add sifted dry ingredients. Slowly add liquid, and mix batter until smooth.

Divide batter among prepared pans, and cover each timbale with foil. Steam in water bath for 30 to 35 minutes.

Puddings are best removed from molds when completely cool.

Granny Sebastian's Bread Pudding

∼ From *If Bread Could Rise to the Occasion* by Paige Shelton ∼

Simply, seriously yummy.

MAKES 9 SMALL SERVINGS OR 6 BIGGER SERVINGS

2 cups whole milk

¼ cup (½ stick) salted butter

⅔ cup brown sugar (light or dark, you choose)

3 eggs

2 teaspoons cinnamon

¼ teaspoon ground nutmeg

1 teaspoon vanilla extract

3 cups bread, torn into small pieces (a harder bread works best—
French, sourdough, even brioche if you have that around; I use
about 20 percent crust and about 80 percent bread innards,
and tearing is important—do not cut into pieces)

⅛ to ¼ cup miniature semisweet chocolate chips (optional)

½ pint unwhipped whipping cream (this might be the most
important ingredient of the recipe, according to Granny
Sebastian)

Preheat oven to 350° F. Grease a 1½-quart casserole dish, and set aside.

In a medium saucepan over medium heat, heat the milk for about 5 to 8 minutes, until a film forms over top. Combine the butter and milk, stirring until the butter is melted, 5 to 7 minutes.

In a separate bowl, combine the sugar, eggs, cinnamon, nutmeg, and vanilla. Beat with an electric mixer at medium speed for about 1 minute. Slowly add the milk mixture, stirring with a spoon.

Place bread in prepared casserole dish, sprinkle with chocolate chips if desired, and pour batter over bread.

Bake for 45 to 50 minutes. Serve warm, either on top of a couple tablespoons of the whipping cream or with the whipping cream poured over the top of the pudding.

Candy Holliday's Blueberry Whipped Cream

⁓ From Town in a Blueberry Jam by B. B. Haywood ⁓

SERVES 12 TO 16

2 cups whipping cream
¼ cup sugar
2 teaspoons vanilla extract
¾ cup Maine wild blueberries, mashed

Mix together all ingredients in a deep bowl (mixture will splatter).

Whip with a mixer for 8 to 10 minutes or until it is a nice whipped-cream consistency.

It will be a beautiful shade of lavender.

Candy loves this on fruit, blueberry gingerbread, or any pie.

Refrigerate if you have any leftovers.

Brie-Blueberry Ice Cream (and Blueberry Sauce)

From *To Brie or Not to Brie* by Avery Aames ~

SERVES 6 TO 8

BRIE-BLUEBERRY ICE CREAM

1 cup half-and-half

1 cup heavy cream

½ cup mascarpone cheese

3 egg yolks

1 cup sugar

1 teaspoon vanilla extract

4 ounces Brie or Fromager d'Affinois, trimmed of its rind

Dash of nutmeg

½ cup blueberries (rinsed and destemmed)

Put the half-and-half, cream, and mascarpone cheese into a saucepan. Place over medium heat and stir occasionally, until steaming.

In a bowl, whisk the egg yolks, sugar, and vanilla together. Once the cream mixture is hot, begin ladling small amounts into the eggs while whisking.

After adding about ½ cup of the hot cream mixture to the eggs, pour the cream mixture back into the saucepan and stir continuously while it thickens. Once the mixture starts steaming gently again, you can turn off the heat. Keep stirring for a few minutes.

Add the Brie in chunks and stir vigorously to melt the cheese into the custard. Add a dash of nutmeg.

THE COZY COOKBOOK

274

Place mixture into a bowl, cover, and chill thoroughly, about 2 hours.

Freeze in an ice cream maker per manufacturer's instructions. (Mine requires 30 minutes of automatic stirring action.)

Five minutes before complete, add in the blueberries. Serve with blueberry sauce.

BLUEBERRY SAUCE

½ cup blueberries

1 tablespoon lemon juice

1 tablespoon water

3 tablespoons sugar

Place all the ingredients in a saucepan and place over medium heat. Bring to a simmer and cook for 5 minutes. Allow to cool and then refrigerate. Reheat gently if you want a warm sauce.

Theodosia's Earl Grey Sorbet

~ From *Gunpowder Green* by Laura Childs ~

An especially refreshing dessert.

MAKES 2 CUPS

1¼ cups water
1 tablespoon sugar
Zest and juice from 2 lemons
2 tablespoons Earl Grey tea leaves
1 egg white

Bring water, sugar, lemon juice, and lemon zest to a boil in sauce-pan and allow to boil for 4 minutes. Add tea leaves, cover, remove from heat, and let steep until cool. Strain into a bowl, cover, and place in freezer until mixture is slushy and half-frozen. Beat egg white until stiff, then fold into mixture. Freeze until sorbet reaches desired consistency. To serve, scoop sorbet into parfait dishes and garnish with fresh fruit or a lemon cookie.

Jenna's Caramel Macchiato Ice Cream (and Sauce)

～ From *Inherit the Word* by Daryl Wood Gerber ～

Knowing how much I love ice cream, my aunt bought me a countertop ice-cream maker. And then Katie, who remembered how much I'd raved about Keller's caramel macchiato ice cream, wheedled this recipe out of him. She said it was a cinch. Yeah, right. Anyway, she walked me through the first batch, and it wasn't that hard. Katie says the trick to making homemade ice cream—which I guess Keller knew, too—is making sure there isn't too much "moisture" in the mixture. Moisture, aka water, turns to ice in the freezer. I guess there's a lot of water in milk. Who knew? Hence, you'll see evaporated milk in these ingredients. I've got to say, yum! If you're really daring, try making your own caramel sauce. Katie included that recipe below.

SERVES 6 TO 8

Caramel Macchiato Ice Cream

1 cup whipping cream

2 tablespoons espresso coffee (brewed, liquid)

¾ cup sugar

⅛ teaspoon salt

1 (12-ounce) can low-fat evaporated milk

3 large egg yolks

¾ cup caramel dessert sauce (I used Smucker's)

In a saucepan set over medium heat, cook cream, brewed espresso, ¼ cup sugar, salt, and evaporated milk. Cook for 3 to 5 minutes, until tiny bubbles form around the edges. Do not boil.

Remove from heat and let stand 10 minutes. In a medium bowl, combine the remaining ½ cup sugar and egg yolks. Stir well. Gradually add the hot milk mixture to the egg mixture, stirring constantly.

Return the mixture to the saucepan. Cook over medium heat for 3 to 5 minutes, until tiny bubbles form again. Do not boil.

Remove the pan from the heat. Cool at room temperature and then set in the refrigerator for 2 hours. Pour chilled mixture into ice-cream maker and freeze according to manufacturer's instructions.

Transfer half of the ice cream to a freezer-safe container, then spread half of the caramel sauce on top. Top with remaining ice cream, then remaining caramel sauce. Using a knife, swirl the caramel through the ice cream.

Cover and freeze for at least 2 hours.

Caramel Sauce à la Katie

Making caramel is a fast process, so have everything ready . . . right next to the pan. You don't want the sugar to burn. Promise! Also, the sugar gets really hot, so wear oven mitts. Okay? Ready . . . go.

MAKES 1 CUP

2 tablespoons water

1 cup sugar

6 tablespoons butter

½ cup whipping cream

In a 2- to 3-quart saucepan, heat the water and sugar over medium heat. Stir constantly. As soon as all the sugar has melted—the color will be a warm amber—add the butter. Whisk until the butter has melted. You will see bubbles around the edge of the pan.

Remove the pan from the heat and add the cream in a steady stream, whisking the whole time. Note: This mixture will foam. It's so pretty.

Whisk until the mixture is smooth, then cool a few minutes and pour into a glass heatproof container and let cool completely. Remember, the glass container will be hot until the mixture is completely cool. Store in the refrigerator for up to 2 weeks.

Baileys Irish Cream and Caramel-Nut Fudge

~ From *Billionaire Blend* by Cleo Coyle ~

Yes, this is the very buttery caramel fudge (with an Irish Cream kick) that Clare used to bribe NYPD Bomb Squad Lieutenant DeFasio and his crew. That night, she made it in an 8-inch-square pan and cut it into bite-size pieces for sharing. If you don't expect to consume it in one night, however, Clare suggests making the fudge in a loaf pan. Then you can remove the fudge block, wrap it in plastic, and store it in the fridge. Over the course of many evenings, you can take out the block, cut off slices to enjoy with coffee, and rewrap it to keep fresh for the next time you'd like a wee nip of edible joy.

MAKES ONE 8-INCH-SQUARE PAN OF FUDGE

⅔ cup evaporated milk

1 cup light brown sugar

⅓ cup sugar

2 tablespoons unsalted butter

½ teaspoon coarse sea salt (do not substitute table salt)

2 cups mini marshmallows

1 teaspoon pure vanilla extract

¼ cup Baileys Irish Cream

2 tablespoons pure maple syrup (not pancake syrup, which is
     flavored corn syrup)

1½ cups white chocolate chips (or 9 ounces of white
     chocolate disks)

¾ cup plus ⅓ cup chopped, toasted walnuts

Step 1—Prep pan: Use an 8-inch-square pan or an 8½ × 4½-inch loaf pan. Line the pan completely with parchment paper and allow the paper to extend beyond at least 2 sides to create a sling with handles. You'll use these to easily lift the fudge from the pan.

Step 2—Bring to a boil: Combine evaporated milk, sugars, butter, and salt in a large saucepan. Place over medium heat and stir occasionally to prevent burning. When the mixture comes to a full, rolling boil, set the timer for 5 minutes and stir constantly.

Step 3—Stir in final ingredients: Pour in the mini marshmallows and stir rapidly to melt. Remove from heat and stir in the vanilla extract, Baileys Irish Cream, and maple syrup. Add the white chocolate chips and stir until melted. Fold in ¾ cup chopped walnuts.

Step 4—Pour, garnish, and chill: Pour fudge mixture into prepared pan. Sprinkle the remaining ⅓ cup chopped walnuts across the top to decorate. Allow to cool completely at room temperature.

Step 5—Warning: Do not cover the top of the pan with plastic wrap until the fudge has completely cooled; otherwise, steam will condense and your fudge will become soggy. Once the fudge loaf is cool, loosely cover the top of the pan with plastic wrap or foil and place the pan in the fridge, chilling until firm. Remove pan from fridge and lift the fudge out of the pan using the parchment-paper handles. Slice to enjoy. To store, rewrap the fudge tightly in plastic and place back in the fridge.

Baileys Buying Note: If you're not a big drinker, simply buy 2 mini-bar bottles of Baileys. Inexpensive, single-serving bottles come in sizes of 50 milliliters, and 2 bottles will allow you to measure out the amount needed for this recipe.

Jasmine Tea Truffles

~ From *The Jasmine Moon Murder* by Laura Childs ~

MAKES 36 TO 48 PIECES

8 ounces high-quality bittersweet or semisweet chocolate
½ cup whipping cream
¼ cup (½ stick) unsalted butter
4 teaspoons jasmine tea

Chop chocolate into coarse pieces and melt with whipping cream in a heavy saucepan set over low heat, stirring occasionally until chocolate melts. Add butter and continue stirring until completely melted in. Remove from heat and let cool to room temperature, then mix in jasmine tea. Chill in refrigerator until hard, about 8 hours. To form truffles, scoop out mixture using a melon baller and form into balls. Roll balls in finely chopped walnuts or almonds, cocoa, or coconut.

Substitute Earl Grey, spiced chai, or your favorite tea if you want to experiment.

Cake Pops

~ From *Red Velvet Revenge* by Jenn McKinlay ~

A cake-and-frosting confection dipped in candy coating and served on a stick.

MAKES 30 CAKE POPS

1 cake (9 × 13) or 18 cupcakes (out of liners)
2 cups buttercream or cream cheese frosting
2 packages candy melts
30 lollipop sticks (large, thick ones)
1 large foam block

Line a cookie sheet with wax paper, and set aside.

In a large bowl, crumble up the cake into very small pieces. Using a rubber spatula, stir in the frosting until it is well mixed; mixture should be the consistency of truffles. Roll the mixture into walnut-size balls and place on prepared cookie sheet.

Once all the cake has been rolled, put it in the fridge to harden a bit. Melt the candy in a double boiler or a microwave, according to the manufacturer's instructions.

Take the cake balls out of the fridge and dip the end of a lollipop stick into the melted candy. Slide a cake ball about ½ inch down onto the candy-tipped stick. Now dip the whole cake ball into the melted candy, tapping it very gently on the side of the bowl to get rid of the excess.

Stand the cake pop up by pushing the non-cake end into the foam block. If you're decorating with sprinkles, sugars, or coconut now is the time to do it, as the candy will harden fairly quickly. Repeat until you're out of cake balls and melted candy.

A Deadly Grind

by Victoria Hamilton

Jaymie and Becca had some lunch and then, to relax a bit from the horrors of the night, Jaymie began her Queen Elizabeth cake, turning the sticky dates into a newer glass bowl, boiling the kettle and pouring one cup over the dates and baking soda, which fizzed up. She would never pour boiling water into a vintage bowl; an unseen hairline crack could cause it to shatter. Nor did she ever use her vintage bowls in the microwave. That would be like putting her grandmother in a rocket ship to the moon.

"What is that all about, boiling water and baking soda?" Becca asked, looking over her shoulder.

"I think you do this to soften the dates, so they blend well with the moist cake batter," Jaymie said, lifting down her favorite Pyrex bowls, a vintage "Primary Colors" set, from the open shelf over the sink. She set the oven to preheat while Becca sat down at the kitchen table to make a list of things to do before the next day.

There was silence for a moment, other than the sounds of Jaymie mixing and Becca scratching items on her list.

"I can't stop thinking about that poor guy . . . the dead man," Becca said, tapping her pen against her pad of paper.

"I know," Jaymie said. She worked the moist ingredients together in the red bowl, the second smallest in the graduated nesting set, while her sister watched.

Queen Elizabeth Cake

~ From *A Deadly Grind* by Victoria Hamilton ~

Modernized recipe.

Feel free to experiment with what is essentially a simple date-nut cake. Perhaps you could change out the "topping" for a cream cheese icing, or bake it in a round pan, turn it out, and slice the cake horizontally, then fill it with raspberry preserves. It is a very rich, moist tea cake, though, and doesn't really need any fancying up!

MAKES 16 GOOD-SIZE PIECES

CAKE

1 cup dates (I packed the dates down to fill the cup measure)
1 cup boiling water
1 teaspoon baking soda
¼ cup shortening
1 cup sugar
1 egg, beaten
½ scant teaspoon vanilla extract
1½ cups flour
1 teaspoon baking powder
¼ scant teaspoon salt
½ cup chopped nuts (walnuts, pecans, hazelnuts)

TOPPING

5 tablespoons brown sugar
3 tablespoons butter
2 tablespoons cream
¼ cup shredded coconut

Preheat oven to 350° F. Spray an 8-inch-square pan with nonstick cooking spray, and set aside.

Mix dates, boiling water, and baking soda together and let stand. This softens the dates to let them blend with the batter.

Blend together shortening, sugar, beaten egg, and vanilla in large bowl.

Mix together in a separate bowl the flour, baking powder, and salt, then add chopped nuts.

Mix flour mixture with shortening mixture until thoroughly combined, then fold in the softened dates. (I mashed the dates to make them softer, and it helped the batter blend nicely.)

Pour cake batter into prepared pan and bake for about 40 to 45 minutes. Test cake with a toothpick for doneness; inserted toothpick should come out clean.

Meanwhile, mix brown sugar, butter, and cream in a small saucepan. Heat over high heat until boiling; cook for 3 minutes.

Remove cake from oven, and while still warm, pour topping mixture over cake. Sprinkle coconut over and put back in the oven to brown. (I put the cake in the oven for 5 minutes, but the coconut was not browning, so I put it under the broiler for 2 or 3 minutes—4 inches away from the element—to brown the coconut. If you do this step, watch it carefully! The caramel glaze on top will bubble.)

Cut into squares and serve with good, strong tea, on your prettiest cake plates! I would suggest, in honor of the Queen Mother's Scottish origins (she spent her childhood at Glamis Castle in Scotland), that you use a tartan-pattern china like Lenox's Holiday Tartan or a wonderful Canadian original, Newfoundland Tartan dishes made by

Royal Adderley of Ridgway, though the latter are rare and hard to find! Alternately, in honor of Queen Victoria, you could use the Herend pattern "Queen Victoria," a lovely floral china introduced at the first world's fair, the Great Exhibition in 1851, and actually purchased and used by Her Royal Highness!

Death by Chocolate Cupcakes

From Sprinkle with Murder by Jenn McKinlay

Dark chocolate ganache on a chocolate-with-chocolate-chips cake.

MAKES 12 CUPCAKES

1⅓ cups all-purpose flour

¼ teaspoon baking soda

2 teaspoons baking powder

¾ cup unsweetened cocoa powder

⅛ teaspoon salt

3 tablespoons salted butter, softened

1½ cups sugar

2 eggs

¾ teaspoon vanilla extract

1 cup milk

1 bag (12-ounce) semisweet chocolate chips

DARK CHOCOLATE GANACHE

2 cups dark chocolate chips

2 cups heavy cream

2 teaspoons vanilla extract

Preheat oven to 350° F.

Sift together the flour, baking soda, baking powder, cocoa, and salt. Set aside. In a large bowl, cream together the butter and sugar until well blended. Add the eggs one at a time, beating well with each addition, then stir in the vanilla. Add the flour mixture alternately with the milk; beat well. Add the chocolate chips. Spoon batter into prepared tins until each liner is half-full. Bake for 15 to 17 minutes. Cool completely before frosting.

MAKE FROSTING

Place chocolate chips in a large bowl. Pour the cream into a saucepan, and bring to a boil. Once the cream boils, remove it from the heat and pour it over the chips. Let stand for 1 to 2 minutes, then stir with a whisk until smooth. Be sure to scrape the bottom of the bowl occasionally. Stir in the vanilla until well blended. Place a piece of plastic wrap directly on the surface and allow to cool to room temperature. Dip tops of cool cupcakes into mixture and allow to dry.

If Fried Chicken Could Fly

by Paige Shelton

espite my distracted mind and the messy kitchen, the cupcakes turned out to be perfect: the right color red, light, chocolaty, and topped with a cream cheese frosting that Jake would have loved to sample. Gram's recipes were almost fail-proof, and I'd made them all so many times that even distractions didn't throw me off my game.

Gram had never minded sharing her recipes, but writing them down had been one of her biggest challenges when she opened the school. She'd learned to cook by watching her mother and her grandmother. They cooked using their intuition, adding just the right ingredients at just the right time, and all without the use of measuring equipment. "People pay better attention when they have to use their noggins, Betts," she'd say. "If you don't have to think about the proportions of ingredients to each other, you get a lazy brain. I don't abide lazy brains."

So before her students baked one cookie or fried one piece of chicken or mashed one potato, Gram spent some time talking to them about the chemistry of food, of ingredients. She wanted her students to be able to think, to know what to do if something didn't work as it should.

When should you add flour, an egg, more sugar? When should you add less? Why is the secret red velvet cupcake ingredient vinegar?

And she was right. When you had to think about what you were doing, you paid better attention to how things blended together, and when your experience mixed with your intuition, somehow food transformed and became better.

Red Velvet Cake/Cupcakes

~ From *If Fried Chicken Could Fly* by Paige Shelton ~

I think I've tried dozens of red velvet cake recipes. Most of the time, I've been terribly disappointed. They've been too dense, too dark, or just not flavorful enough. Then last year some friends of my son's made him a red velvet cake for his birthday. It was delicious. I was on the phone the next day, asking if I could include the recipe in this book. Thankfully, they agreed. So, thank you, Michael Kennedy-Yoon and Katherine Kennedy, for the best red velvet cake ever!

MAKES 1 CAKE OR ABOUT 24 CUPCAKES

½ cup shortening

1½ cups sugar

2 eggs

2 teaspoons vanilla extract

3 level teaspoons cocoa powder

1½ ounces (3 tablespoons) red food coloring

1 teaspoon salt

2½ cups sifted cake flour

1 cup buttermilk

1 tablespoon apple cider vinegar

1 teaspoon baking soda

MAKES ENOUGH TO FROST ONE 9-INCH,

2-LAYER CAKE OR 24 CUPCAKES

6 ounces cream cheese, softened
¾ cup (1½ sticks) salted butter, softened
2 teaspoons vanilla extract
3 tablespoons cream
4 cups sifted confectioners' sugar
Red sugar sprinkles, for topping

Preheat the oven to 350° F. Grease and lightly flour two 9-inch-round cake pans or line a 24-cup muffin pan with paper liners.

In a medium bowl, cream together the shortening, sugar, eggs, and vanilla. In another medium bowl, mix the cocoa and food coloring together with a spoon until pastelike in consistency. Add it to the shortening mixture.

Combine the salt and flour and add to mixture, alternating with the buttermilk.

In a small bowl mix the baking soda and vinegar, and add it to the batter. Mix until all ingredients are well blended and form a smooth batter.

Pour the batter into prepared pans.

Bake for 25 to 30 minutes for cake, or 17 to 21 minutes for cupcakes. Let cool.

MAKE THE FROSTING

In a large bowl, mix the cream cheese, butter, vanilla, cream, and sugar until smooth. Spread the frosting over the cooled cake or cupcakes, and top with sprinkles.

Orange Dreamsicle Cupcakes

*From *Buttercream Bump Off* by Jenn McKinlay*

An orange cupcake topped with vanilla buttercream and garnished with candied orange peel.

MAKES 18 CUPCAKES

½ cup (1 stick) salted butter, softened

1 cup sugar

2 large eggs, separated and whites beaten until stiff

1 tablespoon orange zest

1 teaspoon orange extract

1½ cups all-purpose flour

½ teaspoon salt

1½ teaspoons baking powder

½ cup orange juice

VANILLA BUTTERCREAM FROSTING

MAKES 3 CUPS OF FROSTING

1 cup (2 sticks) salted butter, softened

1 teaspoon clear vanilla extract

4 cups sifted confectioners' sugar

2 to 3 tablespoons milk (or whipping cream)

Preheat oven to 350° F. Line cupcake pans with paper liners, and set aside.

Combine butter, sugar, egg yolks, orange zest, and orange extract in a large mixing bowl. Cream the ingredients together thoroughly. Sift together flour, salt, and baking powder in a separate mixing bowl. Add dry ingredients to creamed ingredients a third at a time, alternating with the orange juice. Fold in the beaten egg whites. Spoon batter into prepared tins, until each liner is half-full. Bake for 15 minutes or until a toothpick inserted in the center comes out clean. Cool cupcakes completely before frosting.

MAKE FROSTING

In a large bowl, cream butter and vanilla extract. Gradually add sugar, 1 cup at a time, beating well on medium speed. Scrape sides of bowl often. Add milk and beat at medium speed until light and fluffy. For best results, keep icing in refrigerator when not in use. This icing can be stored for up to 2 weeks. Rewhip before using.

Moonlight Madness

～ From *Buttercream Bump Off* by Jenn McKinlay ～

A chocolate cupcake with vanilla buttercream frosting rolled in shred-ded coconut and topped with an unwrapped Hershey's Kiss.

MAKES 12 CUPCAKES

1½ cups flour

¾ cup unsweetened cocoa

1½ cups sugar

1½ teaspoons baking soda

¾ teaspoon baking powder

¾ teaspoon salt

2 eggs, room temperature

¾ cup milk

3 tablespoons oil

1 teaspoon vanilla extract

¾ cup warm water

1 bag shredded coconut, sweetened

12 Hershey's Kisses

Vanilla Buttercream Frosting (page 296)

Preheat oven to 350° F. Line a cupcake pan with paper liners, and set aside.

In a large bowl, whisk together flour, cocoa, sugar, baking soda, baking powder, and salt. Add eggs, milk, oil, vanilla extract, and water. Beat on medium speed with an electric mixer until smooth, scraping the sides of the bowl as needed. Scoop into prepared cupcake pan and bake for 20 minutes, until a toothpick inserted in the center comes out clean. Cool cupcakes completely before frosting.

To finish the Moonlight Madness Cupcakes, spread a generous amount of the vanilla buttercream frosting on top of the cupcake with a rubber spatula, then roll the top of the cupcake in a bowl of shredded coconut before the frosting dries so the coconut will adhere to the frosting. Top with an unwrapped Hershey's Kiss.

Sprinkle with Murder

by Jenn McKinlay

Mel was in the kitchen in the back of the bakery, prepping for their happy hour baking class. Ten students were registered for the four-week session in which they were featuring drink-flavored cupcakes. Each student would bake and then decorate a dozen cupcakes to take home. Tonight's was the piña colada. A pineapple cupcake with coconut buttercream icing, sprinkled with shredded coconut and topped off with a cherry and a pineapple chunk held in place by a paper umbrella. It was one of Mel's favorites.

Angie was manning the front counter. Mel glanced through the doorway to see that it was under control. A group of older ladies was in one booth, enjoying two cupcakes each, while a mom with two boys sat in another. One of the boys had chocolate frosting covering his face from chin to hairline and ear to ear. The other one had flipped his over and was eating just the cake. The mom was watching them with a small smile as if trying to memorize this moment.

Mel turned back to the kitchen, feeling oddly fulfilled as if in a very tiny way she had helped to make a memory. It felt almost as good as that first bite of a freshly frosted cupcake, she thought.

Mojito Cupcakes

∽ From *Sprinkle with Murder* by Jenn McKinlay ∽

A golden cupcake flavored with lime zest and dried spearmint leaves and topped with a rum-flavored icing.

MAKES 12 CUPCAKES

½ cup sugar

1½ cups flour

¼ teaspoon salt

2 teaspoons baking powder

1 beaten egg

¼ cup (½ stick) melted butter

1 cup milk

Juice and zest of 1 lime

2 teaspoons dried spearmint leaves

1 recipe Vanilla Buttercream Frosting (page 296), rum extract
   substituted for vanilla extract

Candy spearmint leaves, mint leaves, and lime wedges, for garnish

Preheat oven to 350° F. Sift all the dry ingredients together in a big bowl. Add the beaten egg to the melted butter. Add that to the dry ingredients, stirring in the milk until smooth. Add lime juice and zest. Add the dried spearmint leaves to the batter, mixing well. Bake for 10 to 12 minutes until golden brown. Cool completely before frosting.

Garnish with candy spearmint leaf, real mint leaves, or lime wedges.

Tinkerbells

⟨ From *Sprinkle with Murder* by Jenn McKinlay ⟩

Lemon cupcakes with raspberry buttercream frosting rolled in pink sugar.

MAKES 2 DOZEN CUPCAKES

1 cup (2 sticks) unsalted butter, softened

2 cups sugar, divided

4 extra-large eggs, at room temperature

⅓ cup grated lemon zest (6 to 8 large lemons)

3 cups flour

½ teaspoon baking powder

½ teaspoon baking soda

1 teaspoon salt

¼ cup freshly squeezed lemon juice

¾ cup buttermilk, at room temperature

1 teaspoon pure vanilla extract

Raspberry Buttercream (see Note, below)

Preheat the oven to 350° F. Line cupcake pans with paper liners, and set aside.

Cream the butter and sugar until fluffy, about 5 minutes. With the mixer on medium speed, add the eggs, one at a time, and the lemon zest. Sift together the flour, baking powder, baking soda, and salt in a bowl. In another bowl, combine lemon juice, buttermilk, and vanilla. Add the flour and buttermilk mixtures alternately to the batter, beginning and ending with the flour. Use an ice cream scoop to fill prepared cupcake pans. Bake 20 minutes. Cool completely before frosting with Raspberry Buttercream.

Note: For Raspberry Buttercream, follow directions for Vanilla Buttercream recipe (page 296) but substitute ½ cup of fresh raspberries for milk and vanilla, and cream together with butter and sugar. Be sure to wash and dry raspberries thoroughly before mixing them in. Roll the cupcake in pink decorating sugar before the buttercream has set.

Gluten-Free Chocolate Cupcakes with Ganache Frosting

From Going, Going, Ganache by Jenn McKinlay

MAKES 2 DOZEN CUPCAKES

2 cups blanched almond flour

¼ cup unsweetened cocoa powder

½ teaspoon salt

½ teaspoon baking soda

1 cup sugar

2 large eggs

1 tablespoon pure vanilla extract

GANACHE FROSTING

¾ cup heavy cream

8 ounces dark chocolate chips

1 teaspoon vanilla extract

Pinch sea salt

Pomegranate seeds, for garnish (optional)

Chocolate-dipped strawberries, for garnish (optional)

Preheat oven to 350° F. Line cupcake pans with paper liners, and set aside.

In a large bowl, mix together almond flour, cocoa powder, salt, and baking soda. In a medium-size bowl, combine sugar, eggs, and vanilla. Stir the wet ingredients into the dry mixture until thoroughly combined. Scoop the batter evenly into paper liners. Bake 20 to 25 minutes until a toothpick inserted in the center of the cupcake comes out clean. Let cool before frosting.

MAKE FROSTING

In a medium saucepan, bring the cream to a boil then remove it from the heat. Stir in the chocolate until it is melted and smooth, then stir in the vanilla extract and salt. Let the ganache stand at room temperature for 5 minutes, then move to the refrigerator and chill until the ganache thickens and becomes shiny and spreadable. This could take anywhere from 15 to 30 minutes, depending on the temperature of your refrigerator.

Garnish with pomegranate seeds or a chocolate-dipped strawberry, if desired.

Vegan Vanilla Cupcakes

~ From *Red Velvet Revenge* by Jenn McKinlay ~

A vanilla cupcake with a soy milk base and an organic vanilla frosting.

MAKES 12 CUPCAKES

1 cup vanilla soy milk

1 teaspoon apple cider vinegar

⅔ cup agave nectar

⅓ cup canola oil

2 teaspoons vanilla extract

1 cup all-purpose organic flour

¾ teaspoon baking soda

½ teaspoon baking powder

¼ teaspoon salt

VEGAN VANILLA FROSTING

6 tablespoons vanilla soy milk

2 tablespoons Trader Joe's Vanilla Bean Paste

¼ cup (½ stick) organic margarine

1 (16-ounce) package organic confectioners' sugar, sifted

Preheat oven to 350° F. Line cupcake pans with paper liners, and set aside.

Whisk together soy milk and vinegar in a large bowl and set aside until it curdles. Add the agave nectar, oil, and vanilla extract to the soy milk mixture and beat with an electric mixer until foamy. In another bowl, sift together the flour, baking soda, baking powder, and salt. Add to the wet ingredients and beat until no lumps remain. Fill prepared cupcake liners two-thirds full. Bake 18 to 20 minutes until a knife inserted comes out clean. Cool on wire racks before frosting.

MAKE FROSTING

In a small bowl mix together soy milk, vanilla bean paste, and margarine. Slowly beat in the sugar until frosting is smooth. Spread on top of cupcakes with a rubber spatula.

Pumpkin Cupcakes with Whipped Cream Frosting

~ From *Going, Going, Ganache* by Jenn McKinlay ~

MAKES 2 DOZEN CUPCAKES

2 cups all-purpose flour

1 teaspoon baking soda

1 teaspoon baking powder

1 teaspoon coarse salt

1 teaspoon ground cinnamon

1 teaspoon ground ginger

¼ teaspoon nutmeg

1 cup packed light brown sugar

1 cup sugar

1 cup (2 sticks) unsalted butter, melted

4 large eggs, lightly beaten

1 (15-ounce) can pumpkin puree

WHIPPED CREAM FROSTING

½ cup heavy whipping cream, chilled

4 tablespoons confectioners' sugar

Nutmeg or cinnamon, for garnish (optional)

Preheat oven to 350° F. Line cupcake pans with paper liners, and set aside.

In a medium bowl, whisk together flour, baking soda, baking powder, salt, cinnamon, ginger, and nutmeg. In a large bowl, mix together sugars, melted butter, and eggs. Add dry ingredients, and mix until smooth. Lastly, mix in the pumpkin until thoroughly blended. Scoop the batter evenly into the cupcake liners. Bake 20 to 25 minutes until a toothpick inserted in the center comes out clean. Let cool before frosting.

MAKE FROSTING

In a medium bowl, whip heavy cream on medium-high speed for 3 minutes. In a small bowl, sift confectioners' sugar. Add the sugar to the whipped cream mixture and mix on medium-high speed until stiff peaks form. Frosting should be able to stand on its own.

Garnish with nutmeg or cinnamon, if desired.

Candy Holliday's Pumpkin Cheesecake Swirl

∽ From *Town in a Pumpkin Bash* by B. B. Haywood ∽

SERVES AROUND 8

8 ounces cream cheese, room temperature

8 tablespoons sour cream

¾ cup sugar

2 eggs

1 cup pumpkin, canned or mashed fresh

½ teaspoon cinnamon

¼ teaspoon ginger

1 graham cracker crust

Preheat oven to 375° F. In a large bowl, mix the cream cheese and sour cream until smooth.

Add the sugar and mix. Add the eggs one at a time, and mix.

Remove ⅓ cup of the cream cheese mixture to a smaller bowl, and set aside.

Add the pumpkin and spices to the mixture in the large bowl and mix.

Spread the pumpkin mixture from the large bowl into a graham cracker crust.

Drop tablespoonfuls of reserved cream cheese mixture over the top of the pie.

Use a fork or sharp knife and swirl the drops into the pie mixture.

Bake for 30 minutes, or until the filling is firm in the center when touched.

Cool on a rack or board. Store in the refrigerator.

This pie is great anytime, but especially on Candy's birthday!

Pies and Prejudice

by Ellery Adams

"Hey!" Hugh exclaimed shortly before Reba was due to arrive. "Am I dreaming or are you mixing together ingredients for a shoofly pie?"

Picking up a bottle of King syrup, Ella Mae nodded. "I couldn't make it like your granny did using molasses. I had to send away for some northern syrup."

Hugh abandoned his task of washing lettuce and stepped next to her. He was so close that their shoulders brushed when Ella Mae moved her arms.

"Can I watch or will it break the spell?" he whispered.

"I'll do my best not to mix in any eggshells," she murmured, her voice becoming deep and husky against her will. Luckily, the filling was an uncomplicated blend of syrup, water, baking soda, eggs, and cloves. As Ella Mae stirred, she could feel a tide of desire flow from her body into the grain of her wooden spoon.

Adding measures of flour, brown sugar, and butter to the bowl of her food processor, she pulsed the mixture until it had formed the perfect crumb topping. Scooping the crumbs with her fingers, she spread them across the surface of the dark brown filling. It was difficult to keep her hands steady when all she wanted to do was look into Hugh's eyes. Would she find a reflection of her own need in his blue-green pools?

As though sensing her longing, Hugh slipped directly behind her and placed his hands on her shoulders. "I could watch you bake all day. It's hypnotizing."

Charmed Shoofly Pie

~ From Pies and Prejudice by Ellery Adams ~

SERVES 8

1 Charmed Piecrust (recipe to follow)
1 cup flour
⅔ cup dark brown sugar
3 tablespoons butter
1 cup molasses
1 large egg, beaten
1 teaspoon baking soda
¾ cup boiling water

Preheat oven to 375° F.

Roll out prepared Charmed Piecrust and place on bottom of 9-inch pie dish (Ella Mae recommends a glass pie dish for this pie). Trim off extra dough and pinch sides of dough.

Mix together first three ingredients until butter is integrated (using the pulse button on a food processor works nicely). Reserve ½ cup of crumb mixture.

Add molasses, beaten egg, and baking soda into mixture. Then add boiling water and mix well. Pour the filling into pie dish. Scatter reserved crumb mixture evenly atop pie.

Bake for 18 minutes, then lower temperature to 350° F and bake another 20 minutes until the crust is golden and center of pie is only a bit wobbly. Cool for 1 hour. This pie is very rich, and Ella Mae recommends that you serve it with vanilla ice cream or whipped cream.

CHARMED PIECRUST

2½ cups all-purpose flour, plus extra for rolling

1 teaspoon salt

1 teaspoon sugar

1 cup (2 sticks) unsalted butter, very cold, cut into ½-inch cubes

6 to 8 tablespoons very cold water (put in freezer for 15 minutes before use)

Combine flour, salt, and sugar in a food processor; pulse to mix. Add butter and pulse until mixture resembles coarse meal and you have pea-size pieces of butter. Add ice water 1 tablespoon at a time, pulsing until mixture begins to clump together. Put some dough between your fingers. If it holds together, it's ready. If it falls apart, you need a little more water. You'll see bits of butter in the dough. This is a good thing, as it will give you a nice, flaky crust.

Mound dough and place on a clean surface. Gently shape into 2 disks of equal size. Do not overknead. Sprinkle a little flour around the disks. Wrap each disk in plastic wrap and refrigerate at least 1 hour.

Remove first crust disk from the refrigerator. Let sit at room temperature for 5 minutes or until soft enough to roll. Roll out with a rolling pin on a lightly floured surface to a 12-inch circle (Ella Mae uses a pie mat to help with measurements). Gently transfer into a 9-inch pie plate. Carefully press the pie dough down so that it lines the bottom and sides of the pie plate. Use kitchen shears to trim the dough to within ½ inch of the edge of the pie dish.

Roll out second disk of dough and place on top of the pie filling. Pinch top and bottom of dough firmly together. Trim excess dough with kitchen shears, leaving about an inch of overhang. Fold the edge of the top piece of dough over and under the edge of the bottom piece of dough, pressing together. Flute edges by pinching with thumb and forefinger. Remember to score the center of the top crust with a few small cuts so that steam can escape.

CHARMED EGG WASH

To achieve a golden brown color for your crust, brush the surface with this egg wash before placing the pie in the oven.

1 tablespoon half-and-half
1 large egg yolk

Note: If you're short on time and decide to use the premade piecrusts found in your grocery store's dairy section, you can still use the egg wash on the crusts to give them a homemade flavor.

Peach Pies and Alibis

by Ellery Adams

Reba watched the newlyweds move down the aisle, hugging their loved ones and posing for pictures. "Think of what you did for Mrs. Dower with a single piece of pie. You put color in her gray world. You released her from guilt and grief. She's going to laugh and sing and *live*, all because of you. It is a gift, Ella Mae. As much as it's a burden."

Ella Mae wasn't able to respond because as soon as the recessional music ended, Peter Shaw stood under the arch and invited the guests to gather on the back porch for refreshments. "I don't know about you," he said. "But I can't wait to see my daughter and new son-in-law feed each other some wedding pie."

"All hands on deck," Reba said and took her place at the head of the buffet table. She removed a pair of peach meringue mini tarts garnished with delicate caramel hearts from the small cooler under the table and plated them. These had been made especially for the bride and groom.

Candis swept onto the porch, hugging and kissing Ella Mae and Reba like they were family.

"Rudy and I want everybody to meet the woman responsible for creating this amazing dessert display!" Candis said, beaming at Ella Mae. "If you haven't been to The Charmed Pie Shoppe yet, then you're missing out on a totally life-altering experience."

Blushing, Ella Mae handed Candis the plate with the peach tarts and laughed as Rudy smeared meringue on his bride's nose. Candis returned the favor by pressing her whole pie into his face. He then grabbed her and kissed her, leaving them both covered in meringue.

Charmed Georgia Peach Pie

From Peach Pies and Alibis by Ellery Adams

SERVES 8

1 Charmed Piecrust (page 315)

12 fresh, ripe peaches

½ cup firmly packed dark brown sugar

⅓ cup sugar

1 teaspoon ground cinnamon

¼ cup all-purpose flour

2 tablespoons butter, cut into pieces

1 large egg, beaten

2 tablespoons turbinado sugar (Sugar In The Raw)

Cinnamon, for dusting (optional)

Preheat oven to 425° F. Roll out Charmed Piecrust and place in a 9-inch pie plate.

Peel peaches and cut into slices. Stir together sugars, cinnamon, and flour in a bowl; add peaches, stirring to coat. Immediately spoon peach mixture into piecrust, and dot with pieces of butter.

Carefully place remaining piecrust over filling; press edges of crusts together to seal. Cut off excess crust and crimp edges of pie. Brush top of pie with beaten egg; sprinkle with turbinado sugar and a dusting of cinnamon, if desired. Cut 5 slits in top of pie for steam to escape. Or, create a lattice top by cutting dough disk into strips using a fluted pastry wheel. Place on top of filling and follow the egg/sugar/cinnamon finishing touches. Protect edges of crust with foil or pie shield.

Freeze pie 15 minutes. Meanwhile, heat a cookie sheet covered with a sheet of parchment paper in oven 10 minutes. Place pie on hot cookie sheet.

Bake on lower oven rack 15 minutes. Reduce oven temperature to 375° F; bake 40 minutes. Cover loosely with aluminum foil to prevent over-browning, and bake 25 more minutes or until juices are thick and bubbly (juices will bubble through top but parchment paper will protect your tray). Transfer to a wire rack; cool 2 hours before serving.

Charmed Banana Puddin' Pie

∽ From *Pies and Prejudice* by Ellery Adams ∽

SERVES 6 TO 8

1 Charmed Piecrust (page 315)

¼ cup cold water

2¼ teaspoons unflavored gelatin (1 package)

2 cups whole milk

4 large egg yolks

⅔ cup sugar

¼ cup cornstarch

¼ teaspoon salt

1 teaspoon pure vanilla extract

3 large, very ripe bananas, peeled and sliced

WHIPPED TOPPING

1 cup heavy cream

1 teaspoon dark rum

1 teaspoon vanilla extract

2 tablespoons confectioners' sugar

6 ounces semisweet chocolate, shaved into curls using a vegetable
     peeler, for garnish

Transfer dough to a 9-inch pie dish. Trim and flute the edge. Using a fork, pierce the dough several times, then line with aluminum foil and freeze for 30 minutes. Preheat oven to 450° F.

Place the dough-lined pan on a baking sheet and fill the foil with pie weights. Bake for 12 to 15 minutes. Cool and then remove the foil and weights.

Pour cold water into a small bowl and add gelatin. Let gelatin firm up for about 10 minutes. Next, pour milk into a medium saucepan and warm over low-medium heat until hot (about 10 minutes) but don't allow it to boil. In a large bowl, whisk the egg yolks and sugar. Add cornstarch and salt and blend until there are no lumps. Gradually add the hot milk to the egg mixture, stirring constantly. Add the gelatin to the mix and blend thoroughly. Return entire mixture to saucepan. Cook over medium heat until mixture begins to bubble, whisking constantly. Remove from heat and immediately add vanilla.

Line the banana slices along the cooled piecrust and then spread the custard on top. Put a piece of plastic wrap directly onto the surface of the filling, piercing the plastic a few times with a knife. Cover and refrigerate for 2 to 4 hours.

To make the whipped topping, place a large stainless steel bowl and blender beaters in the freezer for 10 minutes. Remove from freezer and add cream, rum, vanilla, and sugar into chilled bowl. Beat on high speed until stiff peaks form. Spread the topping over chilled pie and garnish with chocolate shavings.

Charmed Chocolate-Bourbon Pecan Pie

〜 From *Pies and Prejudice* by Ellery Adams 〜

MAKES 2 PIES

1 Charmed Piecrust (page 315)

¾ cup sugar

1 cup light corn syrup

½ cup salted butter

4 eggs, beaten

2 tablespoons bourbon

1 teaspoon pure vanilla extract

6 ounces semisweet chocolate chips

1 cup chopped pecans

Preheat oven to 325° F. Roll out piecrusts and place in 9-inch pie plates.

In a medium saucepan, combine sugar, corn syrup, and butter. Cook over medium heat, stirring constantly, until butter melts and sugar dissolves. Cool slightly. In a large bowl blend eggs, bourbon, and vanilla. Mix well. Slowly pour sugar mixture into egg mixture, whisking constantly. Stir in chocolate chips and pecans. Pour mixture into pie shells. Bake in preheated oven for 50 to 55 minutes or until you spot a lovely golden bark.

Charmed Red Hot-Apple Pie

~ From Pecan Pies and Homicides by Ellery Adams ~

SERVES 6 TO 8

1 Charmed Piecrust (page 315)

1 tablespoon lemon juice

¼ cup cinnamon Red Hots candies

1 teaspoon ground cinnamon

⅓ cup honey

4 large Granny Smith apples, peeled and chopped

1 tablespoon cold butter, cut into pieces

Charmed Egg Wash (page 316)

Cinnamon sugar (½ cup sugar and 1 tablespoon cinnamon)

Vanilla ice cream, for serving (optional)

Preheat oven to 350° F. Roll out piecrust and place one crust into pie plate. Gently smooth out any folds and press dough into sides of plate. Trim the pastry edges with a knife or kitchen shears. In small saucepan, cook the lemon juice and cinnamon Red Hots over low heat until the candies melt, approximately 10 minutes. Remove the pan from the heat and stir in the ground cinnamon and honey. Arrange apples in bottom crust and pour the Red Hots mixture over the apples. Dot with pieces of butter.

Cut decorative shapes in the remainder of the piecrust dough with small cookie cutters (Ella Mae prefers hearts). Moisten the edges of the bottom crust with water and then lift the top crust over filling. Trim any extra dough with a knife or kitchen shears and then flute the edges or press them together using the tines of a fork. Brush with Charmed Egg Wash and sprinkle with cinnamon sugar. Bake for 15 minutes. Then cover the edge of the crust with a pie shield or aluminum foil and bake for another 45 minutes or until the crust is golden brown. Cool and serve with vanilla ice cream, if desired.

Charmed Mini Maple-Pecan Pies

~ From *Pecan Pies and Homicides* by Ellery Adams ~

SERVES 10 TO 12

1 Charmed Piecrust (page 315)

1 cup pure Grade A maple syrup

¾ cup packed brown sugar

3 large eggs

¼ cup sugar

3 tablespoons salted butter, melted

1 tablespoon all-purpose flour

1 teaspoon pure vanilla extract

2 cups chopped pecans

Preheat oven to 350° F. Grease a muffin tin, and set aside.

Roll out dough until it is approximately ⅛ inch thick and use a 4-inch-round cookie cutter to cut out circles. Put each circle in prepared muffin tin well. In medium bowl, blend all the ingredients except the pecans. Sprinkle the nuts over crust. Pour the filling over until it nearly reaches the top of each tin. Bake until the filling is set, about 45 minutes. Cool completely and serve with Maple Whipped Cream.

Maple Whipped Cream

1 cup whipping cream

¼ cup pure Grade A maple syrup

¼ teaspoon ground cinnamon

Place a metal bowl and electric mixer beaters in the freezer for 10 minutes. Remove them from the freezer and add the whipping cream to the bowl. Beat until the cream starts to thicken. Add the maple syrup and ground cinnamon, and whip until stiff peaks form.

Charmed Heart-Shaped White Chocolate–Raspberry Cream Two-Bite Pies

~ From Pecan Pies and Homicides by Ellery Adams ~

SERVES 8 TO 10

Charmed Piecrust (page 315)
Charmed Egg Wash (page 316)
8 ounces cream cheese, softened
1 cup fresh raspberries
1 tablespoon pure vanilla extract
2 tablespoons sugar
½ cup white chocolate chips
Finishing sugar, for decorating

Add cream cheese, raspberries, vanilla extract, sugar, and white chocolate chips to a food processor and pulse until smooth. Refrigerate until ready to use.

Preheat oven to 400° F. Line a cookie sheet with parchment paper, and set aside.

Roll out Charmed Piecrust dough to approximately ⅛ inch thick, and cut it with a heart cookie cutter. Transfer the piecrust hearts to the prepared cookie sheet. Add a dollop of filling (amount will depend on size of cookie cutter). Wet the edges of the bottom heart and press another heart gently on top. Seal the edges with the tines of a fork. Brush the hearts with Charmed Egg Wash and add a sprinkle of finishing sugar. For fun, use different-colored sugars like pink, white, and red. Bake for approximately 12 minutes or until the crust turns golden brown.

If Mashed Potatoes Could Dance

by Paige Shelton

Sweet potato pie was one of those desserts that, despite the word sweet, I thought shouldn't taste good. I wasn't a fan of sweet potatoes in any form—except when they were cooked, peeled, and blended with sugar, butter, eggs, vanilla, salt, nutmeg, and milk. And then poured into a piecrust, baked, and finally topped with egg white and marshmallow meringue. The resulting creation was the only form in which I found sweet potatoes palatable.

I'd baked a few sweet potato pies in my day, all of them topped with meringue that I'd made with an electric mixer. Sally insisted that we use a whisk, a copper bowl, and muscle power, as well as precise and perfectly timed ingredient additions. I still wanted to pull out the mixer, but even Gram insisted that I follow Sally's instructions.

Sweet Potato Pie with Marshmallow Meringue

~ From *If Mashed Potatoes Could Dance* by Paige Shelton ~

There is absolutely nothing I like about sweet potatoes—except for sweet potato pie. Those poor sweet potatoes, they sometimes do get a bad rap, but their popularity is growing. They are a healthy food, and cooks and chefs are getting more and more creative developing recipes that include them.

Although I have an aversion to sweet potatoes, many of my family and friends are recommending ideas that are making them more . . . interesting. But without hesitation, I adore sweet potato pie. Hope you enjoy this recipe, too.

SERVES 6 TO 8

CRUST

1 (9-inch) refrigerated piecrust

1 egg yolk, lightly beaten

1 tablespoon whipping cream

FILLING

¼ cup (½ stick) salted butter, melted

1 cup sugar

⅓ teaspoon salt

3 large eggs

3 cups cooked, mashed sweet potatoes, lightly packed
(3 to 4 scrubbed potatoes, each poked with a fork
a few times and baked at 400° F for 45 minutes)

1 cup half-and-half

1 tablespoon lemon zest

3 tablespoons fresh lemon juice

¼ teaspoon ground nutmeg

MARSHMALLOW MERINGUE

3 egg whites

½ teaspoon vanilla extract

⅛ cup salt

¼ cup sugar

1 (7-ounce) jar marshmallow cream (such as Fluff)

MAKE CRUST

Preheat oven to 425° F.

On a lightly floured surface, roll the piecrust into a 13-inch circle. Fit the crust into a 9-inch pie plate, fold the edges under, and crimp. Prick the bottom and sides of the crust with a fork. Line the crust with parchment paper and fill with pie weights or dried beans. Bake 9 minutes. Remove the crust from the oven and take out the weights and parchment. Whisk together the egg yolk and cream, and brush the mixture on the bottom and sides of the crust. Bake for 6 to 8 minutes more or until the crust is golden. Transfer to a wire rack and cool.

Reduce the oven temperature to 350° F.

MAKE FILLING

In a large bowl, stir together the melted butter, sugar, salt, and eggs until well blended. Add the sweet potatoes, half-and-half, lemon zest, lemon juice, and nutmeg. Stir until the mixture is well blended. Pour the mixture into the prepared piecrust.

Shield the exposed crust edge from the heat by covering it with aluminum foil.

Bake for 50 to 55 minutes or until knife inserted in the center comes out clean. Remove the pie to a wire rack and cool completely, about 1 hour.

MAKE MARSHMALLOW MERINGUE

Preheat the oven to 350° F.

In a large metal or glass bowl, beat the egg whites, vanilla extract, and salt with an electric mixer at high speed until foamy. Gradually add the sugar, 1 tablespoon at a time, beating until stiff peaks form. (Note: When making meringue, I prefer to use a heavy-duty stand mixer, but a hand mixer works as well. I always use metal bowls to make meringue as these yield high-volume beaten egg whites; some people use only copper. Glass bowls are also acceptable, but do not use a plastic bowl, as it may contain grease or fat residue, which will inhibit the foaming of the egg whites!)

Beat one-quarter of the marshmallow cream into the egg white mixture. Repeat three more times with the remaining marshmallow cream, beating until smooth. Spread the meringue over the pie. I spread it to about 1 inch away from the sides of the pie and make a pointy peak (or a few) in the middle. I think it's prettier that way.

Bake for 6 to 7 minutes, or until the meringue is lightly browned.

Key Lime–Strawberry Whipped Topping Pie

~ From Town in a Strawberry Swirl by B. B. Haywood ~

SERVES 8

1 can sweetened condensed milk

4 egg yolks

4 ounces key lime juice

1 (9-inch) graham cracker crust

1 cup strawberries, blended in a blender

1 cup whipping cream

1 teaspoon vanilla extract

Preheat oven to 350° F.

In a mixing bowl on low speed, blend the condensed milk and egg yolks.

Add the key lime juice and continue mixing. Mix until blended smoothly.

Pour into the pie shell. Bake for 20 minutes.

Chill until cool enough to cover with the topping.

MAKE THE TOPPING

Mix the blended strawberries, whipping cream, and vanilla with a mixer on Whip for approximately 8 minutes or until soft peaks form.

Drop by large spoonfuls on top of the pie, and smooth out with a knife.

Refrigerate.

The strawberry offsets the strong key lime flavor and makes for a fruity deliciousness!

Sandra Gregoire's Charmed "Customer of the Week" Lime Pie

~ From Pies and Prejudice by Ellery Adams ~

SERVES 8

3 egg yolks, lightly beaten

21 ounces (1½ cans) sweetened condensed milk

¾ cup fresh lime juice or key lime juice

Green and blue food coloring (optional,
    if desired for greener effect)

1 (9-inch) graham cracker crust

2 cups whipping cream

2 tablespoons sugar

Fresh lime slices or candied lime slices,
    for garnish

Preheat oven to 350° F.

Whisk together the egg yolks, sweetened condensed milk, and lime juice. Add food coloring, if desired. Pour into crust. Bake for 15 minutes. Remove from oven and cool on a wire rack. When cool, cover and refrigerate for at least 4 hours.

Place a large stainless steel bowl and blender beaters in the freezer for 10 minutes. Beat whipping cream in chilled bowl at high speed with an electric mixer until foamy. (Note: Start slowly and increase speed in increments over several seconds.)

Gradually add sugar and continue beating until soft peaks form. Spread whipped cream over well-chilled pie or pipe on with a cake decorator. Garnish with fresh lime slices or candied lime slices.

Town in a Strawberry Swirl

by B. B. Haywood

"Wait until you see what Herr Georg has cooked up this time!" Maggie Tremont said as she came breezing through the doorway that led to the bakery shop's kitchen in the back. "He's outdone himself! You'll be amazed."

Candy Holliday dropped into a vacant chair at a small oak table by the front window, set her tote bag down at her feet, and tilted her head upward, sniffing the aromas. "Let me guess. Something with strawberries?"

"Fresh from the berry farm," Maggie confirmed happily. "Miles Crawford dropped them off first thing this morning. You should see how plump and juicy they are. I don't know what he does out at that farm of his, but he grows the biggest, tastiest berries in the region."

"I bet Herr Georg had a field day with those. So," Candy said, as her nose caught some disparate scents, causing her to crane her head around, "what exactly *is* he cooking up back there?"

Maggie smiled slyly at her friend. "You used to work for him, so you're familiar with a lot of his recipes. Why don't you take a guess?"

"I think," Candy said, as her cornflower-blue eyes twinkled devilishly, "that I detect a hint of cinnamon."

Maggie scrunched up her nose. "That's no fair. You're too good at this. But you have to be more specific. What else?"

"Well, let me see." She paused a moment, still sniffing the air. "The most obvious possibility is a strawberry shortcake, but that seems too simple for Herr Georg. So is a traditional strawberry pie. He could be making a strawberry Black Forest cake, which is scrumptious, but I don't think he uses cinnamon in that. So my guess is it's some type of *obstkuchen*—a torte or multilayered cake, using some type of fruit—in this case strawberry, of course. And maybe with a few tablespoons of cinnamon sugar added in?" She opened her eyes and raised an eyebrow. "So how'd I do?"

Maggie looked impressed. "I guess you haven't lost your detecting skills."

"And there's something else, too. Homemade whipped cream?"

"Key lime strawberry whipped cream," Maggie admitted, letting out a breath, as if she'd been deflated. "You peeked!"

"Actually," Candy said with a sly smile, "he made it two years ago when I worked here. And if I remember correctly, it was fantastic. I can't wait to taste it again."

As if on cue, Herr Georg Wolfsburger, the mustachioed proprietor of the Black Forest Bakery, emerged from the back kitchen carrying a glass platter high in the air, held up by his splayed fingers. On it was the strawberry *obstkuchen*.

"Ah, Candy, *meine liebchen*, here you are," the baker said to her with a toothy grin. "You are here just in time to taste my latest creation!"

It was almost too pretty to eat, still warm from the oven and topped by a circle of small, perfectly ripened berries set delicately into the whipped cream.

Herr Georg cut her a delicate slice, topped with a dollop of whipped cream and a strawberry, and set it down in front of her. She was just about to dig in when she was distracted by the sound of a siren. A moment later, her cell phone rang in her back pocket . . .

Herr Georg's Obstkuchen: German Strawberry Torte

~ From *Town in a Strawberry Swirl* by B. B. Haywood ~

SERVES 8 TO 12

CAKE/CRUST

Fine bread crumbs

3 eggs

⅜ cup (¼ cup plus 2 tablespoons) sugar

⅜ cup (6 tablespoons) butter, softened

Pinch salt

1⅓ cups flour

1 teaspoon baking powder

3 tablespoons cinnamon sugar (see Note, below)

FILLING

2 pints strawberries

3 tablespoons strawberry jam

MAKE THE CAKE/CRUST

Preheat oven to 400° F. Grease a baking pan, sprinkle the bottom with bread crumbs, and set aside.

In a large bowl and using a hand mixer on high speed, blend the eggs, sugar, butter, and salt. Mix until the mixture is foamy.

Add the flour and baking powder. Mix until blended.

Pour the dough into prepared baking pan, spreading it to the edges. Bake for 12 to 15 minutes or until golden brown.

Remove the cake and cool.

Hull the strawberries and place the whole fruits on the cake top.

In a small saucepan, heat the strawberry jam over low heat.

Using a pastry brush, spread the warm jam over the strawberries. This makes a glaze. *Guten appetit!*

Note: To make cinnamon sugar, add 1 teaspoon cinnamon powder to 3 tablespoons of sugar and mix together.

Chocolate Stout Brownie Torte

~ From *Death by the Dozen* by Jenn McKinlay ~

A chocolate stout brownie served in a chocolate shell and topped with a thin layer of chocolate mousse between layers of brownie and a dollop of whipped cream on top.

MAKES 32 BROWNIES

12 ounces chocolate stout

1 cup cocoa powder, unsweetened

2 cups sugar

½ cup butter, melted

2 teaspoons vanilla extract

4 eggs

2 cups all-purpose flour

¾ teaspoon salt

1 cup semisweet chocolate chips

Preheat oven to 350° F. Line a 13 × 9-inch baking pan with aluminum foil, and set aside.

In a large bowl, whisk together the stout and cocoa powder until blended and smooth. Whisk in the sugar, butter, vanilla extract, and eggs, one at a time. Blend well. Add the flour and salt, mixing until the batter is smooth. Stir in the chocolate chips. Spread the mixture in the prepared pan. Bake 35 to 42 minutes until a knife inserted in the center comes out clean or with just a few crumbs. Set aside to cool.

Chocolate Mousse

8 ounces bittersweet chocolate, chopped
10 ounces heavy whipping cream

Place the chocolate in the top of a double boiler, or in a microwave-safe bowl; stir occasionally until melted and smooth. Allow to cool slightly. Whip the cream in a large bowl with an electric mixer until soft peaks barely form. Fold the chocolate into the cream and chill 30 minutes in the refrigerator, until set.

To make Mel's torte, use a premade chocolate shell and cut 2 × 2-inch brownies so that you now have 2 layers. Put one layer in the chocolate shell then spread chocolate mousse over it. Place the second layer on top and garnish with a dollop of whipped cream.

Deep-Fried Bananas with Baked Plantains

From Death by the Dozen by Jenn McKinlay

Bananas with brown sugar, wrapped in a spring roll and deep-fried, served with chocolate sauce and baked plantain chips.

SERVES 8

2 large bananas
8 (7-inch-square) spring roll wrappers
1 cup brown sugar
1 quart hot oil for deep frying

Preheat the oil in a deep fryer to 375° F. Peel the bananas and slice them in half lengthwise and then across to make 4 pieces. Place 1 piece of banana on a spring roll wrapper and sprinkle with brown sugar to taste. Roll up the spring roll wrapper; as you roll, fold up the edges to seal the ends, as you don't want the banana to get saturated with oil. Wet the final edge of the spring roll wrapper to seal it. Repeat with remaining bananas. Fry a few banana rolls at a time in the hot oil until evenly browned. Place on paper towels to drain.

Plantain Chips

2 green plantains (green ones bake better than yellow)

Preheat oven to 400° F. Coat a nonstick cookie sheet with cooking spray, and set aside.

Cut the ends off the plantains and peel. Cut each plantain on the diagonal into ½-inch-wide slices. Arrange in a single layer on prepared baking sheet and coat the tops with cooking spray. Bake 15 to 17 minutes, turning after 8 minutes.

Chocolate Sauce

⅔ cup unsweetened cocoa
1⅔ cups sugar
1¼ cups water
1 teaspoon vanilla extract

In a medium saucepan over medium heat, combine the cocoa, sugar, and water. Bring to a boil and let boil 1 minute. Remove from heat and stir in the vanilla.

Charmed Apple, Pear, and Cherry Crisp

~ From *Peach Pies and Alibis* by Ellery Adams ~

SERVES 8

2 Granny Smith apples, peeled, cored, and chopped

2 Anjou pears, peeled, cored, and chopped

¾ cup frozen cherries (you can substitute fresh cranberries or
raisins)

¼ cup sugar

3 teaspoons ground cinnamon

1 teaspoon ground nutmeg

⅓ cup quick-cooking oats

⅓ cup all-purpose flour

½ cup packed light brown sugar

¼ cup (½ stick) unsalted butter, cut into pieces

½ cup chopped pecans

Preheat oven to 375° F. Butter an 8-inch-square pan, and set aside. In a large bowl, mix together the apples, pears, cherries, sugar, cinnamon, and nutmeg. Spread the mixture evenly in the prepared baking dish. In the same bowl or in a food processor, combine the oats, flour, and brown sugar. Mix in the butter until crumbly. (If using food processor, use the pulse button to crumble.) Stir in the pecans. Sprinkle the mixture over the apples. Bake for approximately 45 minutes or until the topping is golden brown.

Index

Aames, Avery
  Clobbered by Camembert, 3, 12, 26, 111
  Days of Wine and Roquefort, 108
  Long Quiche Goodbye, The, 209, 235–36, 237
  Lost and Fondue, 76, 148
  To Brie or Not to Brie, 67, 163–64, 165, 274
Adams, Ellery
  Peach Pies and Alibis, 317–18, 319, 347
  Pecan Pies and Homicides, 14–15, 16, 175, 324, 326, 328
  Pies and Prejudice, 19, 312–13, 314, 321, 323, 336
Affairs of Steak (Hyzy), 156–58, 159, 161, 171, 181
Agony of the Leaves (Childs), 160
Aioli, Paprika, 175–76
Almond, Chicken, and Apricot Salad, 98
amaretto syrup/liqueur in Orange-Spice Yule Latte, 138
Anginetti (Glazed Lemon Cookies), 250–52
Aphrodisiac Brownies, 262–64
appetizers, 143–67
  Affairs of Steak excerpt (Hyzy), 156–58
  Baked Crab Rangoon, 155
  Blue Cheese and Garlic Fondue, 148
  Book, Line, and Sinker excerpt (McKinlay), 152–53
  Charlene's Cucumber Cups Stuffed with Feta, 154
  Cranberry-Pecan Brie en Croûte, 161–62
  Crostini Times Two, 149–50
  Death al Dente excerpt (Budewitz), 145–46
  Deviled Eggs, 151
  Fennel and Shrimp Prosciutto Wraps, 147
  Morel Sauté, 150
  Olive Tapenade, 149
  Parmesan Crisps, 160
  Pastry-Wrapped Asparagus Spears with Prosciutto, 159
  Ricotta-Stuffed Mushrooms, 165

  Smoked Salmon Florets, 166
  Stuffed Cherry Tomatoes, 167
  To Brie or Not to Brie excerpt (Aames), 163–64
apples
  Aunt Vera's Brie, Apple, and Turkey Grilled Cheese, 105–6
  Beet-Mushroom-Barley Soup, 87
  Charmed Apple, Pear, and Cherry Crisp, 347
  Charmed Red Hot-Apple Pie, 324–25
  Maggie Tremont's German Strawberry-Apple Pancakes, 28–29
  Max's Blue Cheese, Apple, and Walnut Salad, 99–100
  Nanna Tibbetts's Moose Mincemeat, 265
Apricot, Chicken, and Almond Salad, 98
Archer, Connie
  Broth of Betrayal, A, 91–92, 93, 95, 98
  Ladle to the Grave, 79–80, 81, 110, 118
  Roux of Revenge, A, 46, 66, 84–85, 87
  Spoonful of Murder, A, 21–22, 23, 86, 88, 89, 107
asparagus
  Pastry-Wrapped Asparagus Spears with Prosciutto, 159
  Penne Rigate with Asparagus and Sesame-Chile Shrimp, 207–8
Assault and Pepper (Budewitz), 141, 205–6, 207
Aunt Vera's Brie, Apple, and Turkey Grilled Cheese, 105–6
Aunt Vera's Gluten-Free Orange-Chocolate Biscotti, 255–57
Avocado and Roasted Red Pepper Sandwich, 110

bacon
  Bacon-Cheddar Muffins, 62
  Charmed Bacon-Lattice Breakfast Pie, 16
  Charmed Pancetta and Gruyère Tart, 19–20
  Clare's Fully Loaded Colcannon for Mike, 222–23

bacon (*cont.*)
    Delilah's Grilled Cheese with Bacon and
      Fig Jam, 108–9
    Goat Cheese and Pancetta Sandwich, 107
    Skillet Potatoes, 30
    Twice-Baked Potatoes, 229–30
Bailey's Irish Cream and Caramel-Nut Fudge,
    280–81
Baked Crab Rangoon, 155
baked goods. *See* breads, muffins, and other
    baked goods; desserts
Balsamic Vinaigrette, 99–100
bananas
    Betts's Best Banana Bread, 40
    Charmed Banana Puddin' Pie, 321–22
    Deep-Fried Bananas with Baked Plantains,
      345–46
    Fit for the King Muffins (Banana-Peanut
      Butter-Chocolate Chip Muffins), 60–61
    Golden Acres Banana-Bran Muffins, 49–50
Barbara's Bake Shop, Iowa, 248
Barley-Beet-Mushroom Soup, 87
Baschnagel, Heidi, 248
basil
    Polenta with Taleggio and Basil, 237
    Watermelon, Basil, and Feta Salad, 95
Bean (Two) and Pesto Salad, Erin's, 96–97
beef
    Beef Wellington, 171–72
    Charmed Meat Pies with Paprika Aioli,
      175–76
    Clare Cosi's Skillet Lasagna (for Mike),
      211–12
    Grilled Flank Steak, 173–74
    Nanna Tibbetts's Moose Mincemeat, 265
Beet-Mushroom-Barley Soup, 87
Betts's Best Banana Bread, 40
Betty Crocker, 197, 199
Billionaire Blend (Coyle), 211, 280
Biscotti, Aunt Vera's Gluten-Free Orange-
    Chocolate, 255–57
Biscuits, Rosemary, 66
Black Orchid Cocktail, 117
Blood Orange and Fennel Salad, 101–2
blueberries
    Blueberry Gingerbread, 43–44
    Blueberry-Lemon Shortbread, 247
    Blueberry Sauce, 275
    Brie-Blueberry Ice Cream, 274–75
    Candy Holliday's Blueberry Whipped
      Cream, 273
    Jake's Favorite Blueberry-Orange Muffins, 57

blue cheese
    Blue Cheese and Garlic Fondue, 148
    Max's Blue Cheese, Apple, and Walnut Salad,
      99–100
blue curaçao liqueur in Black Orchid
    Cocktail, 117
Book, Line, and Sinker (McKinlay),
    152–53, 154
Bourbon-Chocolate Pecan Pie, Charmed, 323
Bowled Over (Hamilton), 226, 227
Bran-Banana Muffins, Golden Acres, 49–50
Bran New Death (Hamilton), 47–48, 49, 62
Bread Pudding, Granny Sebastian's, 271–72
breads, muffins, and other baked goods,
    31–76
    Bacon-Cheddar Muffins, 62
    Betts's Best Banana Bread, 40
    Blueberry Gingerbread, 43–44
    Bran New Death excerpt (Hamilton),
      47–48
    Brew to a Kill, A excerpt (Coyle), 53
    Cherry Scones, 76
    Cinnamon Bread, 37–38
    Clare Cosi's Classic Coffee Cake Muffins
      with Streusel Topping and Vanilla Glaze,
      54–56
    Clare Cosi's Doughnut Muffins, 51–52
    Cliff's Pear Bread, 45
    Dandy Devonshire Cream, 72
    Easy Cream Scones, 69
    Fit for the King Muffins (Banana-Peanut
      Butter-Chocolate Chip Muffins), 60–61
    Gluten-Free Popovers, 67
    Golden Acres Banana-Bran Muffins, 49–50
    Gram's Instant Miracle Rolls, 65
    Hail to the Chef excerpt (Hyzy), 33–36
    Haley's Lemon Curd, 75
    Holly Holliday's Pumpkin Chocolate Chip
      Bread, 39
    If Bread Could Rise to the Occasion excerpt
      (Shelton), 64
    Jake's Favorite Blueberry-Orange Muffins, 57
    Muffin but Murder excerpt (Hamilton),
      58–59
    Old-Fashioned Crumpets, 68
    Rosemary Biscuits, 66
    Savory Herb Muffins, 63
    Shades of Earl Grey excerpt (Childs), 73–74
    Streusel (Crumb) Topping, 56
    Sweet Tea Revenge excerpt (Childs), 70–71
    Town in a Blueberry Jam excerpt
      (Haywood), 41–42

Vanilla Glaze, 55–56
Zucchini Bread, 46
See also desserts; sandwiches
breakfast, 1–30
    Charmed Bacon-Lattice Breakfast Pie, 16
    Charmed Pancetta and Gruyère Tart,
       19–20
    Delilah's Grilled Breakfast Sandwich, 3–4
    Eggs Benedict, 8–9
    Fat-Free, Cheese-Free, Yolk-Free, High-
       Fiber Omelet, 10–11
    French Toast Sandwich, 23
    Grandmother's Pancake Mix, 26–27
    Jenna's Monte Cristo Sandwich, 24–25
    Maggie Tremont's German Strawberry-Apple
       Pancakes, 28–29
    Pancakes with Gouda and Figs, 26–27
    Pecan Pies and Homicides excerpt (Adams),
       14–15
    San Simon Frittata, 12–13
    Skillet Potatoes, 30
    Spinach Quiche, 17–18
    Spoonful of Murder, A excerpt (Archer),
       21–22
    State of the Onion excerpt (Hyzy), 5–7
Brew to a Kill, A (Coyle), 53, 54, 182, 222
Brie cheese
    Aunt Vera's Brie, Apple, and Turkey Grilled
       Cheese, 105–6
    Brie-Blueberry Ice Cream, 274–75
    Cranberry-Pecan Brie en Croûte, 161–62
    Delilah's Grilled Breakfast Sandwich,
       3–4
broccoli in Fat-Free, Cheese-Free, Yolk-Free,
    High-Fiber Omelet, 10–11
Broth of Betrayal, A (Archer), 91–92, 93,
    95, 98
brownies
    Aphrodisiac Brownies, 262–64
    Chocolate Stout Brownie Torte, 343–44
Budewitz, Leslie
    Assault and Pepper, 141, 205–6, 207
    Butter Off Dead, 101, 120–21, 122, 134
    Crime Rib, 96, 99, 173, 184–85, 186
    Death al Dente, 94, 145–46, 147, 149, 213
Buffalo West Wing (Hyzy), 203, 220
buttercream
    Raspberry Buttercream Frosting, 303
    Vanilla Buttercream Frosting, 296–97
Buttercream Bump Off (McKinlay), 296, 298
Butter Off Dead (Budewitz), 101, 120–21,
    122, 134

cabbage in Clare's Fully Loaded Colcannon for
    Mike, 222–23
caffeine as aphrodisiac, 262
cakes
    Cake Pops, 283–84
    Queen Elizabeth Cake, 287–89
    Red Velvet Cake/Cupcakes, 294–95
    Sandy's Favorite Whoopie Pies, 260–61
cál ceannann (white-headed cabbage), 222
Candy Cane Latte, 137–38
Candy Holliday's Blueberry Whipped
    Cream, 273
Candy Holliday's Pumpkin Cheesecake Swirl,
    310–11
candy melts in Cake Pops, 283–84
Caprese Salad, 94
caramel
    Bailey's Irish Cream and Caramel-Nut
       Fudge, 280–81
    Caramel Sauce à la Katie, 279
    Jenna's Caramel Macchiato Ice Cream,
       277–79
carrots
    Chicken Pot Pie Soup with Dumplings,
       81–82
    Individual Chicken Pot Pies, 181
    Jaymie's Fourth of July Potato Salad, 227–28
    Potato-Yam Soup, 86
    Tomato-Spinach Soup, 89
Cauliflower and Cheddar Soup, 83
celery
    Chicken, Apricot, and Almond Salad, 98
    Chicken Pot Pie Soup with Dumplings,
       81–82
    Jaymie's Fourth of July Potato Salad,
       227–28
Champagne Cookies, 248–49
Charlene's Cucumber Cups Stuffed with
    Feta, 154
Charmed Apple, Pear, and Cherry Crisp, 347
Charmed Bacon-Lattice Breakfast Pie, 16
Charmed Banana Puddin' Pie, 321–22
Charmed Chocolate-Bourbon Pecan Pie, 323
Charmed "Customer of the Week" Lime Pie,
    Sandra Gregoire's, 336–37
Charmed Egg Wash, 316
Charmed Georgia Peach Pie, 319–20
Charmed Heart-Shaped White Chocolate-
    Raspberry Cream Two-Bite Pies, 328–29
Charmed Meat Pies with Paprika Aioli,
    175–76
Charmed Mini Maple-Pecan Pies, 326

Charmed Pancetta and Gruyère Tart, 19–20
Charmed Piecrust, 315–16
Charmed Red Hot-Apple Pie, 324–25
Charmed Shoofly Pie, 314–16
Cheddar cheese
    Bacon-Cheddar Muffins, 62
    Cauliflower and Cheddar Soup, 83
    Charmed Bacon-Lattice Breakfast Pie, 16
    Clare's Fully Loaded Colcannon for Mike,
        222–23
    Funeral Potatoes, 224–25
    Skillet Potatoes, 30
    Spinach Quiche, 17–18
    Twice-Baked Potatoes, 229–30
cheese
    Aunt Vera's Brie, Apple, and Turkey Grilled
        Cheese, 105–6
    Bacon-Cheddar Muffins, 62
    Blue Cheese and Garlic Fondue, 148
    Brie-Blueberry Ice Cream, 274–75
    Caprese Salad, 94
    Cauliflower and Cheddar Soup, 83
    Charlene's Cucumber Cups Stuffed with
        Feta, 154
    Charmed Bacon-Lattice Breakfast Pie, 16
    Charmed Pancetta and Gruyère Tart, 19–20
    Clare Cosi's Skillet Lasagna (for Mike),
        211–12
    Clare's Fully Loaded Colcannon for Mike,
        222–23
    Cranberry-Pecan Brie en Croûte, 161–62
    Delilah's Grilled Breakfast Sandwich, 3–4
    Delilah's Grilled Cheese with Bacon and Fig
        Jam, 108–9
    Fennel and Shrimp Prosciutto Wraps, 147
    French Toast Sandwich, 23
    Funeral Potatoes, 224–25
    Goat Cheese and Pancetta Sandwich, 107
    Jenna's Monte Cristo Sandwich, 24–25
    Max's Blue Cheese, Apple, and Walnut Salad,
        99–100
    Pancakes with Gouda and Figs, 26–27
    Parmesan Crisps, 160
    Pesto Sauce, 110
    Polenta with Taleggio and Basil, 237
    Ricotta-Stuffed Mushrooms, 165
    San Simon Frittata, 12–13
    Skillet Potatoes, 30
    Smoked Salmon and Mascarpone
        Risotto, 209
    Spinach Quiche, 17–18
    Torpedo Sandwich, 111

Twice-Baked Potatoes, 229–30
    Watermelon, Basil, and Feta Salad, 95
    See also cream cheese; specific cheeses
Cheesecake Swirl, Candy Holliday's Pumpkin,
    310–11
Cheese-Free, Fat-Free, Yolk-Free, High-Fiber
    Omelet, 10–11
cherries
    Candy Cane Latte, 137–38
    Charmed Apple, Pear, and Cherry Crisp, 347
    Cherry Scones, 76
cherry tomatoes
    Ladybug Tea Sandwiches, 114
    Stuffed Cherry Tomatoes, 167
chicken
    Chicken, Apricot, and Almond Salad, 98
    Chicken Pot Pie Soup with Dumplings,
        81–82
    Clare Cosi's Skillet Lasagna (for Mike),
        211–12
    Clare's Chicken Marsala for Mike, 188–90
    Clare's Roasted Chicken with Rosemary and
        Lime for Mike, 182–83
    Fake Fried Chicken, 195–96
    Fried Chicken, 193–94
    Individual Chicken Pot Pies, 181
    World's Best Grilled Chicken Breasts, The,
        186–87
chicken stock/broth
    Beet-Mushroom-Barley Soup, 87
    Creamed Spinach with Olive Oil and
        Shallots, 220
    Potato-Yam Soup, 86
    Smoked Salmon and Mascarpone
        Risotto, 209
Childs, Laura
    Agony of the Leaves, 160
    Dragonwell Dead, 117
    English Breakfast Murder, The, 202
    Gunpowder Green, 276
    Jasmine Moon Murder, The, 124, 282
    Scones and Bones, 68
    Shades of Earl Grey, 69, 73–74, 75
    Steeped in Evil, 90, 112–13, 114, 155
    Sweet Tea Revenge, 70–71, 72, 125, 126
    Teaberry Strangler, The, 166
Chilled Cucumber, Yogurt, and Walnut
    Soup, 93
Chilled Mango Summer Soup, 90
Chilly Choco Latte, The Village Blend's, 130
china dishes, 288–89
Chips, Plantain, 346

chocolate
 Aphrodisiac Brownies, 262–64
 Aunt Vera's Gluten-Free Orange-Chocolate
  Biscotti, 255–57
 Bailey's Irish Cream and Caramel-Nut
  Fudge, 280–81
 Charmed Chocolate-Bourbon Pecan
  Pie, 323
 Charmed Heart-Shaped White Chocolate-
  Raspberry Cream Two-Bite Pies, 328–29
 Chocolate Mousse, 344
 Chocolate Sauce, 346
 Chocolate Soufflé, 267–68
 Chocolate Stout Brownie Torte, 343–44
 Chocolate Zombie Clusters, 258–59
 Dark Chocolate Ganache, 290–91
 Death by Chocolate Cupcakes, 290–91
 Fit for the King Muffins (Banana-Peanut
  Butter-Chocolate Chip Muffins), 60–61
 Gluten-Free Chocolate Cupcakes with
  Ganache Frosting, 304–5
 Holly Holliday's Pumpkin Chocolate Chip
  Bread, 39
 Jasmine Tea Truffles, 282
 Marjorie Coffin's White Moose Hot
  Cocoa, 133
 Melody's Chocolate Mousse, 269
 Moonlight Madness, 298–99
 Village Blend's (The) Chilly Choco Latte,
  130
 Whipped Topping, 321–22
 White Chocolate "Snowflake" Latte,
  136–37
cinnamon as aphrodisiac, 262
Cinnamon Bread, 37–38
Clare Cosi's Classic Coffee Cake Muffins with
  Streusel Topping and Vanilla Glaze,
  54–56
Clare Cosi's Doughnut Muffins, 51–52
Clare Cosi's Skillet Lasagna (for Mike), 211–12
Clare's Chicken Marsala for Mike, 188–90
Clare's Fully Loaded Colcannon for Mike,
  222–23
Clare's Roasted Chicken with Rosemary and
  Lime for Mike, 182–83
Classic Coffee Cake Muffins with Streusel
  Topping and Vanilla Glaze, Clare Cosi's,
  54–56
Cleopatra, 262
Cliff's Pear Bread, 45
Clobbered by Camembert (Aames), 3, 12,
  26, 111

cocktails
 Black Orchid Cocktail, 117
 Cocktails with the Murphy Girls, 122–23
 See also drinks
Cocoa, Marjorie Coffin's White Moose
  Hot, 133
coconut in Moonlight Madness, 298–99
coffee
 caffeine as aphrodisiac, 262
 Coffee Milk and Coffee Syrup, 127–28
 Homemade Coffee Syrup, 127–28
 Jenna's Caramel Macchiato Ice Cream,
  277–79
 Mexican Coffee, 141
 Nanna Tibbetts's Moose Mincemeat, 265
 Old-Fashioned Iced Coffee, 129
 Pumpkin Spice Coffee Blend, 134
 See also lattes
Coffee Cake Muffins (Clare Cosi's Classic) with
  Streusel Topping and Vanilla Glaze,
  54–56
Colby cheese in Charmed Bacon-Lattice
  Breakfast Pie, 16
Colcannon for Mike, Clare's Fully Loaded,
  222–23
cookies
 Anginetti (Glazed Lemon Cookies),
  250–52
 Aunt Vera's Gluten-Free Orange-Chocolate
  Biscotti, 255–57
 Blueberry-Lemon Shortbread, 247
 Champagne Cookies, 248–49
 Chocolate Zombie Clusters, 258–59
 Nancy's Raspberry Petit Fours, 245–46
 Nanna Tibbetts's Moose Mincemeat
  Cookies, 266
Coyle, Cleo
 Billionaire Blend, 211, 280
 Brew to a Kill, A, 53, 54, 182, 222
 Decaffeinated Corpse, 127
 Espresso Shot, 250
 Holiday Grind, 135
 Holliday Buzz, 188
 Murder by Mocha, 177–78, 179, 258, 262
 Murder Most Frothy (Coyle), 129, 130
 Roast Mortem, 51
Crab Rangoon, Baked, 155
Cranberry-Pecan Brie en Croûte, 161–62
Cream, Dandy Devonshire, 72
cream cheese
 Aunt Vera's Brie, Apple, and Turkey Grilled
  Cheese, 105–6

cream cheese (*cont.*)
  Baked Crab Rangoon, 155
  Cake Pops, 283–84
  Candy Holliday's Pumpkin Cheesecake
    Swirl, 310–11
  Champagne Cookies, 248–49
  Charmed Heart-Shaped White
    Chocolate-Raspberry Cream
    Two-Bite Pies, 328–29
  Delilah's Grilled Breakfast Sandwich, 3–4
  Delilah's Grilled Cheese with Bacon and Fig
    Jam, 108–9
  Ladybug Tea Sandwiches, 114
  Pastry-Wrapped Asparagus Spears with
    Prosciutto, 159
  Red Velvet Cake/Cupcakes, 294–95
  Smoked Salmon Florets, 166
  Stuffed Cherry Tomatoes, 167
Creamed Spinach with Olive Oil and
  Shallots, 220
Cream Scones, Easy, 69
creme de menthe liqueur in Candy Cane Latte,
  137–38
Crime Rib (Budewitz), 96, 99, 173,
  184–85, 186
Crisp, Charmed Apple, Pear, and
  Cherry, 347
Crisps, Parmesan, 160
Crostini Times Two, 149–50
Crumb (Streusel) Topping, 56
Crumpets, Old-Fashioned, 68
cucumbers
  Charlene's Cucumber Cups Stuffed with
    Feta, 154
  Cucumber, Yogurt, and Walnut Soup
    (Chilled), 93
cupcakes
  Death by Chocolate Cupcakes,
    290–91
  Gluten-Free Chocolate Cupcakes with
    Ganache Frosting, 304–5
  Mojito Cupcakes, 301
  Moonlight Madness, 298–99
  Orange Dreamsicle Cupcakes, 296–97
  Pumpkin Cupcakes with Whipped Cream
    Frosting, 308–9
  Red Velvet Cake/Cupcakes, 294–95
  Tinkerbells, 302–3
  Vegan Vanilla Cupcakes, 306–7
Curd, Haley's Lemon, 75
"Customer of the Week" Lime Pie, Sandra
  Gregoire's, 336–37

Dandy Devonshire Cream, 72
Dark Chocolate Ganache, 290–91
dark rum in Black Orchid Cocktail, 117
dates in Queen Elizabeth Cake, 287–89
Days of Wine and Roquefort (Aames), 108
Deadly Grind, A (Hamilton), 285–86, 287
Death al Dente (Budewitz), 94, 145–46, 147,
  149, 213
Death by Chocolate Cupcakes, 290–91
Death by the Dozen (McKinlay), 343, 345
Decaffeinated Corpse (Coyle), 127
Deep-Fried Bananas with Baked Plantains,
  345–46
Delilah's Grilled Breakfast Sandwich, 3–4
Delilah's Grilled Cheese with Bacon and Fig
  Jam, 108–9
Denver the Crabby Tabby, 201
desserts, 239–347
  Anginetti (Glazed Lemon Cookies), 250–52
  Aphrodisiac Brownies, 262–64
  Aunt Vera's Gluten-Free Orange-Chocolate
    Biscotti, 255–57
  Bailey's Irish Cream and Caramel-Nut
    Fudge, 280–81
  Blueberry-Lemon Shortbread, 247
  Blueberry Sauce, 275
  Brie-Blueberry Ice Cream, 274–75
  Cake Pops, 283–84
  Candy Holliday's Blueberry Whipped
    Cream, 273
  Candy Holliday's Pumpkin Cheesecake
    Swirl, 310–11
  Caramel Sauce à la Katie, 279
  Champagne Cookies, 248–49
  Charmed Apple, Pear, and Cherry
    Crisp, 347
  Charmed Banana Puddin' Pie, 321–22
  Charmed Chocolate-Bourbon Pecan
    Pie, 323
  Charmed Egg Wash, 316
  Charmed Georgia Peach Pie, 319–20
  Charmed Heart-Shaped White Chocolate-
    Raspberry Cream Two-Bite Pies, 328–29
  Charmed Mini Maple-Pecan Pies, 326
  Charmed Piecrust, 315–16
  Charmed Red Hot-Apple Pie, 324–25
  Charmed Shoofly Pie, 314–16
  Chocolate Mousse, 344
  Chocolate Sauce, 346
  Chocolate Soufflé, 267–68
  Chocolate Stout Brownie Torte, 343–44
  Chocolate Zombie Clusters, 258–59

Dark Chocolate Ganache, 290–91
Deadly Grind, A excerpt (Hamilton), 285–86
Death by Chocolate Cupcakes, 290–91
Deep-Fried Bananas with Baked Plantains, 345–46
Final Sentence excerpt (Gerber), 253–54
Ganache Frosting, 304–5
Gluten-Free Chocolate Cupcakes with Ganache Frosting, 304–5
Granny Sebastian's Bread Pudding, 271–72
Herr Georg's *Obstkuchen:* German Strawberry Torte, 341–42
If Fried Chicken Could Fly excerpt (Shelton), 292–93
If Mashed Potatoes Could Dance excerpt (Shelton), 330
Jasmine Tea Truffles, 282
Jenna's Caramel Macchiato Ice Cream, 277–79
Key Lime-Strawberry Whipped Topping Pie, 334–35
Lemon Steamed Pudding, 270
Maple Whipped Cream, 327
Marshmallow Meringue, 332, 333
Melody's Chocolate Mousse, 269
Mojito Cupcakes, 301
Moonlight Madness, 298–99
Nancy's Raspberry Petit Fours, 245–46
Nanna Tibbetts's Moose Mincemeat, 265
Nanna Tibbetts's Moose Mincemeat Cookies, 266
Orange Dreamsicle Cupcakes, 296–97
Peach Pies and Alibis excerpt (Adams), 317–18
Pies and Prejudice excerpt (Adams), 312–13
Plantain Chips, 346
Pumpkin Cupcakes with Whipped Cream Frosting, 308–9
Queen Elizabeth Cake, 287–89
Raspberry Buttercream Frosting, 303
Read It and Weep excerpt (McKinlay), 243–44
Red Velvet Cake/Cupcakes, 294–95
Sandra Gregoire's Charmed "Customer of the Week" Lime Pie, 336–37
Sandy's Favorite Whoopie Pies, 260–61
Sprinkle with Murder excerpt (McKinlay), 300
Sweet Potato Pie with Marshmallow Meringue, 331–33
Theodosia's Earl Grey Sorbet, 276

Tinkerbells, 302–3
Town in a Strawberry Swirl excerpt (Haywood), 338–40
Vanilla Buttercream Frosting, 296–97
Vegan Vanilla Cupcakes, 306–7
Whipped Topping, 321–22
Deviled Eggs, 151
Devonshire Dandy Cream, 72
Doughnut Muffins, Clare Cosi's, 51–52
Dragonwell Dead (Childs), 117
Drayton's Green Tea Tippler, 124
Dreamsicle Orange Cupcakes, 296–97
drinks, 115–41
  Black Orchid Cocktail, 117
  Butter Off Dead excerpt (Budewitz), 120–21
  Candy Cane Latte, 137–38
  Cocktails with the Murphy Girls, 122–23
  Coffee Milk and Coffee Syrup, 127–28
  Drayton's Green Tea Tippler, 124
  Eggnog Latte, 136
  Fa-La-La-La Lattes, 135–40
  froth, creating without an espresso machine steam wand, 139–40
  Gingerbread Latte, 135–36
  Homemade Coffee Syrup, 127–28
  Homemade Gingerbread Syrup, 135–36
  Huckleberry Margaritas, 123
  Huckleberry Vodka, 122
  Killer Sweet Tea, 126
  Marjorie Coffin's White Moose Hot Cocoa, 133
  May Wine, 118–19
  Mexican Coffee, 141
  Old-Fashioned Iced Coffee, 129
  Orange-Spice Yule Latte, 138
  Pumpkin Spice Coffee Blend, 134
  Simple Sugar Syrup, 129
  Summer Tea Sparkler, 125
  Town in a Wild Moose Chase excerpt (Haywood), 131–32
  Village Blend's (The) Chilly Choco Latte, 130
  White Chocolate "Snowflake" Latte, 136–37
Dumplings, Chicken Pot Pie Soup with, 81–82

Earl Grey Sorbet, Theodosia's, 276
Easy Cream Scones, 69
Eggnog Latte, 136

eggs
Charmed Bacon-Lattice Breakfast Pie, 16
Charmed Pancetta and Gruyère Tart, 19–20
Chocolate Soufflé, 267–68
Delilah's Grilled Breakfast Sandwich, 3–4
Deviled Eggs, 151
Eggs Benedict, 8–9
French Toast Sandwich, 23
Haley's Lemon Curd, 75
Jaymie's Fourth of July Potato Salad, 227–28
Jenna's Monte Cristo Sandwich, 24–25
Marshmallow Meringue, 332, 333
San Simon Frittata, 12–13
Spinach Quiche, 17–18
See also specific baked goods and desserts
Eggsecutive Orders (Hyzy), 8, 10, 17, 151, 267
Egg Wash, Charmed, 316
English Breakfast Murder, The (Childs), 202
English muffins in Eggs Benedict, 8–9
Erin's Two-Bean and Pesto Salad, 96–97
espresso coffee in Jenna's Caramel Macchiato
Ice Cream, 277–79
Espresso Shot (Coyle), 250

Fake Fried Chicken, 195–96
Fa-La-La-La Lattes, 135–40
Fat-Free, Cheese-Free, Yolk-Free, High-Fiber
Omelet, 10–11
fennel
Fennel and Blood Orange Salad, 101–2
Fennel and Shrimp Prosciutto Wraps, 147
Pasta with Strawberry, Leek, and
Fennel, 210
feta cheese
Charlene's Cucumber Cups Stuffed with
Feta, 154
Spinach Quiche, 17–18
Watermelon, Basil, and Feta Salad, 95
Fettucine with Minted Tomato Sauce, aka
Fettucine a La Fresca, 213–14
figs
Delilah's Grilled Cheese with Bacon and
Fig Jam, 108–9
Goat Cheese and Pancetta Sandwich, 107
Pancakes with Gouda and Figs, 26–27
Final Sentence (Gerber), 253–54, 255
Fish, Planked, 202
Fit for the King Muffins (Banana-Peanut
Butter-Chocolate Chip Muffins),
60–61
Flank Steak, Grilled, 173–74
Fondue, Blue Cheese and Garlic, 148

Fourth of July Potato Salad, Jaymie's,
227–28
French Toast Sandwich, 23
Fresca, Fettucine a La (Fettucine with Minted
Tomato Sauce), 213–14
Fried Chicken, 193–94
Frittata, San Simon, 12–13
frosting
Ganache Frosting, 304–5
Pumpkin Cupcakes with Whipped Cream
Frosting, 308–9
Raspberry Buttercream Frosting, 303
Vanilla Buttercream Frosting, 296–97
Vegan Vanilla Frosting, 306–7
froth, creating without an espresso machine
steam wand, 139–40
Fudge, Bailey's Irish Cream and Caramel-Nut,
280–81
Fully Loaded Colcannon for Mike, Clare's,
222–23
Funeral Potatoes, 224–25

Galium odoratum (sweet woodruff), 118
ganache
Dark Chocolate Ganache, 290–91
Ganache Frosting, 304–5
Garlic and Blue Cheese Fondue, 148
Georgia Peach Pie, Charmed, 319–20
Gerber, Daryl Wood
Final Sentence, 253–54, 255
Inherit the Word, 24, 103–4, 105, 277
German Strawberry-Apple Pancakes, Maggie
Tremont's, 28–29
German Strawberry Torte, Herr Georg's
Obstkuchen, 341–42
ginger
Blueberry Gingerbread, 43–44
Gingerbread Latte, 135–36
Homemade Gingerbread Syrup, 135–36
Summer Tea Sparkler, 125
Glaze, Vanilla, 55–56
Glazed Lemon Cookies (*Anginetti*), 250–52
gluten-free
Aunt Vera's Gluten-Free Orange-Chocolate
Biscotti, 255–57
Gluten-Free Chocolate Cupcakes with
Ganache Frosting, 304–5
Gluten-Free Popovers, 67
Goat Cheese and Pancetta Sandwich, 107
Going, Going, Ganache (McKinlay), 304, 308
Golden Acres Banana-Bran Muffins, 49–50
Gouda and Figs, Pancakes with, 26–27

Gram's Instant Miracle Rolls, 65
Grand Marnier liqueur in Orange-Spice Yule
    Latte, 138
Grandmother's Pancake Mix, 26–27
Granny Sebastian's Bread Pudding, 271–72
Great Exhibition in 1851, 289
green beans in Erin's Two-Bean and Pesto
    Salad, 96–97
Green Tea Tippler, Drayton's, 124
Grilled Breakfast Sandwich, Delilah's, 3–4
grilled cheese sandwiches
    Aunt Vera's Brie, Apple, and Turkey Grilled
        Cheese, 105–6
    Delilah's Grilled Cheese with Bacon and Fig
        Jam, 108–9
Grilled Chicken Breasts, The World's Best,
    186–87
Grilled Flank Steak, 173–74
Gruyère and Pancetta Tart, Charmed, 19–20
Gunpowder Green (Childs), 276

Hail to the Chef (Hyzy), 33–36, 167
Haley's Lemon Curd, 75
ham
    Eggs Benedict, 8–9
    Fat-Free, Cheese-Free, Yolk-Free, High-Fiber
        Omelet, 10–11
    Fennel and Shrimp Prosciutto Wraps, 147
    Jenna's Monte Cristo Sandwich, 24–25
    Pastry-Wrapped Asparagus Spears with
        Prosciutto, 159
    Torpedo Sandwich, 111
Hamilton, Victoria
    Bowled Over, 226, 227
    Bran New Death, 47–48, 49, 62
    Deadly Grind, A, 285–86, 287
    Muffin but Murder, 58–59, 60, 63, 83
    No Mallets Intended, 197–98, 199
hands, meaning of, 255
Haywood, B. B.
    Town in a Blueberry Jam, 41–42, 43,
        247, 273
    Town in a Pumpkin Bash, 39, 232–33,
        234, 310
    Town in a Strawberry Swirl, 28, 210, 334,
        338–40, 341
    Town in a Wild Moose Chase, 131–32, 133,
        260, 265, 269
Heart-Shaped White Chocolate-Raspberry
    Cream Two-Bite Pies, Charmed, 328–29
Herb Muffins, Savory, 63
Herend's Queen Victoria china, 289

Herr Georg's Obstkuchen: German Strawberry
    Torte, 341–42
Hershey's Kisses in Moonlight Madness,
    298–99
High-Fiber Omelet, Fat-Free, Cheese-Free,
    Yolk-Free, 10–11
Holiday Grind (Coyle), 135
Holiday Tartan china by Lenox, 288
Holliday Buzz (Coyle), 188
Holly Holliday's Pumpkin Chocolate Chip
    Bread, 39
Homemade Coffee Syrup, 127–28
Homemade Gingerbread Syrup, 135–36
Home of the Braised (Hyzy), 217–19, 231, 270
Hot Cocoa, Marjorie Coffin's White Moose, 133
huckleberries
    Huckleberry Margaritas, 123
    Huckleberry Vodka, 122
Hyzy, Julie
    Affairs of Steak, 156–58, 159, 161, 171, 181
    Buffalo West Wing, 203, 220
    Eggsecutive Orders, 8, 10, 17, 151, 267
    Hail to the Chef, 33–36, 167
    Home of the Braised, 217–19, 231, 270
    State of the Onion, 5–7, 37

ice cream
    Brie-Blueberry Ice Cream, 274–75
    Jenna's Caramel Macchiato Ice Cream,
        277–79
Iced Coffee, Old-Fashioned, 129
If Bread Could Rise to the Occasion (Shelton),
    40, 45, 57, 64, 65, 271
If Fried Chicken Could Fly (Shelton), 191–92,
    193, 248, 292–93, 294
If Mashed Potatoes Could Dance (Shelton), 30,
    221, 224, 229, 330, 331
Inaugural Luncheon (2005), 270
Inaugural Luncheon (2009), 231
Individual Chicken Pot Pies, 181
Inherit the Word (Gerber), 24, 103–4,
    105, 277
Instant Miracle Rolls, Gram's, 65

Jake's Favorite Blueberry-Orange Muffins, 57
Jarlsberg cheese in Torpedo Sandwich, 111
Jasmine Moon Murder, The (Childs), 124, 282
Jasmine Tea Truffles, 282
Jaymie's Fourth of July Potato Salad, 227–28
Jenna's Caramel Macchiato Ice Cream,
    277–79
Jenna's Monte Cristo Sandwich, 24–25

Kahlúa in Mexican Coffee, 141
Kalamata olives
    Charlene's Cucumber Cups Stuffed with
        Feta, 154
    Ladybug Tea Sandwiches, 114
    Olive Tapenade, 149
Katie, Caramel Sauce à la, 279
Kennedy, Katherine, 294
Kennedy-Yoon, Michael, 294
Key Lime-Strawberry Whipped Topping Pie,
    334–35
Killer Sweet Tea, 126
kirsch in Candy Cane Latte, 137–38

Ladle to the Grave (Archer), 79–80, 81, 110, 118
Ladybug Tea Sandwiches, 114
Lasagna (for Mike), Clare Cosi's Skillet,
    211–12
lattes
    Candy Cane Latte, 137–38
    Eggnog Latte, 136
    Fa-La-La-La Lattes, 135–40
    froth, creating without an espresso machine
        steam wand, 139–40
    Gingerbread Latte, 135–36
    Homemade Gingerbread Syrup, 135–36
    Orange-Spice Yule Latte, 138
    Village Blend's (The) Chilly Choco
        Latte, 130
    White Chocolate "Snowflake" Latte,
        136–37
Leek, Strawberry, and Fennel, Pasta with, 210
lemons
    Anginetti (Glazed Lemon Cookies), 250–52
    Blueberry-Lemon Shortbread, 247
    Haley's Lemon Curd, 75
    Lemon Steamed Pudding, 270
    Roasted Rock Cornish Game Hens with
        Rosemary and Lemon Butter, 179–80
    Tinkerbells, 302–3
Lenox's Holiday Tartan china, 288
lettuce
    Chicken, Apricot, and Almond Salad, 98
    Watermelon, Basil, and Feta Salad, 95
Lilly Wallace New American Cook Book,
    The, 226
limes
    Clare's Roasted Chicken with Rosemary and
        Lime for Mike, 182–83
    Mojito Cupcakes, 301
    Sandra Gregoire's Charmed "Customer of
        the Week" Lime Pie, 336–37

Long Quiche Goodbye, The (Aames), 209,
    235–36, 237
Lost and Fondue (Aames), 76, 148

Maggie Tremont's German Strawberry-Apple
    Pancakes, 28–29
main courses, 169–214
    Assault and Pepper excerpt (Budewitz),
        205–6
    Beef Wellington, 171–72
    Charmed Meat Pies with Paprika Aioli,
        175–76
    Clare Cosi's Skillet Lasagna (for Mike),
        211–12
    Clare's Chicken Marsala for Mike, 188–90
    Clare's Roasted Chicken with Rosemary and
        Lime for Mike, 182–83
    Crime Rib excerpt (Budewitz), 184–85
    Fake Fried Chicken, 195–96
    Fettucine with Minted Tomato Sauce, aka
        Fettucine a La Fresca, 213–14
    Fried Chicken, 193–94
    Grilled Flank Steak, 173–74
    If Fried Chicken Could Fly excerpt
        (Shelton), 191–92
    Individual Chicken Pot Pies, 181
    Murder by Mocha excerpt (Coyle), 177–78
    Nantucket Sea Scallops, 203–4
    No Mallets Intended excerpt (Hamilton),
        197–98
    Paprika Aioli, 175–76
    Pasta with Strawberry, Leek, and Fennel, 210
    Penne Rigate with Asparagus and
        Sesame-Chile Shrimp, 207–8
    Planked Fish, 202
    Roasted Rock Cornish Game Hens with
        Rosemary and Lemon Butter, 179–80
    Smoked Salmon and Mascarpone
        Risotto, 209
    Turkey Roulettes, 199–201
    World's Best Grilled Chicken Breasts,
        The, 186–87
Mango Summer Soup, Chilled, 90
maple
    Charmed Mini Maple-Pecan Pies, 326
    Maple Whipped Cream, 327
Margaritas, Huckleberry, 123
Marjorie Coffin's White Moose Hot Cocoa, 133
Marsala for Mike, Clare's Chicken, 188–90
Marshmallow Meringue, 332, 333
mascarpone cheese
    Brie-Blueberry Ice Cream, 274–75

Charmed Pancetta and Gruyère Tart, 19–20
Smoked Salmon and Mascarpone
    Risotto, 209
Mashed Potatoes, 221
Max's Blue Cheese, Apple, and Walnut Salad,
    99–100
May Wine, 118–19
McKinlay, Jenn
    Book, Line, and Sinker, 152–53, 154
    Buttercream Bump Off, 296, 298
    Death by the Dozen, 343, 345
    Going, Going, Ganache, 304, 308
    Read It and Weep, 243–44, 245
    Red Velvet Revenge, 283, 306
    Sprinkle with Murder, 290, 300, 301, 302
Meat Pies (Charmed) with Paprika Aioli,
    175–76
Melody's Chocolate Mousse, 269
Meringue, Marshmallow, 332, 333
Mexican Coffee, 141
mincemeat
    Nanna Tibbetts's Moose Mincemeat, 265
    Nanna Tibbetts's Moose Mincemeat
        Cookies, 266
Mini Maple-Pecan Pies, Charmed, 326
Minted Tomato Sauce, Fettucine with
    (aka Fettucine a La Fresca), 213–14
Mojito Cupcakes, 301
molasses
    Charmed Shoofly Pie, 314–16
    Molasses Whipped Sweet Potatoes, 231
Monte Cristo Sandwich, Jenna's, 24–25
Monterey Jack cheese in Charmed
    Bacon-Lattice Breakfast Pie, 16
Montezuma, 262
Moonlight Madness, 298–99
moose mincemeat
    Nanna Tibbetts's Moose Mincemeat, 265
    Nanna Tibbetts's Moose Mincemeat
        Cookies, 266
Morel Sauté, 150
mousse
    Chocolate Mousse, 344
    Melody's Chocolate Mousse, 269
mozzarella cheese
    Caprese Salad, 94
    Clare Cosi's Skillet Lasagna (for Mike),
        211–12
Muffin but Murder (Hamilton), 58–59, 60,
    63, 83
muffins
    Bacon-Cheddar Muffins, 62

Clare Cosi's Classic Coffee Cake Muffins
    with Streusel Topping and Vanilla
    Glaze, 54–56
Clare Cosi's Doughnut Muffins, 51–52
Fit for the King Muffins (Banana-Peanut
    Butter-Chocolate Chip Muffins), 60–61
Golden Acres Banana-Bran Muffins, 49–50
Jake's Favorite Blueberry-Orange Muffins, 57
Savory Herb Muffins, 63
See also breads, muffins, and other baked
    goods
Murder by Mocha (Coyle), 177–78, 179,
    258, 262
Murder Most Frothy (Coyle), 129, 130
Murphy Girls, Cocktails with the, 122–23
mushrooms
    Beef Wellington, 171–72
    Beet-Mushroom-Barley Soup, 87
    Clare Cosi's Skillet Lasagna (for Mike),
        211–12
    Clare's Chicken Marsala for Mike, 188–90
    Fat-Free, Cheese-Free, Yolk-Free, High-Fiber
        Omelet, 10–11
    Individual Chicken Pot Pies, 181
    Morel Sauté, 150
    Ricotta-Stuffed Mushrooms, 165
    Spinach Quiche, 17–18
    Wild Mushroom Soup, 88
    Wild Rice and Pumpkin Pilaf, 234

Nancy's Raspberry Petit Fours, 245–46
Nanna Tibbetts's Moose Mincemeat, 265
Nanna Tibbetts's Moose Mincemeat
    Cookies, 266
Nantucket Sea Scallops, 203–4
Newfoundland Tartan china by Royal Adderley
    of Ridgway, 288–89
No Mallets Intended (Hamilton), 197–98, 199
nonpareils (confetti), 250
Nutella in Chocolate Zombie Clusters, 258–59
nuts
    Chocolate Zombie Clusters, 258–59
    Nanna Tibbetts's Moose Mincemeat
        Cookies, 266
    Queen Elizabeth Cake, 287–89
    toasting nuts tip, 259
    See also almonds; peanut butter; pecans;
        walnuts

Obstkuchen: German Strawberry Torte, Herr
    Georg's, 341–42
Old-Fashioned Crumpets, 68

Old-Fashioned Iced Coffee, 129
Olive Tapenade, 149
Omelet (High-Fiber), Fat-Free, Cheese-Free,
    Yolk-Free, 10–11
oranges
    Aunt Vera's Gluten-Free Orange-Chocolate
        Biscotti, 255–57
    Fennel and Blood Orange Salad, 101–2
    Grilled Flank Steak, 173–74
    Jake's Favorite Blueberry-Orange
        Muffins, 57
    Orange Dreamsicle Cupcakes, 296–97
    Orange-Spice Yule Latte, 138

pancakes
    Maggie Tremont's German Strawberry-Apple
        Pancakes, 28–29
    Pancakes with Gouda and Figs, 26–27
pancetta
    Charmed Pancetta and Gruyère Tart, 19–20
    Goat Cheese and Pancetta Sandwich, 107
Paprika Aioli, 175–76
Parmesan cheese
    Parmesan Crisps, 160
    Pesto Sauce, 110
    San Simon Frittata, 12–13
pasta
    Clare Cosi's Skillet Lasagna (for Mike),
        211–12
    Fettucine with Minted Tomato Sauce, aka
        Fettucine a La Fresca, 213–14
    Pasta with Strawberry, Leek, and Fennel, 210
    Penne Rigate with Asparagus and Sesame-
        Chile Shrimp, 207–8
    Tomato-Spinach Soup, 89
Pastry-Wrapped Asparagus Spears with
    Prosciutto, 159
Peach Pie, Charmed Georgia, 319–20
Peach Pies and Alibis (Adams), 317–18, 319, 347
Peanut Butter-Banana-Chocolate Chip
    Muffins, Fit for the King, 60–61
pears
    Charmed Apple, Pear, and Cherry Crisp, 347
    Cliff's Pear Bread, 45
peas
    Chicken Pot Pie Soup with Dumplings,
        81–82
    Individual Chicken Pot Pies, 181
Pecan Pies and Homicides (Adams), 14–15, 16,
    175, 324, 326, 328
pecans
    Charmed Chocolate-Bourbon Pecan Pie, 323

Charmed Mini Maple-Pecan Pies, 326
    Cranberry-Pecan Brie en Croûte, 161–62
Penne Rigate with Asparagus and Sesame-Chile
    Shrimp, 207–8
peppermint in Candy Cane Latte, 137–38
pesto
    Erin's Two-Bean and Pesto Salad, 96–97
    Pesto Sauce, 110
Petit Fours, Nancy's Raspberry, 245–46
Piecrust, Charmed, 315–16
pies
    Charmed Banana Puddin' Pie, 321–22
    Charmed Chocolate-Bourbon Pecan Pie, 323
    Charmed Georgia Peach Pie, 319–20
    Charmed Heart-Shaped White Chocolate-
        Raspberry Cream Two-Bite Pies, 328–29
    Charmed Mini Maple-Pecan Pies, 326
    Charmed Red Hot-Apple Pie, 324–25
    Charmed Shoofly Pie, 314–16
    Key Lime-Strawberry Whipped Topping Pie,
        334–35
    Sandra Gregoire's Charmed "Customer of
        the Week" Lime Pie, 336–37
    Sweet Potato Pie with Marshmallow
        Meringue, 331–33
    Pies and Prejudice (Adams), 19, 312–13, 314,
        321, 323, 336
Pilaf, Wild Rice and Pumpkin, 234
Planked Fish, 202
plantains
    Deep-Fried Bananas with Baked Plantains,
        345–46
    Plantain Chips, 346
Polenta with Taleggio and Basil, 237
Popovers, Gluten-Free, 67
pork in Clare Cosi's Skillet Lasagna (for Mike),
    211–12
potatoes
    Clare's Fully Loaded Colcannon for Mike,
        222–23
    Funeral Potatoes, 224–25
    Jaymie's Fourth of July Potato Salad, 227–28
    Mashed Potatoes, 221
    Potato-Yam Soup, 86
    Skillet Potatoes, 30
    Twice-Baked Potatoes, 229–30
pot pies
    Chicken Pot Pie Soup with Dumplings,
        81–82
    Individual Chicken Pot Pies, 181
prosciutto
    Fennel and Shrimp Prosciutto Wraps, 147

Pastry-Wrapped Asparagus Spears with
   Prosciutto, 159
pudding
   Granny Sebastian's Bread Pudding, 271–72
   Lemon Steamed Pudding, 270
puff pastry
   Beef Wellington, 171–72
   Cranberry-Pecan Brie en Croûte, 161–62
   Individual Chicken Pot Pies, 181
   Pastry-Wrapped Asparagus Spears with
      Prosciutto, 159
pumpkin
   Candy Holliday's Pumpkin Cheesecake
      Swirl, 310–11
   Holly Holliday's Pumpkin Chocolate Chip
      Bread, 39
   Pumpkin Cupcakes with Whipped Cream
      Frosting, 308–9
   Pumpkin Spice Coffee Blend, 134
   Wild Rice and Pumpkin Pilaf, 234

Queen Elizabeth Cake, 287–89
Queen Victoria china by Herend, 289
Quiche, Spinach, 17–18

raisins in Nanna Tibbetts's Moose
   Mincemeat, 265
Rangoon, Baked Crab, 155
raspberries
   Charmed Heart-Shaped White Chocolate-
      Raspberry Cream Two-Bite Pies, 328–29
   Nancy's Raspberry Petit Fours, 245–46
   Raspberry Buttercream Frosting, 303
   Tinkerbells, 302–3
Raspberry Buttercream Frosting, 303
Read It and Weep (McKinlay), 243–44, 245
Red Hot-Apple Pie, Charmed, 324–25
Red Pepper (Roasted) and Avocado
   Sandwich, 110
Red Velvet Cake/Cupcakes, 294–95
Red Velvet Revenge (McKinlay), 283, 306
Rhode Island, 127
rice
   Cucumber, Yogurt, and Walnut Soup
      (Chilled), 93
   Smoked Salmon and Mascarpone
      Risotto, 209
   Wild Rice and Pumpkin Pilaf, 234
ricotta cheese
   Clare Cosi's Skillet Lasagna (for Mike),
      211–12
   Ricotta-Stuffed Mushrooms, 165

Risotto, Smoked Salmon and Mascarpone, 209
Roasted Rock Cornish Game Hens with
   Rosemary and Lemon Butter, 179–80
Roast Mortem (Coyle), 51
Rock Cornish Game Hens (Roasted) with
   Rosemary and Lemon Butter, 179–80
Rolls, Gram's Instant Miracle, 65
Romans, 262
rosemary
   Clare's Roasted Chicken with Rosemary and
      Lime for Mike, 182–83
   Roasted Rock Cornish Game Hens with
      Rosemary and Lemon Butter, 179–80
   Rosemary Biscuits, 66
Roulettes, Turkey, 199–201
Roux of Revenge, A (Archer), 46, 66,
   84–85, 87
Royal Adderley of Ridgway's Newfoundland
   Tartan china, 288–89

salads
   Caprese Salad, 94
   Chicken, Apricot, and Almond Salad, 98
   Erin's Two-Bean and Pesto Salad, 96–97
   Fennel and Blood Orange Salad, 101–2
   Jaymie's Fourth of July Potato Salad,
      227–28
   Max's Blue Cheese, Apple, and Walnut
      Salad, 99–100
   Watermelon, Basil, and Feta Salad, 95
   See also soups, salads, and sandwiches
salmon
   Planked Fish, 202
   Smoked Salmon and Mascarpone
      Risotto, 209
   Smoked Salmon Florets, 166
Sandra Gregoire's Charmed "Customer of the
   Week" Lime Pie, 336–37
sandwiches
   Aunt Vera's Brie, Apple, and Turkey Grilled
      Cheese, 105–6
   Avocado and Roasted Red Pepper
      Sandwich, 110
   Delilah's Grilled Breakfast Sandwich,
      3–4
   Delilah's Grilled Cheese with Bacon and Fig
      Jam, 108–9
   Fennel and Shrimp Prosciutto Wraps, 147
   French Toast Sandwich, 23
   Goat Cheese and Pancetta Sandwich, 107
   Jenna's Monte Cristo Sandwich, 24–25
   Ladybug Tea Sandwiches, 114

sandwiches (*cont.*)
  Torpedo Sandwich, 111
  See also soups, salads, and sandwiches
Sandy's Favorite Whoopie Pies, 260–61
San Simon Frittata, 12–13
sauces
  Blueberry Sauce, 275
  Caramel Sauce à la Katie, 279
  Chocolate Sauce, 346
  Fettucine with Minted Tomato Sauce, aka
    Fettucine a La Fresca, 213–14
  Pesto Sauce, 110
Savory Herb Muffins, 63
Scallops, Nantucket Sea, 203–4
scones
  Cherry Scones, 76
  Easy Cream Scones, 69
Scones and Bones (Childs), 68
Sea Scallops, Nantucket, 203–4
Sesame-Chile Shrimp and Asparagus, Penne
  Rigate with, 207–8
Shades of Earl Grey (Childs), 69, 73–74, 75
Shallots and Olive Oil, Creamed Spinach
  with, 220
Shelton, Paige
  If Bread Could Rise to the Occasion, 40, 45,
    57, 64, 65, 271
  If Fried Chicken Could Fly, 191–92, 193,
    248, 292–93, 294
  If Mashed Potatoes Could Dance, 30, 221,
    224, 229, 330, 331
Shoofly Pie, Charmed, 314–16
Shortbread, Blueberry-Lemon, 247
shrimp
  Fennel and Shrimp Prosciutto Wraps, 147
  Penne Rigate with Asparagus and Sesame-
    Chile Shrimp, 207–8
side dishes, 215–37
  Bowled Over excerpt (Hamilton), 226
  Clare's Fully Loaded Colcannon for Mike,
    222–23
  Creamed Spinach with Olive Oil and
    Shallots, 220
  Funeral Potatoes, 224–25
  Home of the Braised excerpt (Hyzy),
    217–19
  Jaymie's Fourth of July Potato Salad,
    227–28
  Long Quiche Goodbye, The excerpt (Aames),
    235–36
  Mashed Potatoes, 221
  Molasses Whipped Sweet Potatoes, 231

Polenta with Taleggio and Basil, 237
Town in a Pumpkin Bash excerpt (Haywood),
  232–33
Twice-Baked Potatoes, 229–30
Wild Rice and Pumpkin Pilaf, 234
Silva, Dante, 127
Simple Sugar Syrup, 129
Skillet Lasagna (for Mike), Clare Cosi's,
  211–12
Skillet Potatoes, 30
Smoked Salmon and Mascarpone Risotto, 209
Smoked Salmon Florets, 166
"Snowflake" White Chocolate Latte, 136–37
Sorbet, Theodosia's Earl Grey, 276
Soufflé, Chocolate, 267–68
soups, salads, and sandwiches, 77–114
  Aunt Vera's Brie, Apple, and Turkey Grilled
    Cheese, 105–6
  Avocado and Roasted Red Pepper
    Sandwich, 110
  Balsamic Vinaigrette, 99–100
  Beet-Mushroom-Barley Soup, 87
  Broth of Betrayal, A excerpt (Archer), 91–92
  Caprese Salad, 94
  Cauliflower and Cheddar Soup, 83
  Chicken, Apricot, and Almond Salad, 98
  Chicken Pot Pie Soup with Dumplings,
    81–82
  Chilled Mango Summer Soup, 90
  Cucumber, Yogurt, and Walnut Soup
    (Chilled), 93
  Delilah's Grilled Cheese with Bacon and Fig
    Jam, 108–9
  Erin's Two-Bean and Pesto Salad, 96–97
  Fennel and Blood Orange Salad,
    101–2
  Goat Cheese and Pancetta Sandwich, 107
  Inherit the Word excerpt (Gerber), 103–4
  Ladle to the Grave excerpt (Archer), 79–80
  Ladybug Tea Sandwiches, 114
  Max's Blue Cheese, Apple, and Walnut
    Salad, 99–100
  Potato-Yam Soup, 86
  Roux of Revenge, A excerpt (Archer), 84–85
  Steeped in Evil excerpt (Childs), 112–13
  Tomato-Spinach Soup, 89
  Torpedo Sandwich, 111
  Watermelon, Basil, and Feta Salad, 95
  Wild Mushroom Soup, 88
sour cream
  Candy Holliday's Pumpkin Cheesecake
    Swirl, 310–11

Clare Cosi's Classic Coffee Cake Muffins with Streusel Topping and Vanilla Glaze, 54–56
Funeral Potatoes, 224–25
Skillet Potatoes, 30
Twice-Baked Potatoes, 229–30
soy milk in Vegan Vanilla Cupcakes, 306–7
Sparkler, Summer Tea, 125
spearmint in Mojito Cupcakes, 301
spinach
    Creamed Spinach with Olive Oil and Shallots, 220
    Fat-Free, Cheese-Free, Yolk-Free, High-Fiber Omelet, 10–11
    Spinach Quiche, 17–18
    Tomato-Spinach Soup, 89
Spoonful of Murder, A (Archer), 21–22, 23, 86, 88, 89, 107
Sprinkle with Murder (McKinlay), 290, 300, 301, 302
State of the Onion (Hyzy), 5–7, 37
Steamed Pudding, Lemon, 270
Steeped in Evil (Childs), 90, 112–13, 114, 155
Stout Brownie Chocolate Torte, 343–44
strawberries
    Herr Georg's *Obstkuchen:* German Strawberry Torte, 341–42
    Key Lime-Strawberry Whipped Topping Pie, 334–35
    Maggie Tremont's German Strawberry-Apple Pancakes, 28–29
    May Wine, 118–19
    Pasta with Strawberry, Leek, and Fennel, 210
Streusel (Crumb) Topping, 56
Stuffed Cherry Tomatoes, 167
Sugar Syrup, Simple, 129
Summer Soup, Chilled Mango, 90
Summer Tea Sparkler, 125
sweet potatoes
    Molasses Whipped Sweet Potatoes, 231
    Sweet Potato Pie with Marshmallow Meringue, 331–33
Sweet Tea, Killer, 126
Sweet Tea Revenge (Childs), 70–71, 72, 125, 126
sweet woodruff *(Galium odoratum)*, 118
Swiss cheese
    Charmed Bacon-Lattice Breakfast Pie, 16
    Delilah's Grilled Cheese with Bacon and Fig Jam, 108–9
    French Toast Sandwich, 23
    Jenna's Monte Cristo Sandwich, 24–25

Taleggio and Basil, Polenta with, 237
Tapenade, Olive, 149
Tart, Charmed Pancetta and Gruyère, 19–20
tea
    Drayton's Green Tea Tippler, 124
    Jasmine Tea Truffles, 282
    Killer Sweet Tea, 126
    Summer Tea Sparkler, 125
    Theodosia's Earl Grey Sorbet, 276
Teaberry Strangler, The (Childs), 166
Tea Sandwiches, Ladybug, 114
tequila
    Huckleberry Margaritas, 123
    Mexican Coffee, 141
Theodosia's Earl Grey Sorbet, 276
Tinkerbells, 302–3
Tippler, Drayton's Green Tea, 124
toasting nuts tip, 259
To Brie or Not to Brie (Aames), 67, 163–64, 165, 274
tomatoes
    Caprese Salad, 94
    Clare Cosi's Skillet Lasagna (for Mike), 211–12
    Erin's Two-Bean and Pesto Salad, 96–97
    Fat-Free, Cheese-Free, Yolk-Free, High-Fiber Omelet, 10–11
    Fettucine with Minted Tomato Sauce, aka Fettucine a La Fresca, 213–14
    Ladybug Tea Sandwiches, 114
    Stuffed Cherry Tomatoes, 167
    Tomato-Spinach Soup, 89
Tomme Crayeuse cheese in Delilah's Grilled Breakfast Sandwich, 3–4
Torpedo Sandwich, 111
tortes
    Chocolate Stout Brownie Torte, 343–44
    Herr Georg's *Obstkuchen:* German Strawberry Torte, 341–42
Town in a Blueberry Jam (Haywood), 41–42, 43, 247, 273
Town in a Pumpkin Bash (Haywood), 39, 232–33, 234, 310
Town in a Strawberry Swirl (Haywood), 28, 210, 334, 338–40, 341
Town in a Wild Moose Chase (Haywood), 131–32, 133, 260, 265, 269
Truffles, Jasmine Tea, 282
turkey
    Aunt Vera's Brie, Apple, and Turkey Grilled Cheese, 105–6
    Jenna's Monte Cristo Sandwich, 24–25

turkey (*cont.*)
  San Simon Frittata, 12–13
  Turkey Roulettes, 199–201
Turkish culture, 262
Twice-Baked Potatoes, 229–30
Two-Bean and Pesto Salad, Erin's, 96–97
Two-Bite Pies, Charmed Heart-Shaped White
    Chocolate-Raspberry Cream, 328–29

U.S. Food and Drug Administration, 118

vanilla
  Vanilla Buttercream Frosting, 296–97
  Vanilla Glaze, 55–56
  Vegan Vanilla Cupcakes, 306–7
vegetable stock/broth
  Tomato-Spinach Soup, 89
  Wild Mushroom Soup, 88
  Wild Rice and Pumpkin Pilaf, 234
Village Blend in Rhode Island, 127
Village Blend's Chilly Choco Latte, 130
Vinaigrette, Balsamic, 99–100
vodka
  Drayton's Green Tea Tippler, 124
  Huckleberry Vodka, 122

walnuts
  Bailey's Irish Cream and Caramel-Nut
    Fudge, 280–81
  Cucumber, Yogurt, and Walnut Soup
    (Chilled), 93
  Max's Blue Cheese, Apple, and Walnut
    Salad, 99–100
Watermelon, Basil, and Feta Salad, 95
Whipped Topping, 321–22
whipping cream
  Candy Holliday's Blueberry Whipped
    Cream, 273
  Caramel Sauce à la Katie, 279
  Chocolate Mousse, 344
  Granny Sebastian's Bread Pudding, 271–72
  Jasmine Tea Truffles, 282
  Jenna's Caramel Macchiato Ice Cream,
    277–79

Maple Whipped Cream, 327
Sandra Gregoire's Charmed "Customer of
    the Week" Lime Pie, 336–37
Whipped Cream Frosting, 308–9
Whipped Topping, 334–35
white beans in Erin's Two-Bean and Pesto
    Salad, 96–97
white chocolate
  Charmed Heart-Shaped White Chocolate-
    Raspberry Cream Two-Bite Pies,
    328–29
  Marjorie Coffin's White Moose Hot
    Cocoa, 133
  White Chocolate "Snowflake" Latte,
    136–37
Whoopie Pies, Sandy's Favorite, 260–61
Wild Mushroom Soup, 88
Wild Rice and Pumpkin Pilaf, 234
wine
  Clare's Chicken Marsala for Mike, 188–90
  Creamed Spinach with Olive Oil and
    Shallots, 220
  May Wine, 118–19
  Morel Sauté, 150
  Smoked Salmon and Mascarpone
    Risotto, 209
wonton skins in Baked Crab Rangoon, 155
World's Best Grilled Chicken Breasts, The,
    186–87
Wraps, Fennel and Shrimp Prosciutto, 147

Yam-Potato Soup, 86
yogurt
  Charlene's Cucumber Cups Stuffed with
    Feta, 154
  Chicken, Apricot, and Almond Salad, 98
  Cucumber, Yogurt, and Walnut Soup
    (Chilled), 93
Yolk-Free, Fat-Free, Cheese-Free, High-Fiber
    Omelet, 10–11
Yule Orange-Spice Latte, 138

Zombie Chocolate Clusters, 258–59
Zucchini Bread, 46

Series Lists

If you want to read more in any of these tasty series, here are full lists of titles in each:

CHEESE SHOP MYSTERIES BY AVERY AAMES

The Long Quiche Goodbye

Lost and Fondue

Clobbered by Camembert

To Brie or Not to Brie

The Days of Wine and Roquefort

As Gouda as Dead

COOKBOOK NOOK MYSTERIES BY DARYL WOOD GERBER

Final Sentence

Inherit the Word

Stirring the Plot

CHARMED PIE SHOPPE MYSTERIES BY ELLERY ADAMS

Pies and Prejudice

Peach Pies and Alibis

Pecan Pies and Homicides

Lemon Pies and Little White Lies

SOUP LOVER'S MYSTERIES BY CONNIE ARCHER

A Spoonful of Murder

A Broth of Betrayal

A Roux of Revenge

Ladle to the Grave

FOOD LOVERS' VILLAGE MYSTERIES BY LESLIE BUDEWITZ

Death al Dente

Crime Rib

Butter Off Dead

SEATTLE SPICE SHOP MYSTERIES BY LESLIE BUDEWITZ

Assault and Pepper

TEA SHOP MYSTERIES BY LAURA CHILDS

Death by Darjeeling

Gunpowder Green

Shades of Earl Grey

The English Breakfast Murder

The Jasmine Moon Murder

Chamomile Mourning

Blood Orange Brewing

Dragonwell Dead

The Silver Needle Murder

Oolong Dead

The Teaberry Strangler

Scones and Bones

Agony of the Leaves

Sweet Tea Revenge

Steeped in Evil

Ming Tea Murder

COFFEEHOUSE MYSTERIES BY CLEO COYLE

On What Grounds

Through the Grinder

Latte Trouble

Murder Most Frothy

Decaffeinated Corpse

French Pressed

Espresso Shot

Holiday Grind

Roast Mortem

Murder by Mocha

A Brew to a Kill

Holiday Buzz

Billionaire Blend

Once Upon a Grind

VINTAGE KITCHEN MYSTERIES BY VICTORIA HAMILTON

A Deadly Grind

Bowled Over

Freezer I'll Shoot

No Mallets Intended

MERRY MUFFIN MYSTERIES BY VICTORIA HAMILTON

Bran New Death

Muffin But Murder

Death of an English Muffin

CANDY HOLLIDAY MURDER MYSTERIES BY B. B. HAYWOOD

Town in a Blueberry Jam

Town in a Lobster Stew

Town in a Wild Moose Chase

Town in a Pumpkin Bash

Town in a Strawberry Swirl

Town in a Sweet Pickle

WHITE HOUSE CHEF MYSTERIES BY JULIE HYZY

State of the Onion

Hail to the Chef

Eggsecutive Orders

Buffalo West Wing

Affairs of Steak

Fonduing Fathers

Home of the Braised

All the President's Menus

CUPCAKE BAKERY MYSTERIES BY JENN MCKINLAY

Sprinkle with Murder

Buttercream Bump Off

Death by the Dozen

Red Velvet Revenge

Going, Going, Ganache

Sugar and Iced

LIBRARY LOVER'S MYSTERIES BY JENN MCKINLAY

Books Can Be Deceiving

Due or Die

Book, Line, and Sinker

Read It and Weep

On Borrowed Time

COUNTRY COOKING SCHOOL MYSTERIES BY PAIGE SHELTON

If Fried Chicken Could Fly

If Mashed Potatoes Could Dance

If Bread Could Rise to the Occasion

If Catfish Had Nine Lives

If Onions Could Spring Leeks

Author Bios

AVERY AAMES/DARYL WOOD GERBER

Daryl Wood Gerber writes the nationally bestselling Cookbook Nook Mysteries. As Avery Aames, she pens the nationally bestselling, Agatha Award–winning Cheese Shop Mysteries. Daryl is an avid foodie. She loves to cook. As a girl, she sold chocolate cream pies around the neighborhood. Prior to her breakout as an author, she catered, ran a restaurant, and even did some short-order cooking. Now, every week, she shares recipes on the Mystery Lovers' Kitchen blog. To find out more, visit averyaames.com and darylwoodgerber.com.

ELLERY ADAMS

Ellery Adams is the *New York Times* bestselling author of the Books by the Bay Mysteries, the Charmed Pie Shoppe Mysteries, and the Book Retreat Mysteries. She has had a lifelong love affair with both stories and food. As a child, she used to make mud pies and eat them. Over the years, she became more adept in the kitchen, and when she's not writing, she loves to don an apron and fill her home with the sweet, buttery scent of baking pies. Ms. Adams has held many jobs, including caterer, retail clerk, car salesperson, teacher, tutor, and tech writer, all while penning poems, children's books, and novels. She writes and creates culinary delights from her home in central Virginia. Visit the author at elleryadamsmysteries.com.

CONNIE ARCHER

Connie Archer is the national bestselling author of the Soup Lover's Mysteries set in Snowflake, Vermont. Connie was born and raised in New England and now lives on the other coast. Visit her website at conniearchermysteries.com and her blog at conniearchermysteries.com/blog. You can also find Connie on Facebook at facebook.com/ConnieArcherMysteries.

LESLIE BUDEWITZ

Leslie Budewitz is passionate about food, great mysteries, and her native Montana. She is the author of the Food Lovers' Village Mysteries and the new Spice Shop Mysteries. Also a lawyer, her first book, *Books, Crooks & Counselors: How to Write Accurately About Criminal Law and Courtroom Procedure*, won the 2011 Agatha Award for Best Nonfiction and was nominated for the 2012 Anthony and Macavity awards. Leslie loves to cook, eat, hike, travel, garden, and paint—not necessarily in that order. She lives in northwest Montana with her husband, Don Beans, a doctor of natural medicine, and their Burmese cat, Ruff, an avid bird watcher. Visit Leslie at lawandfiction.com and lesliebudewitz .com. Her characters check in monthly at the group mystery blog killerchar acters.com.

LAURA CHILDS

Laura Childs is the *New York Times* bestselling author of the Tea Shop Mysteries, the Scrapbooking Mysteries, and the Cackleberry Club Mysteries, and was a recent recipient of the RT Book Reviewers' Choice Award for Best Amateur Sleuth. In her previous life, she was CEO and creative director of her own marketing firm and authored several screenplays. She is married to a professor of Chinese art history, loves to travel, rides horses, enjoys fund-raising for various nonprofit organizations, and has two Chinese shar-pei dogs. Visit Laura online at laurachilds.com.

CLEO COYLE

Cleo Coyle is a pseudonym for Alice Alfonsi, writing in collaboration with her husband, Marc Cerasini. In addition to their *New York Times* bestselling Coffeehouse Mysteries, their Haunted Bookshop Mysteries, published under the name Alice Kimberly, are national bestselling works of amateur-sleuth fiction for Berkley Prime Crime. Alice and Marc were born and raised in small towns near Pittsburgh, Pennsylvania. They met in New York City, where both began their postcollege careers, and married in Nevada's Little Church of the West. Now they live and work in New York City, where they write independently and together. When not haunting coffeehouses or hunting ghosts, Alice writes young adult and children's books; Marc writes thrillers and nonfiction—and both are *New York Times* bestselling media tie-in writers who have penned properties for Lucasfilm, NBC, Fox, Disney, Imagine, and MGM.

Cleo enjoys hearing from readers. Visit her online coffeehouse at coffee housemystery.com, where she posts recipes and coffee picks. You can also connect with her on facebook.com/CleoCoyle and at twitter.com/cleocoyle.

VICTORIA HAMILTON

As Victoria Hamilton, Donna Lea Simpson is the national bestselling author of the Vintage Kitchen Mysteries, as well as the Merry Muffin Mysteries, including *Muffin but Murder* and *Bran New Death*. She is also a collector of vintage cookware, recipes and old cookbooks, as well as teapots and teacups. Visit her at victoriahamiltonmysteries.com and facebook.com/AuthorVictoria Hamilton.

B. B. HAYWOOD

B. B. Haywood is the author of the *New York Times* bestselling Candy Holliday Murder Mysteries. You can read more at hollidaysblueberryacres.com.

JULIE HYZY

New York Times bestselling author Julie Hyzy writes the White House Chef Mysteries and the Manor House Mysteries for Berkley Prime Crime. She has won both the Anthony and the Barry awards for her mystery fiction. Learn more about her at juliehyzy.com.

JENN McKINLAY

Jenn McKinlay will work for food. No seriously, pretty much anything having to do with food will get her motivated. So whether it's creating a recipe, sharing a recipe, or taste-testing a recipe, she is all in! Jenn is the *New York Times* bestselling author of the Cupcake Bakery Mysteries, the Library Lover's

Mysteries, and the Hat Shop Mysteries. When she's not toiling over her stories, you can usually find her in the kitchen. Visit her online at jennmckinlay.com.

PAIGE SHELTON

Paige Shelton is the *New York Times* bestselling author of the Farmers' Market Mysteries and the Country Cooking School Mysteries. She spent lots of years in advertising but now writes novels full time. She lives in Salt Lake City, Utah, with her husband and son. When she's up early enough, one of her favorite things is to watch the sun rise over the Wasatch Mountains. Visit her website at paigeshelton.com.